# THE EDGE OF SLEEP

# THE EDGE OF SLEEP

JAKE EMANUEL
AND
WILLIE BLOCK
WITH
JASON GURLEY

ST. MARTIN'S PRESS
NEW YORK

First published in the United States by St. Martin's Press, an imprint of St. Martin's Publishing Group

THE EDGE OF SLEEP. Copyright © 2023 by Jake Emanuel and Willie Block with Jason Gurley. All rights reserved. Printed in the United States of America. For information, address St. Martin's Publishing Group, 120 Broadway, New York, NY 10271.

www.stmartins.com

Designed by James Sinclair

Endpaper art by Ehren Salazar

The Library of Congress Cataloging-in-Publication Data is available upon request.

ISBN 978-1-250-28493-8 (hardcover)
ISBN 978-1-250-28492-1 (ebook)

Our books may be purchased in bulk for promotional, educational, or business use. Please contact your local bookseller or the Macmillan Corporate and Premium Sales Department at 1-800-221-7945, extension 5442, or by email at MacmillanSpecialMarkets@macmillan.com.

First Edition: 2023

10  9  8  7  6  5  4  3  2  1

*The worlds we attend to in our dreams are real.*
*We, their inventors, are also their gods:*
*We create them fully-formed as we slumber,*
*and violently extinguish them as we wake.*
*Dreams are criminal acts: murder, genocide.*
*How delicious they are; how terrible.*

—Hayden Aldridge Percy, *Journeys of the Unconscious Mind*

# THE EDGE OF SLEEP

# Prologue

## I

Dave Torres doesn't know where he is.

A darkness, not quite total, enfolds him; the cold of it jars his bones. Something flickers before his eyes, too near for him to focus on it. Just as quickly, it's gone again. A silky, nervous shape wriggles against his fingertips. At the periphery of his vision, dozens of murky shapes hover in the shadows, studying him.

The darkness flares golden, bringing with it a sudden heat that relieves his aches, then threatens to sear him alive; a terrible whine, loud as the front row at a Jetpacks show, sends needles into his ears. A moment later, the shredded wing of an aircraft carves through space, rippling the darkness. Dave reels backward as a buckled fuselage missiles past, its fractured windows glowing, flashing with bright flames. The wreckage of the plane tumbles away from him, disappearing into a swirling void beneath Dave's feet.

*What is going on?*

The shadow observers venture closer. Fish, all sorts of them. Striped ones, dotted ones, sleek and spiny ones. Some of them bioluminescent smears in the dark.

*I'm underwater?*

The fish scatter as a heavy shadow blots out the light above.

For a moment Dave thinks it might be a ship—but, no, it's larger, broader, and it twists through the water like a ribbon. Twists deeper. Toward Dave.

Dave cries out. A flurry of bubbles rushes from his mouth, rising skyward, but they never reach the distant surface. Instead, they collect and break against the belly of that ominous, massive beast—

## 2

With a shock, Dave finds himself on land again. His legs liquefy, and he's on his knees in a second, coughing up gallons of seawater. His lungs sizzle, as though he's breathed in sparks from a bonfire. Water sluices down his body and onto parched soil. His eyes, stung with salt, twitch involuntarily.

He collapses, rolls onto his back, sucks in air like a man who hasn't tasted it in weeks.

The shadow passes over him again. Dave shields his eyes against a watery sun. The dark silhouette of a whale spirals down through high clouds. Larger. Closer.

*I'm dead*, Dave understands. *I'm actually fucking dead.*

The whale hangs its enormous body in the sky, weightless as dandelion fluff. The whale's fins gently stir the air. Its flukes rise and fall.

A geyser of seawater issues from the whale's blowhole, raining a fine, salty mist upon Dave.

The whale's heavy-lidded eye, black as polished obsidian, regards him.

*Not dead. Not yet, I'm afraid.*

The words are soundless, but vibrate at a nauseating frequency. Dave's heart flutters like a bird's, defibrillated. His organs quiver. He lies prone, struck down by the voice of a god.

*Dave.* The whale blinks its enormous eye slowly. *What did you bring me, Dave?*

Dave keeps his mouth resolutely shut, afraid he might vomit again. The entire sea seems to roil in his guts.

*What did you bring me?*

I don't have anything, Dave croaks.

*Check your pockets, please.*

My pockets?

The whale dips its giant head. *Your pockets.*

I'm being mugged by a flying fish.

The whale spouts again, displeased.

Mist rains down on Dave as he pats first the left pocket of his drenched jeans. It's empty. But not the right. He struggles to withdraw the object from his shrunken pocket, then looks dubiously up at the whale.

It's just a bottle of Somalcya, he reports. Sleeping pills.

*Give it to me.*

You . . . want my sleeping pills?

*Give it to me.*

Dave opens his palm, holds the bottle up to the whale.

*Open it, please.*

Dave struggles with the cap. I'm sorry. My hands are so . . . fucking . . . *slick—*

The lid pops free. Before Dave can shake the pills into his hand, they take flight, rising from the little orange bottle like bubbles.

The whale opens its vast mouth, baleen gleaming.

*Dave.*

Not the whale. Who—?

*Wake up, Dave! Wake up—*

# The Whale

## I

—*wake up.*

*Wake up, Dave—*

"—wake up!"

Dave's eyes snap open.

"What the hell, bro?" Matteo swims into view, thick brow knitted in concern. "Jesus. Stay right there. Don't move. There's glass . . . well, it's everywhere."

The room flexes, shivers. Dave blinks, trying to clear his head, to orient himself. The bank of closed-circuit TV monitors. The smoke detector's blinking battery light. The crimson glow of the exit sight. The steady red indicator on the security camera. All of it familiar, but not from this angle.

*I'm on the floor*, Dave realizes. *Why am I on the floor?*

Dave runs his hand through his hair. "Ouch," he mutters. He inspects his hand in the dim light. It's streaked with ink. No. Blood. He plants his hand on the floor, intending to push himself upright, but snatches it back in pain. "Fuck!"

"I told you not to move, man," Matteo says, reappearing with a plastic first aid kit. He crouches next to Dave. "All the glass, remember? Give me your hand."

"My head, not my hand," Dave says. The words come out cottony and heavy. "Shit."

"Yeah, you tore yourself up. Hand."

Dave winces as Matteo brushes glass fragments from his palm. Then he sucks air over his teeth as Matteo pours hydrogen peroxide onto his skin. An array of tiny cuts bubble and froth.

"Chill," Matteo says, annoyingly calm. "It's hardly a scratch. A paper cut."

"A flesh wound," Dave says on autopilot.

"Yo, I love that movie. 'My name is Enrique Montego. You sworded my dad. Prepare to be killed.'"

Dave doesn't correct him. "What happened?"

Matteo dabs Dave's palm dry, clucking his tongue. "Check this. I go out for a smoke, right? Hank told me he thought someone tagged the Daxalab sign on day shift. So, I take a walk, right? To investigate."

"Someone tagged the sign?"

"Hank's full of shit. Sign's fine. So, I have my smoke. I come back, and the card reader won't read my access card."

"I thought Hank said they fixed that."

"Full of shit," Matteo repeats. "Like I said. Point is, I couldn't get in, right? So, I knock on the glass, trying to get you off your ass to come get the door for me. But I could see right into the security office, right? And there you were, lurching around like a goddamn zombie." He laughs to himself, then leans over Dave to grab something. He rocks back onto his heels, waggling an empty prescription bottle. "You were shaking this around like a champagne bottle. Pills like a fountain. *Everywhere*, bro."

Dave scans the room. Matteo's right. There are small pills scattered among the shards of glass.

"So, like, I finally get in—you gotta sorta *press* the card against the scan strip while you slide it, that's the trick—"

"Matteo."

"I'm getting there." Matteo strips open a gauze packet, then straps it to Dave's palm with a roll of medical tape. "So, I get inside and I'm, like, yo, Dave, and you, like, flinched. You shouted some nonsense about elephants. And then—" Matteo breaks off, laughing at the memory. "And then! Then you tried to fucking make a *break* for it. But you tripped over the chair. You squawked like a chicken. Literally, bro. *B'gawk!* And you broke Hank's favorite glass. Which he will make you pay for."

"Elephants?"

"I felt a little bad for laughing. Seeing how you cracked your head and all." A grin splits his face. "Shit was funny, though. It's on tape, too! I can play it back for you."

"Let's not—"

But Matteo's already shifted his attention to the desk. "Right about *here*," he says, and taps a key. Black-and-white footage of the security office appears on the computer monitor.

It's a strange feeling, Dave thinks, watching himself on TV. He doesn't remember doing any of this. On-screen, Dave drums restlessly on the arms of his chair. He yawns, then sharply pats first one cheek, then the other.

"That never works," Matteo offers. "Trust me. You wanna stay awake, you gotta move your legs." He probes Dave's scalp. "Jesus, bro, you weren't kidding. You've got a bump already. There's a cut. Feels small, though. Probably you won't need stitches."

Matteo pours more hydrogen peroxide onto Dave's head.

On the monitor, Dave watches himself rest his head on the desk. Almost immediately, he appears to be asleep.

"Am I talking?" he asks, pointing at the screen.

Matteo squints at the screen while pressing a fresh gauze pad to Dave's wound. "Sure looks it. Probably dreaming about . . . Shit. What was the name of that elephant in the picture books? Bob? No. Barber."

"Babar," Dave corrects, without thinking. "He was French."

"Yo, this is my favorite part," Matteo says. "Watch, watch. Look, you can even see my shadow at the outer door."

In the footage, Dave abruptly shoves back from the desk. The chair corkscrews away while Dave fumbles the pill bottle from his pocket.

"Here goes, man. Look at your crazy ass."

Cradling the pill bottle in his cupped palms, Dave extends both arms skyward.

Matteo cackles. "Like you're the Lion King or something, bro."

Dave watches his TV self pull the bottle close to his chest and struggle to open it. When he finally manages to pop the cap—

"This is my favorite part," Matteo howls. "You crazy idiota. Shit belongs on TikTok. I gotta find my memory stick."

Dave shakes the bottle at the ceiling. Little green pills geyser all over the room. He's shouting something. Matteo was right. It's unintelligible nonsense. The word *elephant* is definitely there.

"You ever see that one chick who records her sleepwalking episodes?" Matteo asks, scouring the desk for a thumb drive. "There's this one where she sleepwalks to the fridge in her footie pajamas— footie pajamas!—and collects all of her beers, then goes outside and throws them all over the lawn. Whole time she's narrating. Like she's Richard Atten-bro or some shit."

"David."

Matteo glances at Dave. "What's that?"

"Richard Atten*borough* was the crazy billionaire from *Jurassic Park*. And *David* Attenborough is the voice of the nature docu— Who gives a shit, Matteo? Help me find my pills."

"Ew, bro, you don't want those pills. Hank walks his nasty boots on this floor. Besides, you don't seem to have any problem sleeping. What do you need them for?"

*You don't know the half of it.*

Dave spots one of the pills on the chair cushion and scoops it up. Matteo looks on in horror as Dave blows lightly on the green capsule, then dry-swallows it.

"Man, Hank's meaty *ass* is parked there all day."

"You're not going to help me, are you?"

"How much of that shit are you taking? They aren't Tic Tacs, bro."

"Yeah, and what do you care? Long as you get more snaps for your Instagram."

Matteo clutches his pearls. "I care, *David*, because I can't get you laid tonight if you're slack-jawed and glazed over." He spots a pill and covers it with his boot. "Don't take any more. In fact, cough up the one you already—"

"Move your foot."

"I don't think so."

Dave grips Matteo's ankle. "Lift up, asshole."

Matteo leans forward, grinding the pill into the thin office carpet.

"Goddammit." Dave falls back on his knees. "I don't need to get *laid*. I need *sleep*. And I don't need a fucking *mother*."

"What you *need* is someone to sleep *with*," Matteo corrects. "I believe I can help with that."

Dave plucks a pill from beneath the desk chair, then pops it into his mouth defiantly.

"You're an animal," Matteo says, watching as Dave chews the pill. "Yo, that rich fucker's party is tonight. And we're going, even if I have to drag you around like *Weekdays with Barney*—"

"*Weekend at Bernie's*, you lunkhead."

"And I'm going to hook you up with the first chick I see. She'll be blisteringly hot, and really into—" Matteo frowns, looks Dave up and down. "—guys with bandages. With frog voice. Who likes . . . elephants. Fuck, are you ever not giving me much to work with."

Dave inspects the pill bottle. A few loose pills rattle around inside. He drops the handful he's found on the floor in with them.

"Look, you go," Dave says. "I'll finish out the shift. I'll cover for you, even."

"Nobody's even gonna know we *left*," Matteo argues. "Ain't like anyone ever watches the footage." He waggles the USB stick. "At least not *most* of it."

"Hand it over."

"You know what you are? You're a stick, David Torres. A skinny little stick in the funky-ass mud." Matteo closes his fingers around the USB stick. "I'll make you a deal: You come to the party with me, and when you wake up in the morning, you'll be so thoroughly fucked you won't care when this pops up on YouTube."

"I come with, you give me the stick."

"Or that."

Dave sighs. "Fuck you. Fine."

"Right on." Matteo turns to the security camera, thrusts his hips as elegantly as possible, and waves both middle fingers like he's guiding a plane to the tarmac. "Yo, Daxalab! Fourth of July, mofos. We is out!"

2

In Matteo's Camaro, Dave rests his head on the window and closes his eyes.

"Yo, no, dude. Two things," Matteo says. "One, you're gonna get blood on my window. I just had this sweet honey detailed. Two, wake the fuck up!"

"I'm *tired*. I just want to lie down—"

"Nope."

"—and sleep until next July Fourth."

Matteo pats the wheel. "This car? This car's on a rail, and that rail goes only one place: rich motherfucker's party." He reverses out of the parking space, even though the whole lot is empty.

"Look. I get it. *Katie* might be there. So what? Girl did you dirty, ghosted your ass. Welcome to the real world. Anyway, it's been three weeks. Tonight, you'll find some fresh thing, and you'll forget all about her."

"She didn't ghost me. She just needed—"

"Space." Matteo scoffs. "That's what they all say. Right before they ghost your ass."

"It isn't like that." Dave pushes his features around, trying to wake himself up. "I'm happy to give her space when she needs—"

"It's a *breakup*, Dave. You're not *giving* her space. She *made* it. She took it. She threw your clueless ass overboard."

"Whatever, man. Just take me home."

"I ever tell you about my buddy Spinks?"

"Spinks."

"Like the pharaohs."

"You mean Sphinx."

"*That's what I said*," Matteo insists. "Spinks got the PTSD, my friend. Combat flavor, worst you can get, and in a hella bad way. But what did he do? He didn't lay down and take it. He came home, came right to my door, said, 'Matteo, do me right,' and you know what I did? Took him out, bro. Introduced him to this girl, Sonya. You know what?"

"He's magically fine now."

"Motherfucker got some booty. He's *fine* now." Matteo punches Dave's thigh. "That's you in twelve hours."

"Ouch." Dave rubs his leg. "I don't think you know anything about PTSD. Don't hit me again."

"Barber Elephant," Matteo singsongs. "Don't murder me in my little green suit."

"Babar wore the suit. You're wearing your security uniform. Girls love the rent-a-cop vibe."

"Barber Elephant, you're such a downer," Matteo trills. "Barber Elephant, you're bumming me out."

# 3

*Ooh-wee, my stomach's grumbling. Hey, Dina! How about some hot dogs here in the studio, huh? I'll have one Chicago-style. With the pickles. Hey! That's right. If you're just tuning in, I and all of your friends here at KPWG are celebrating this nation's independence all night long, and you're invited! Thanks for sticking it out with me, your ol' pal Late Night Larry, as we keep this shindig humming.*

"This guy's a joke," Dave grumbles. "I can't believe you listen to this."

"Yo, Larry's a dork, yeah, but he's cool. Sometimes he has this ex-navy guy who calls in, rants about all sorts of conspiracy shit. Dude is legit crazy."

"What kind of conspiracies?"

"Like how Edwards AFB is built on top of an alien city."

"Oh, you mean for real crazy," Dave says. "Alien city. Jesus."

Matteo takes a corner too fast in the Camaro, throwing Dave hard against the passenger door. "Yo, you like that? Little drifting action?"

"I don't think you know what drifting is," Dave complains.

"Shit, bro, this baby *glides*."

Dave slides down in the seat. The throbbing in his skull has abated, but the sleeping pills aren't working. The last few months have been a perfect storm: not only are the nightmares getting worse, but he's also developed a serious tolerance to the one thing that helps him sleep. Maybe Matteo's right. He just needs to move his legs.

*We're coming up on 4:15 a.m. here, and it just occurs to me it's a little early for hot dogs. What's that, Ern? It's*

*never too early for hot dogs? Is there such a thing as a*
*breakfast hot dog? I could go for a . . .*

Matteo swings the Camaro up the steep driveway of a three-story mission-style house.

"Shit. Driveway parking. Not a good sign."

Party lights are strung from the roof to the hedge surrounding the property, illuminating a perfectly coiffed lawn strewn with crumpled red cups, a single lonely flip-flop, a forgotten purse, an overturned keg. Music swells from open windows, but there isn't a soul in sight.

"I knew we should've bailed on Dax earlier," Matteo says, yanking the hand brake. As they get out of the car, he says, "How do you know this rich fool, anyway?"

"Randy? Just high school."

The heavy oak front door stands open. Matteo goes through, but Dave pauses to grind out a still-smoldering cigarette on the welcome mat. Inside, the party is past its sell-by date. In the sunken living room, a scrawny guy with a pile of dreads tucked into a beaded cap is passed out, still bent over a cloudy bong. Scrabbling sounds come from the kitchen, but when they investigate, they find only a slender Dalmatian licking the crusty dishes in an open dishwasher.

"Well, this is a bust," Matteo grumbles.

"Snap! Dave Torres in the house, y'alls!"

Dave and Matteo turn toward the voice and find Abbott and Costello leaning on a wet bar. The short, wide one holds his arms out, grinning broadly. The tall, angular one regards them coolly.

"You know these clowns?" Matteo stage-whispers.

"Unfortunately." Dave lifts a hand half-heartedly. "Connor. What's up?"

Connor and the stringy guy wander over.

"You missed a hell of a hoedown, my man," Connor says,

cradling an open bottle of Don Julio. He holds his free fist out for a bump, but Dave leaves him hanging. "Whatever, homes. You missed Rands, you know. Lightweight bitch is already asleep."

*Homes?* Matteo mouths to Dave.

Dave shrugs.

"Beers in the fridge," Connor says, and Matteo excuses himself to scrounge up drinks. When he returns, he knocks two bottles open against the counter and passes one to Dave.

"This is my homey Gus from Huntington Beach," Connor goes on. "Say sup, Gus."

"Sup," Gus says, arms folded.

"Gus from Huntington," Matteo says, regarding the man skeptically. "So how do you two know Dave?"

"Man, it's been a *minute* since high school," Connor says, ignoring Matteo. "You livin'? You workin'?" He looks Dave up and down, noticing the uniform. "Torres," he reads from Dave's badge. "Leon," he reads from Matteo's. His eyes narrow. "You gentlemen cops now?"

"They rent-a-cops," Gus offers. "No offense."

"Night watchmen." Dave shrugs. "It's a paycheck."

Connor nods sagely. "Respect, homes. Can't be easy, with your disability and all." He turns to Gus. "See, my man Dave here suffers from . . . from . . ." He snaps his fingers, the word out of reach. "What'd you call it again? I want to say, like, 'crazy sleep,' but that ain't PC, right?"

"Parasomnia," Dave answers.

"Parsomonia, right, right." To Gus, Connor explains, "In high school, man, this guy was a *freak*. This one time, freshman year, I think, we had a—"

"Nobody needs to hear this story, Connor."

"Whoa, it's cool, it's cool," Connor says, palms raised. But he continues anyway. "We had this all-night rager—"

"It was a sleepover."

"We were watching some movie. What movie was it we were watchin'?"

"Wasn't a movie," Dave says flatly. "It was Noah's 'Best of *Saturday Night Live*' tapes."

Gus's eyebrows rise appreciatively. "What era we talkin' here? Hartman? Lovitz?"

"It don't matter what era, you fuckin' nerd," Connor says.

"I'm just saying, the original cast years are the only good ones." Gus nods, totally mellow. "Belushi is God."

"Point is, *Gus*, we all wake up in the middle of the night because *this* fool"—Connor whacks Dave's chest with the back of his hand—"pissed his sleeping bag, then started screaming and bashing his head on the floor."

"You want me to shut this pencil-dick up?" Matteo glances at Dave. "It would be my pleasure."

"Whoa, now, Officer Leon. We just reminiscing." Then Connor's face shifts, and he turns to Dave, eyes bright. "Hey! You and Katie, right? Man, I heard something about how that went down. Sorry, homes. She was here, you know, couple hours ago."

"Was Katie the one doing body shots?" Gus asks. "Right on that table over th—"

"No, dumb shit. Doesn't matter. Katie's the pretty one." Connor holds a hand above his own head. "Real tall. Solid junk in the tr—"

"The junkie?" Gus clarifies.

Dave takes a sudden step into Gus's airspace. "Say it again. Call her that again."

Matteo tightens like a spring beside him.

"Yo, what?" Connor cries. "Whoa, homes. Whoa, we all comrades here. See?" He slides a hand between Dave and Gus. "Chill, yo. You don't want to piss yours—"

Matteo stumbles unconvincingly, splashing his beer on Connor.

"Oh shit, *homes*," Matteo says. He scoops up a pile of damp party napkins and dabs forcefully at Connor's wrinkled Kurt Cobain sweater. "Shit, homes, is this angora?"

"Fuckin'—" Connor takes a halting step backward.

"Now, Chevy Chase, he could fall like a pro," Gus observes, eyes glassy. "This guy, he telegraphed his fall. That shit was weak, bro."

"I am *so* sorry," Matteo bubbles. "I swear, Connor, I did not mean to do that. I have this condition, see, where anytime I'm close to a *total douchebag*, I burn real hot, see—"

Startling himself as much as everyone, Connor plants one foot and shoves Matteo, hard. Dave feels all of Matteo's coiled energy unwind and instinctively takes a step back. Gus does the same, taking the Don Julio from Connor and hugging it to his chest.

"It's like that, huh?" Matteo says. "We going, fool?"

"Homes, I will motherfuckin' *merc* you—" Connor's voice cracks. He clears his throat. "Fuckin' *merc*, homes."

"Oh, we going," Matteo says, passing his beer to Dave. "Let's go, you silly-ass clown *bitch*."

Connor lunges. Matteo steps aside, captures Connor in a half nelson. "You're gonna cool it, yeah?" he says right in Connor's ear. "Gus, you want to tell your boy to cool his punk ass?"

"Cool your punk," Gus deadpans. "Ass. Your punk ass."

Connor struggles, but Matteo keeps him in a tight lock. Until Connor manages to get a foot onto the wall, then the other. He pistons backward, driving both men out of the dining room and into the living room.

The sunken living room.

They hit the floor and separate, both wheezing.

"Matteo, man," Dave says, "let's just go, all right?"

Connor pushes upright first. "Ooh, did Officer Leon get a boo-boo?"

Matteo rolls over, then springs at Connor like a receiver coming off the line. The two of them crash into the L-shaped leather couch, which scrapes shrilly across the terra-cotta tile.

On the sofa, the unconscious guy in the beaded hat pitches forward. Dave leaps, but he's too late. The bong hits the floor first, exploding with a watery bang. Couch guy follows, plunging face-first into broken glass. He doesn't put up his hands to break his fall; his nose hits the tile with an awful crunch. The guy lies prone and bleeding, unmoving.

Matteo shoves Connor away. While Matteo vaults the couch, Connor pushes his stringy hair back and smooths his sweater, breathing hard.

"Bro, you all right?" Matteo asks, sliding through shattered glass to scoop the guy up and roll him onto his back. "You hear me?"

Time downshifts for Dave. Connor backs away from the scene in slo-mo; Matteo administers first aid in a field of broken glass for the second time that night. What the hell was he thinking, letting Matteo talk him into a party? He should be home, staring at the ceiling, trying to sleep. Instead, he's here, in some yuppie's house, with its twenty-thousand-dollar sofa, with its floor-to-ceiling windows, with its rare art—

Dave's eyes fall on a painting just behind Matteo. A jungle scene, the undergrowth parting to reveal a hidden glade, warm with sunlight. Two small figures, glowing in the glare, stretch their arms out to something large and ominous looming in the shadow of vines and twisted kapok trees.

Elephant.

*Elephant.*

*Beware the eleph—*

"Dave, this guy isn't breathing!" Matteo shouts, and the world snaps to speed again.

"I didn't do shit," Connor says, now behind Dave.

"What did he take?" Dave asks, turning around.

"Nothin', homes. Just—" Connor shoots a frantic look at Gus. "Just weed, right?"

"Just grocery-store weed," Guys says, unruffled.

"Just harmless fuckin' weed," Connor echoes. "I'm not this homes's keeper, homes."

Matteo rolls the stranger over. "What's his name?"

"He's a stranger to me," Gus says, patting his pockets. He finds a lighter, then looks around for a cigarette.

"Name!" Matteo repeats. "Douchebag, his name!"

Connor stutters, "Uh—To-Tony. It's Tony."

"Tony! Hey, yo, Tony, you with me?" Matteo brushes glass from Tony's pallid face. Wincing, he tugs a shard out of Tony's lip. Blood trickles down the man's chin.

"Someone needs to call 911," Dave says.

"One. Two. Three," Matteo counts, beginning chest compressions. Dave watches as Matteo delivers thirty sharp presses, then leans in and breathes into Tony's slack mouth. He starts again: "One. Two. Three . . ."

Connor and Gus exchange a look. Connor edges back a step.

"Don't do it," Dave warns, putting down the beers. He fumbles for his phone, nearly drops it, then hits the Emergency icon. To Connor, he says, "Bitch, at least go get Randy."

Matteo starts counting out compressions again.

"He's *asleep*, Dave," Connor protests. "That would be *so* rude."

Dave listens to the phone a second, then swears. "911 is fucking busy!"

"That," Gus says, lighted half cigarette dangling from his lips, "is not normal."

"No, Gus, it most certainly *isn't* normal," Dave snaps.

"Try again," Matteo says, breathlessly compressing Tony's chest.

Dave dials again, switches the phone to speaker. All sound drains out of the living room for a moment. Then the pulse of a busy signal leaks from the phone.

"Connor!" Dave yells. "Randy! Wake him up!"

"Bro, let the dude chill. He threw a bangin' party. He deserves a good night's sleep. Anyway, he's with Beck."

"Motherfuck—Where is he? Show me!"

Connor shrugs, then points at the staircase in the foyer. "I don't know what room, though. Biggest one, probs."

"Doors are generally the same size," Gus observes. "A door isn't larger or smaller based on room size." To Dave, he says, "You'll have to *open* each door to see if the room on the other side is big or little."

"Shut the fuck up, Gus." To Matteo, Dave says, "Be right back, I'm going for help." He sprints up the stairs, shouting Randy's name.

Matteo glances up from his work to see Connor backing away. "Bitch, where're you going?"

"My man here has a misdemeanor," Gus says. "Can't really be hanging around when the fuzz arrives. We regret we have to leave, but this was a fine party, Officer." He snaps a laconic salute. "We do appreciate the invitation."

"Yo!" Matteo bellows, watching Connor and Gus disappear through the back door. "Fucking pendejos!"

# 4

Dave has no luck locating Randy on the second floor. He climbs to the third, which reveals itself to be a warren of heavy oak doors and iron hinges. *Feels like a goddamn luxury hotel, not someone's house*, Dave thinks, throwing open door after door. Several empty bedrooms, a library, a home theater, and four bathrooms later, he finds a bedroom that's actually occupied.

"Randy?" Dave calls into the darkness. "I'm coming in, man."

He throws a light switch, then startles at the sight of his own reflection in a glossy bank of windows.

*Keep it together, Dave.*

"Hey, it's real shitty of me to wake you, I know, but we've got a crisis downstairs," Dave says loudly.

In the center of the room is a large four-poster bed. Through the gauzy canopy, Dave sees two people, seemingly undisturbed by the blazing lights, cuddled close beneath the sheets.

"Randy?" he repeats.

Facing Dave is Becka, Randy's longtime girlfriend: eyes closed, lips parted, a smear of pale lipstick on the bone-white pillowcase. Behind her, one arm loosely draped over her waist, is Randy, face buried in Becka's dark hair.

Dave tries to ignore the twinge in his chest. He used to sleep just like this with Katie, the smell of her lavender shampoo guiding him into sleep. He always slept better at her apartment, in her bed; it was a world where his nightmares didn't exist.

Until they did.

"Yo, Randy," Dave says again. "You really gotta get up, man. It's Dave."

He reaches through a part in the canopy and shakes Randy's shoulder.

Randy's skin is cool and firm.

"Randy?" Dave shakes Randy again. "Man, don't play. Wake up."

# 5

Matteo is slumped on the couch, cradling a fresh beer, when Dave returns. He looks up, shakes his head. "This guy, Tony, he's . . ."

"Dead," Dave finishes. He sniffs the air. "Do you smell anything? Something funny?"

"That Connor prick smelled like my nephew." Matteo wrinkles his nose. "He's thirteen months old. He's got so much skin it folds up. Like the Michigan Man."

"Michelin," Dave corrects absently. He trails his fingers across the couch, still sniffing.

"You gotta, like, clean inside those folds, you know. Little kids grow this funky mold in there. My sister, she calls it 'neck cheese.'" Matteo shudders. "Shit *reeks*. Connor smelled like neck cheese. Fuckin' smell's on me now, too."

"You smell gas?"

"The hell you mean, gas?"

"I mean Tony," Dave says. He pulls his shirt over his nose and mouth. "Tony's dead, you said. And upstairs . . ."

"What's upstairs?"

"I'm saying maybe there's a gas leak or—"

"Wait, wait, whoa." Matteo twists around on the couch, sloshing beer onto the leather. "You're saying they're—?"

"That's what I'm saying."

Matteo lunges off the sofa and disappears into the guest bathroom. Dave can hear him banging open cabinet doors.

"These goddamn animals don't have any hand towels!" Matteo calls out.

"Use your shirt."

Matteo comes out of the bathroom, the neck of his undershirt pulled over his face. "What do we do now? Try 911 again?"

"Your turn."

Matteo dials with his free hand while Dave searches the first floor. Dave finds what he's looking for in a second living room, behind an overturned Eames lounger.

"Still busy!" Matteo shouts from the other room.

Dave drags a parachute-sized curtain to the sunken living room.

"Help me get him on this," he says, unfurling the fabric on the stained carpet.

"Fuck no." Matteo shakes his head. "I am *not* burying these people. In their own curtains? That's cold—"

"We're not burying anybody, you hillbilly," Dave says. "If 911 won't send someone here, we'll deliver the bodies to them."

Matteo's eyes widen. "Motherfucker, my car is not a hearse."

"Grab his feet," Dave says, lacing his arms through Tony's armpits.

"I just had her detailed, man!"

# 6

"Hey, it's Katie. Maybe I'll call you back."

Wind shears over the Camaro's open windows. Dave can barely hear the tone when it sounds. "Katie!" he cries. "Katie, Katie, hey, listen—Um, it's me. Listen, listen. Did you take any-thing at the party tonight? I swear I'm not trying to be your—Just—Look, if you did, call 911. Right now. I'm not trying to scare you, but—"

"It's busy, remember?" Matteo interjects.

"Fuck. Right. Um—Look, just call me," Dave goes on. "We were just there. Bad shit went down, Katie. I don't know wh—"

"Dave thinks the drugs were laced with something!" Matteo yells.

"Just call me back. Please. *Please.*"

The three curtain-wrapped bodies shift in the back seat as Matteo takes a curve too fast. Someone's skull *thwacks* against the passenger window.

"Swear to God, Dave, if I have to scrub blood out of my seats—"

"Just drive!"

"Roger that, Drill Ser*geant*! Whatever you say, *sir*!"

"I'm calling her again," Dave says, tapping the screen. He grabs the dash as Matteo whips through another turn. "Pick up, honey—come on, baby. Pick up, pick up!"

# 7

The red letters of the ER sign slide across the Camaro's windshield. The tires smoke as Matteo skids to a stop in the ambulance lane. Air escapes one of the passengers in a hollow gurgle.

"They sound like my toilet after my upstairs neighbor takes a big—"

"Matteo. Let's get them out of here, yeah?"

But Matteo's bent over the wheel, squinting at the hospital doors. "Something's off here, bro."

"Yeah, we've got three—"

*BEEEEP!* Matteo leans on the horn.

"Cool it!"

Dave throws open his door, but Matteo puts a hand on his arm.

"Something's off," he repeats. "When have you ever seen a hospital this . . . chill? Look around, man."

Dave climbs out of his seat into the dawn air. There's no activity on the sidewalks. He can't see anyone moving around inside the lighted building.

"It's early?" he offers.

"Not one patient waiting for help? Not one nurse grabbing a smoke? Man, I've *been* to this ER before. It's never a ghost town." He lays on the horn: *BEEEEEEEEEEEEEEEEEP!*

"Knock that shit off."

"Exactly. Someone should be running out here to tell me to cut that shit out. Shit's sick here, man. This is not good."

Dave bends back into the car and wrestles with the passenger seat. "Then fucking help me get them out of the car and inside," he grunts. "I gotta check on Katie." The seat doesn't release. "The hell's wrong with your car?"

"Go easy, bro, she's sensitive," Matteo warns.

# 8

Matteo's right, Dave notices right away. The lobby of the emergency room is deserted. Nobody's manning the admittance desk. On every wall, strobes flash in sync, giving the whole room a horror-movie vibe.

Matteo twists his hair in his fists. "Shit's *fucked*, man. I'm not staying here."

"Wait," Dave says.

"Hey! A little help out here?" Matteo yells, pounding his palm on the admittance counter. He shoves off and paces back and forth, venturing near a pair of automatic doors. Printed on the glass is a warning:

SURGERY WING

NO ADMITTANCE

HOSPITAL PERSONNEL ONLY

Matteo takes a big step forward. The doors hiss open. The corridor yawns ahead of him, receding into the distance like a bottomless pit.

"Help!" Matteo hollers, his voice bouncing off the walls. "Need some help down here!"

"Shh," Dave says. "You hear that?"

Matteo cocks his head. "Someone's crying. Let's go."

"Dude, the sign."

"Yeah, something tells me ain't no security waiting to throw us out," Matteo says. "Come on. I want to get those people out of my car as much as you do."

They head into the corridor. Along the way, they pass little half rooms to the right and left. Dave pauses in front of one, then pulls back its curtain.

There's someone in the bed. A white sheet has been drawn over their face.

"Oh, fuck me," Matteo breathes. He roots himself to the floor and watches as Dave throws back curtain after curtain. Almost every bed contains a dead body.

"Matteo," Dave breathes. "I think you were right. Something really bad's going down."

# 9

They find the source of the sobs deeper in the corridor and around a corner, where the hallway opens up into a cluttered nurses' station. A stout middle-aged woman is bent over the desk, face buried in her hands, shoulders shaking.

"Ma'am," Dave says gently. "Can you help us—?"

*"Yo, what the fuck is happening here?"* Matteo demands shakily.

The nurse doesn't look up. It's as though she doesn't hear them at all.

Matteo leans over the desk. "Lady, come on, you gotta—"

"Doesn't matter." Dave puts his hand flat against Matteo's chest. "Listen."

Shouts echo from deeper in the building.

Matteo snaps into motion, and Dave trots in his wake. At the end of another hallway, Matteo shoulders through a pair of swinging double doors, then pulls up short. Dave nearly collides with him, then stops when he sees what Matteo's found.

A large room, lined with storage bins and shelves, has been transformed into a morgue. Shoved along the west wall are gurneys bearing zippered white bags. Human-sized bags, arranged haphazardly, as though they were rolled into the room and released to drift where they may.

Which is exactly what happens next: An orderly in a white

smock bangs into the room through an adjacent door, back first, then drags a fresh gurney into the room, pivots, and releases it, sending it spinning across the floor. It thumps into another gurney, and both roll in separate directions. The orderly, not pausing to admire his handiwork, disappears through the door again.

Dave exchanges a look with Matteo.

They follow.

In the next room they find a nurse frantically working a respirator unit, trying to resuscitate a gray-skinned man in a baseball cap. Across the room, a mustached doctor in a knotted blue surgeon's cap, a mask hanging uselessly around his neck, is backed against the wall by a nurse in navy scrubs. She thrusts her finger against his chest; his hands go up reflexively, in protest. She's yelling something about backup staff.

"I'm having flashbacks." Matteo stares blankly at the chaotic scene. "Dios mío." He crosses himself.

"Excuse me," Dave says loudly, and when nobody looks up, Dave waves his arms. "Hey! Can we get a little help over here? Anyone?"

Navy Scrubs turns toward Dave. The surgeon, seeing an opportunity, yanks the cap from his head and slides out of the room.

"I don't know how you got back here, but you can't be here," Scrubs says. "Out."

"No, you don't understand, we've got—"

"Out," she repeats. "I'm serious. You can't be back here. Off you go." She shoos them toward an exit.

"What happened here?" Matteo asks. His skin has drained of color.

"Come with me," Scrubs says again, firmly. "Out. Out."

Dave scans her uniform, spots her name tag. "Look. Linda? Linda, we have an emergency. This is an ER still, right?"

Linda sighs. She loops her hair in her fist and knots it loosely behind her head. "Yes, of course it is," she begins, but then she notices Matteo sag and lunges, getting an arm behind him. "Whoa, there. All right, buddy, let's—"

"He said something about flashbacks," Dave offers. "He just needs some water. Or coffee. It's been a—"

"A long night," Linda finishes. "Yeah, tell me about it." She guides Matteo out of the room, and Dave falls in behind them. To Matteo, she says, "All right, sir, hang tight there."

She leads them back to the nurses' station, then drops Matteo into a spare wheelchair. "Sit. There you go." Then Linda turns to the desk and says, "Britney, come over here, would you?"

The weeping woman wipes her eyes, then pumps sanitizer onto her palms and wrings them out. She trots over listlessly.

"Brit, this is—" Linda looks at Dave for help.

"His name's Matteo."

"Brit, Matteo. He needs your help right now."

"Copy," Britney says. She sniffles once, draws a deep breath, and seems to transform in front of Dave's eyes. Her eyes are still red, but her shoulders square, and her voice takes on that familiar caregiver's tone. "Matteo? Hi, there. I'm Britney. Let's have a look at you, huh?"

Satisfied, Linda takes Dave by the elbow and walks him a few feet away. "All right," she says. "Let's hear it. What are you and your friend doing in an off-limits area?"

Dave maps the seriousness in her expression and says, "It's easier if I show you. Come with me? Please."

10

Dave sits on the curb, listening once again to Katie's voice mail greeting. He hangs up and shoves his phone back into his pocket.

Linda studies the shrouded bodies in the back seat. "Why are they wrapped in a—? What is that, a duvet?"

"A very expensive drapery."

"And you found them. Like this."

Dave's head suddenly weighs sixty pounds. A powerful yawn rises from his belly. He rubs his eyes with the heel of his palm, drops his chin to his chest.

"Sir." Linda snaps her fingers twice at him.

"I'm up. I'm—What?"

"I said, you just found them this way?"

"Well, not in the car," Dave answers, squinching his eyes tight and blinking hard to clear the cobwebs. "And not in the curtain. But . . . dead? Yes. They were all dead."

Linda tugs a corner of one body's wrapping. "There's blood on this."

"It's a really long story."

"You understand we'll have to notify the authorities, yes?" She turns away from the bodies. "That's nonnegotiable. They'll want to ask you and your friend questions, and they'll probably want more detail than you just gave me." She runs her fingers through her hair, pulls the knot free, re-lashes it in place. "If they answer, that is."

"It'd be a relief," Dave says. "We tried already—911."

"Circuits down?"

"Busy signal."

"Same thing," Linda says. She pats her scrubs, then frowns. "Shit. Do you have a cigarette?"

"Don't smoke," Dave says. "You didn't ask me about the long story."

"It's been a very long night," Linda says, dropping her hands into her waist pockets and leaning against the Camaro. "Forget it. Life of an ER nurse. Your friend . . ."

"He's in shock, right?"

"That's not exactly how shock works. You know him well?"

"We work together."

"So, that's a—?"

"A yes. I guess."

"You said 'flashback' before. Did he—?"

"Serve? He did. I don't know much about it. Air force, I think?"

"That helps," Linda says. She pushes off the car. "I need to let Brit know."

"You think he'll be okay?"

"What I think is you ought to find a seat in the lobby," she says. "You look pretty wrecked yourself. Maybe grab a little shut-eye if you can. I'll come find you when your friend's squared away."

"I just leave . . . *them*?" Dave nods at the car. "I mean, car's in the ambulance lane. You didn't even say anything."

Linda releases a weary sigh. "What was your name?"

"David. Dave. Torres."

"Dave Torres," she says gently, "my team is . . . understaffed tonight. We've lost a few patients we didn't plan to lose."

"Looked like more than a few. What I saw in there . . . What happened?"

"I shouldn't have said anything. Listen, you look like you're about to fall over."

Linda puts her hand on Dave's back and steers him toward the sliding doors. He feels exhaustion in every step as he crosses the room; he could crumple and doze right here in the middle of the floor.

The strobes pulse like a nightclub.

"I'll turn those off," Linda says. "Grab a chair against that wall. They're softest, I hear. I'll come find you soon."

II

"Dad, I told you: You have to stay off the leg. Dr. Washington was very clear about that. No walking on your own, not yet."

Dave blinks in surprise. He breaks away from the lobby TV and its futuristic vacuum cleaner infomercial. While he's been spacing out, the lobby has gained a few new guests: a young woman wearing a T-shirt that reads WE ALL DESERVE LOVE!!! sits beside an old man with wispy white hair and skin like baked leather.

The old man wears an elaborate mechanical brace on his left knee. The woman—his daughter? Dave wonders—wears a worn-down expression not unlike Dave's own.

The old guy struggles to stand up, reaching with bony fingers for his walker. The woman tugs him down again, with not much effort. The guy looks as if he weighs eighty pounds, Dave realizes.

The woman notices Dave watching. "He doesn't like hospitals," she offers with a shrug.

"I don't trust anyone who does," Dave says.

Perhaps noticing that his daughter is distracted, the old guy lunges again for his walker.

"All right, Daddy, all right!" The woman reaches into her purse, producing a bronzed flask. "I hope you don't mind," she says to Dave. "It's the only thing that helps him relax."

"As long as you offer us some," Matteo says, shuffling into the lobby on Britney's arm.

Dave leaps up. "You're—?"

"Freshly hydrated?" Matteo asks. "Full of fluids? Why, yes, Dave. Yes, I am." He waves a sheet of paper. "I also have an appointment to see someone named Dr. Corningbaumerstein on Tuesday." His brow wrinkles as he inspects the paper again. "No. Corning-Baumerstein."

"Did you actually want—?" the young woman asks, still holding out the flask.

"Keep it for your old man," Dave says. "My friend doesn't need it right now."

Britney says, "He definitely does not. I, however . . ." She notices the woman's expression change. "All right. Kidding, kidding. I'm on duty. Just don't let anyone else see that, all right?" To Matteo, she says, "A couple Advil when you get home, a couple more when you wake up. Get some good rest."

Matteo thanks Britney, who disappears into the personnel corridor again.

The young woman passes the flask to her father. "Only if you agree to stay put," she says. "I just need to close my eyes for two godforsaken minutes . . ."

## 12

Back in the storage room, Britney wrestles with the traffic jam of gurneys, arranging them as neatly as she can to make space for more. Just in time, the orderly returns, pushing a new one.

"No," Britney says, a hand over her heart. "That's not—?"

The orderly reads his clipboard. "Arjun Chakrabarti."

"Oh, damn it. Poor Mr. Chakrabarti." Britney's eyes well up. "He was just so sweet."

"Please don't start crying again," the orderly says.

Across the room, Linda yanks her gloves off, balls them up, and sinks them in a waste bin. She turns to help Britney, but movement catches her eye. Dr. Gordon emerges from the staff corridor, tugging his windbreaker on over street clothes.

"Brit," Linda says, "I'll be right back."

She follows Gordon around a corner.

"Not a word," Dr. Gordon says over his shoulder, not stopping.

"You're not *leaving*," Linda demands.

"I made an announcement," Gordon says, turning around. He smooths his mustache with his thumbs, something Linda's noticed he does when distressed. "I made an announcement. You'd have heard it if you hadn't disappeared."

"I was outside with that patient's friend," she says. "You wouldn't believe what's in the back seat of their—"

"I've dismissed everyone," Gordon interrupts. "You should head home, too."

"Wait, you—? What the hell, Jack?"

"I've ordered the staff," Gordon repeats more slowly, "to go home."

"In the middle of a Level One MCI. You're insane. Are you *insane*?"

"Nobody's said anything about a mass casualty incident, Linda, Jesus."

"That pile of bodies back there says otherwise, *Jack*." Linda's fists ball against her hips. "What else *could* it be? Those two guys we just helped? There are dead people in their back seat. From *outside* the hospital."

"Enough!" Gordon kicks the floor, leaving a short black scuff mark. "We don't know anything. And nobody's coming to help. I can't get Dr. Laghari on the phone, or anyone from the board, for that matter. The emergency lines are all down. Rose has been back there, trying them all night. Every time, same thing: No answer. Busy signals. Police, fire department. The goddamned CDC. The FBI. Nothing."

"Well, shit, Jack, it sure sounds like an MCI to me."

"Go home, Linda," Gordon repeats. He zips his windbreaker, smooths his hair, and turns on his heel. "There's nothing we can do."

"Santa Mira is the only hospital in thirty miles, Jack, we can't just—"

"You want to stay, stay." Gordon pauses at the exit. "Rose tried my house, too, okay? Five times. Nobody answered."

"We can't function without a doctor, Jack. We just lost nineteen patients in less than a full shift."

"I'm sorry. I'm going to make sure Jim and the girls are okay." Gordon offers her a weak shrug, then pushes through the door.

"Coward!" Linda screeches after him.

The door falls shut again.

"God fucking *damn* it!" Linda kicks the wall, denting it. "I don't believe this."

"Don't believe what?"

Britney stands at the end of the short hallway, holding Mr. Chakrabarti's clipboard.

"I just—Jack just—" Linda stops and takes a deep, cleansing breath. Then she claps her hands together, as if she's arrived at a decision. "Britney, listen, I—"

"Uh-uh. Don't ask."

"Jack just bailed. He ditched us. Everyone's gone."

"Lin, I've been on since yesterday," Britney says, shaking her head. "*Morning.* I'm a literal zombie right now."

"There's no shift change coming. It's you and me, Brit. That's it. Well, maybe the orderly. What's his name? Paolo?"

"Pietro. No, he's gone, too."

"Of course he is."

"Lin, this is a nightmare. I keep going on autopilot." Her lip quivers. "If I stop for a second and think about what's happened tonight—I just can't. I can't."

Linda turns and shoves through the exit door. When it falls shut behind her, she thrusts her fists toward the ground and screams. No words, just emotion.

At the horizon, the sky has imperceptibly begun to lighten. Linda stays where she is until her breathing is controlled. Then she turns and goes back inside.

Britney is still there.

"Look," Brit says. "Ten minutes. Give me a quick ten, let me close my eyes, splash my face—"

Linda embraces the older nurse. "Thank you. Oh God, thank you, thank you, Britney."

"Ten minutes," Britney repeats, words muffled by Linda's hair.

"Take twenty," Linda says. "We've got this, right?"

"We've got this. I hope."

## 13

"Know what I hate?"

"Are we talking everyday hate, or epic, bring-the-universe-to-its-knees hate?"

"The latter," Matteo says.

"Spiders. Climate change."

"I hate—"

"Little balls of lint in your socks. Splinters."

"I hate when someone offers you a drink," Matteo says emphatically, "and someone *else* declines it for you."

"Matteo."

"It's called consent, bro."

"It was probably Rutgers Mill in that flask, man. I saved you."

Matteo chews his lip thoughtfully. "Yeah. Old guys do love the cheap shit. Why is that, you think?" Then he stops. "Fuck. Why are we still here?"

"Because your hearse needs unloading. Linda's coming back to help."

"Linda?"

"The other nurse. The boss lady one."

"Oh." Matteo's eyebrows go up. "The scary one."

"The lady was right about the whiskey," Dave says, nodding toward the pair. The old man's chin is dipped to his chest. A string of spittle hangs from his lip. "Knocked the old dude right out."

"She's out cold, too. Bet you wish you could sleep like her. Wherever you're at, just—*bam*—asleep."

"It's a gift I don't have."

"I can see the flask from here."

"Don't do it. You just got jacked up on electrolytes or whatever."

"But it's right *there*."

"Watch TV, bro," Dave says, giving Matteo's knee a grandfatherly pat.

Matteo watches the infomercial. Ten seconds pass. He says, "Fuck it, I can't take it," and crouch-walks across the lobby.

"Don't do it," Dave warns.

"What if it isn't Rutgers, though?" Matteo whispers back. "It might be Pappy O'Daniel's in there."

"Pappy Van Winkle's," Dave corrects. "Man, don't steal her dad's booze."

Matteo slides the flask out of the woman's half-open purse, keeping his eyes on her and the old man the whole time. He unscrews the flask slowly, then takes a sip. His nose wrinkles, then smooths out again.

*Not bad*, he mouths to Dave.

Dave waves both hands at him: *Shut up.*

Matteo takes a long last swig, then replaces the cap and slides the flask back into the purse. He crawls away, then pauses, a perplexed expression crumpling his brow.

"Whatever you're about to do, don't," Dave mutters to himself.

But Matteo goes up on his knees and waves one hand in front of the woman's face.

*"Matteo!"* Dave warns.

Matteo waves in front of the old guy's face, too. Then, to Dave's horror, he snaps his fingers loudly beside the guy's ears. He claps his palms an inch from the woman's nose.

"Goddammit, Matteo!" Dave says, no longer whispering.

Matteo looks toward Dave, eyes wide. He circles the woman's wrist with his fingers, lifts her arm, then releases it.

It thuds heavily to the seat.

The woman doesn't stir.

"Maldito Cristo!" Matteo exclaims. "Dave!"

Matteo presses two fingers to the woman's neck. Dave leaps up and rushes to help. He repeats the gesture for the old man, whiskers like sandpaper against his hand.

"I got nothing."

"Her, too," Matteo says.

"Fuck me. They were just—She just—"

Matteo scrambles upright. "Help!" he cries out. "Scary Nurse, we need some fucking help out here!" He activates the sliding doors and breaks into a run, shouting as he disappears.

Dave sinks to the floor, looking up at the deceased father and daughter. "I don't understand," he mumbles. To her, he says, "I'm so sorry. You just wanted to sleep, you looked so tir—"

*Tired.*

The woman was exhausted; it had been stamped in the web of lines around her eyes.

Matteo explodes back into the room, Linda on his heels. "Over there!"

Linda takes in the scene, but pauses, gripping Matteo's shoulders. "Listen to me. You've got to sit down. Right here, okay? There you go. If you can't breathe, your head goes between your knees. Understand?"

With Matteo settled, Linda trots over to Dave and takes a knee. She repeats the test Dave and Matteo previously performed, pressing two fingers to the dead pair's necks. Satisfied, she turns to Dave; where he expects to see accusation, he sees only resignation.

"You're not going to ask why there are so many dead people around me tonight?" he says.

"Listen, every single person in this hospital who doesn't have a toe tag has one hell of a body count tonight," Linda says. "No, I'm not going to ask."

Matteo says, "Guys! Oh fuck—They both drank the whiskey! What if it was pois—?" His eyes fly wider. "Dave! Goddammit, Dave, I fucking drank her poison whiskey!"

"Matteo," Linda says, voice patient and warm. She holds one hand at her chest, moving it up, then down. "Breathe. In, out. You see? Head between your knees."

To Dave's surprise, Matteo obeys, still muttering to himself.

Linda slides the flask out of the woman's purse, unscrews it, and sniffs it. "Smells like Rutgers Mill," she says. "It's bad, but it's not poison."

"I knew it," Dave says. He watches Matteo a moment, then says, "Look. I have an idea."

"About?"

"I don't like it. But all five of these people—" He pauses, scrutinizing Linda's eyes, trying to gauge how much she might believe him. He forges on: "They all might have been asleep."

"Everybody sleeps in a waiting room."

"No, check it," Dave says. "Two of those people in my friend's car were in their bed. The other one was—And then these two, they went to sleep, and . . . What if—?"

"No," Linda says. "No. No. No, no—" She lurches to her feet and breaks into a run.

"Stay here," Dave says to Matteo. "I'll be right back."

Matteo's head snaps up. "The fuck you're leaving me with these people," he says.

They chase Linda through the surgery wing, past the nurses' station, through the ad hoc morgue, and into the staff corridor, where Linda elbows through a door marked ON CALL 1.

Just as quickly she bursts back into the hall, running for the next door. Dave pauses to look into ON CALL 1.

"Empty," Matteo says. "What are we looking for?"

Linda throws open ON CALL 2, then freezes. She goes to her knees next to a cot. Dave and Matteo linger in the doorway, watching as Linda shakes the other nurse.

"Brit," she moans. "Come on, honey, open your eyes. We've got a lot to do. I need your help, you promised me."

Linda keeps shaking her.

"Ma'am," Dave says, kneeling next to Britney. He touches her neck, searching for a pulse. He tries again and again while Linda watches.

"She's gone," Linda says. She falls back onto her hands. Eyes damp, she looks at Dave. "We were all that's left. Everyone else is gone."

Matteo turns away from the door, retching.

"Linda," Dave says. "Listen to me a second. All the other patients, the ones we just passed back there . . . What were they doing?" he asks. "When they died tonight. What were they doing? Were they all in their rooms? Watching TV, what?"

Her eyes flash darkly. "It was the middle of the night. What do you think they were doing? They were . . ." Linda trails off, blinking.

"Sleeping," Dave says. "Everyone who died tonight was asleep. Weren't they?"

# Micro-Sleep

## I

The sun breaks over Providence, Rhode Island, like a bomb, detonating in the window of Millie's apartment, throwing a painful glare across her laptop screen.

"Oh, fuck off, sun," she mutters.

She downs the dregs of her coffee, swallowing with it a couple aspirin. Two straight nights of shit sleep has her seeing double: Two cats, staring up at her from a crusty food dish. Two box televisions, which equals four foil-wrapped rabbit ears, four out-of-focus news anchors speaking at her in Klingon. And fourteen coworkers, trapped in little boxes on her screen.

These early weekday meetings, she thinks, will be her end. Up at daybreak to check in with her remote team. She's the only East Coaster among them; the others are scattered around the globe, taking the meeting between making dinner and the kids' bath time, or just before they finally topple into bed themselves.

Millie keeps her laptop's camera covered with a Post-it note. She doesn't like cameras tracking her. It's just a bonus that none of her coworkers can tell if she's paying attention or not.

"Folks, I don't know what to tell you," says the team lead, Martin, a mole-faced man with a whiteboard where his forehead should be. He leans close to his own camera, his face filling the box on Millie's screen. "When we started this week, we had two hundred twenty-three bugs. Somehow we're closing out the week with over three hundred. Why are we even still discussing this?"

"Because it's a holiday weekend," Carolina, somewhere in the central time zone, points out. "Because the last time we had a weeklong crunch, it turned into a month of long hours. Because we know what you're about to say."

"You *are* predictable," says Domhnall, who's dialed in from Dublin. "No offense intended, Marty. Though we don't have the same holiday here, Carolina."

"I can work the weekend," Millie says.

When no one replies to her generous offer, she checks her microphone. Muted. She taps the icon to activate her mic, then says, "I'll do it. Work the weekend, I mean."

"There you have it," says Claudia, who's joined from Sydney. "Millie will save us all."

Millie can't tell if Claudia's being sarcastic or sincere.

Marty's giant mouth turns down at one corner. "Millie, let's you and I sync up offline first."

"I'm just trying to help, asshole," Millie mutters in response.

All the faces on Millie's screen seem to freeze in place. Except Jermaine, who covers his mouth with one hand. Eyes dancing, Jermaine says, "Millie, honey. You're not muted."

"With that," Martin announces, "we're at time. Updates before noon, please. If everyone could give us the room . . . ?" He raises an eyebrow at his camera. "Millie, you stay."

One by one, Millie's coworkers blink out of the meeting. Before long, two Martins are all that is left.

"Millie," they say with one voice. "You may find this conversation . . . less than pleasant."

## 2

Here's what I can say with some certainty. *Something* is happening.

Case in point: WZPE's AM news show usually ends at 8am. Not today. They've basically got the phone lines wide open, and people are calling in by the hundreds. The last caller just sobbed, "They're dead, they're dead, they're dead," and disconnected.

There are TV and radio stations all over the state that just . . . aren't on the air at all.

From my window, if I elevate my chair, I usually have a great view of the mile-long gridlock at the intersection of Monaghan and Wolcott. The traffic lights there aren't even working, but the intersection's just . . . dead. No cars that I've seen.

Usually by now my upstairs neighbor is jazzercising. But the whole building is strangely subdued. I haven't heard a single other person.

Perhaps it's my overactive imagination . . . but I really don't think that's the case.

If you have any information about what might be happening, I'll see you in the comments.

—Posted by Eli Broder, 7/4/25 9:12 a.m.

The blog cross-posts automatically to all his social platforms. It's conceivable some of his audience might respond there, but he'll check for replies in a minute.

Instead, he nudges the joystick on his wheelchair, reversing away from his desk, then makes a 180-degree turn toward the balcony door. He slides it open, then rolls onto the narrow deck.

It's the sort of Boston day he usually loves: overcast, with a smudge of deep gray over the Massachusetts Bay promising rain later in the morning.

Today, though, the gray sky reads menacing, the approaching storm a lumbering threat.

The WZPE anchors carry out to the balcony:

> . . . caution advised for commuters today. Charlie, I don't know if the planets are in retrograde, or God got up on the wrong side of the bed, but it is definitely an off day.
>
> That's an understatement, Helena. Our field reporters are chasing down unconfirmed reports about multiple health and public safety incidents on city transit this morning. We're expecting more details soon.
>
> In the meantime, authorities have strongly encouraged people to consider alternate modes of transportation to their places of business today . . .

A breath of wind stirs the clothes on Mrs. Roderick's line. Aprons and dish towels flutter lightly. It's unusual that she hasn't reeled the laundry in by now, Eli realizes. Especially with the approaching storm. He leans to his left, straining to see through her window. But the light turns the glass opaque, giving him only the reflection of the parking garage across the street.

*Something isn't right at all.*

It reminds him of the holidays, when half of Boston has flown back home, leaving the streets and neighborhoods oddly hollowed out. Those who stay behind, though, always keep the city festive and alive.

Today it's anything but festive. Today feels like a last exhalation before the light leaves the city's eyes.

# 3

"Millie, can you switch on your video, please? This feels like it ought to be a face-to-face conversation."

When she doesn't immediately reply, Martin adds, "Well, suit yourself. Listen, Millie—"

"I apologize for my salty language," Millie says flatly. "It was uncalled-for."

"Well, thanks, I suppose, but—Millie, let's be honest, it's not about the language. I've been called worse by more significant people than you."

"Are you—? Martin, are you firing me?"

Though Millie has no investment in the people with whom she works, the job itself matters a great deal to her. There aren't many remote-work companies lining up to hire a narcoleptic, border-line agoraphobic, socially anxious loner like her. It took two full years of searching to land this gig as a quality assurance engineer, then another six months of walking a wire, trying to learn the gig faster than they could find out she'd never done QA work before.

"I'm not thrilled with your performance," Martin says, strok-ing his nub of a chin. "Your reports lately are full of holes; I've been asking Amelia to validate them for a couple weeks now. And your participation with the team is lacking. Today's a fine example."

"But I just offered to work the—"

"Well, yes. I'll concede you're generous when no one else wants to step up." He releases a pregnant sigh. "What good is that gener-osity, though, if the rest of the team has to re-execute your tests?"

"I'll do better."

Martin's face softens. "Listen, is there something going on I'm not aware of? Anything I can help with?"

Millie's throat tightens; she can feel the episode coming on like a freight train, inevitable and inescapable. Usually she gets the warning a little earlier, but every so often, particularly when she's stressed, they just . . . happen.

Martin's words stretch like taffy. *Miiillllieeee, I caaaaan heelllp iffff youuu lllleettt meeeee—*

She feels suddenly and totally exhausted, which is a bad sign. Over the decades she's learned to identify clues that she's about to crash headlong into sleep, little twitches in her vision or mistakes in her speech. Exhaustion means the episode will be a big—

The desk yanks her face toward it; her eyes flutter shut as she tips forward.

For a moment, there's only quiet, and then there's bedlam:

*Fists hammer the apartment door. FBI, a granite-laced voice roars. You have three seconds to lie down and put your hands behind your head!*

*Millie shouts:* GOOO AWAAAAAYYY!

*The door shudders at the first swing of the battering ram. Millie throws herself over the sofa. As she picks herself up, one of her kitchen cabinet doors explodes open, and a special agent in full body armor and obsidian-black goggles tucks and rolls.*

*Millie throws herself down the hallway as the agent comes up in a firing position. Bullets stitch the wall behind her.*

*She kicks her bathroom door open, then slams it shut behind her and presses the button next to the sink. Steel shutters drop over the small bathroom window and seal the door. In here, she's safe.*

*Her mother always called the bathroom the panic room.*

*Now Millie understands why.*

*She huddles in the bathtub, breathing heavily as she listens to the agents splinter her front door and pour into the apartment. Loud voices move from room to room, shouting, Clear! Clear!*

*No one can get into this room.*

*Water sloshes inside the toilet tank. It trickles over the edge and drips down to the floor.*

*Millie's heart races as the tank wobbles against the wall. The*

*lid bucks upward, then drops heavily back into place. More water*
*spills out. The pipes in the wall groan; tiles pop free from the wall*
*around the toilet.*

STOPP ITTTT! *she cries.*

*The lid of the tank erupts, blasted to the ceiling. It falls again,*
*hard and fast, and shatters on the floor. An agent rises from the*
*tank, water sluicing down his helmet and goggles as he aims his*
*rifle at her.*

*Millie scrambles backward in the tub, but it's deeper now, the*
*walls rising above her like a canyon. The agent kicks his way out of*
*the toilet tank, water geysering all over the bathroom, and looms*
*over the bathtub, bullets exiting his rifle and thudding, sparking,*
*into the cast-iron tub around her—*

WHAM!

Millie's head strikes the desk. Her laptop jumps at the impact.
Martin, who has been saying something about a performance
improvement plan, stops short.

"Millie, what was that?"

She's groggy from the episode, but she's got years and years
of practice snapping back to reality from micro-sleep, and even
more years of practice at lying.

"My dog," she says. "He got excited by a bird at the window, and
just crashed into my desk." She cups a hand over her mouth—is
her nose bleeding?—and calls, "Bad dog! Defect, sit! Sit!"

"You named your dog Defect?" Martin chuckles despite himself. "You might be a legit tester after all, Millie. We've just got to
pull you out of this spin you're in."

While Millie pinches her nose shut, Martin signs off, remind-
ing her to check her mail for a PIP document. "You'll need to
sign that and get it back to me by Monday," he says.

A PIP. Not her first performance improvement plan. She's experienced enough to know that PIPs are never designed to correct
an employee's trajectory; they're legal cover-your-ass documents

for the company to dodge any wrongful termination suits. She wonders how long she has before she's toast.

When Martin's gone, she brews a fresh pot of coffee, then pulls herself onto the kitchen counter. As she waits, she stares at a parallelogram of sunlight drifting slowly across the linoleum floor.

The parallelogram twitches. Millie blinks, and the slant of light has shifted six inches to the left and fractured.

She's lost time. How much?

The blood around her nose has begun to crust over. The coffee has long since finished brewing; it's still somewhat warm, at least. The little digital clock on the old coffeemaker reads 4:11 PM. It doesn't keep time correctly anymore, but if it's saying it's after 4:00 p.m., that means it's—she glances at her phone—been forty minutes since she first walked into the kitchen.

She puts the phone down, but it dings and displays a notification. A new post in the sleep disorder forum she participates in.

Hi, everyone. New to the forum. 16yo and just diagnosed: Narcolepsy with cataplexy.

My mom took me to the neurologist when I went to sleep at a baseball game and missed the whole thing. Nobody could wake me up.

I had to keep a sleep diary, then do all these tests, and now we're trying medications. Zyret didn't work. I'm on something now called Vigilest, which sounds like it's for old guys whose junk doesn't work anymore.

I just needed to talk to people like me. The neurologist told me all the things I didn't know. That I might never get a driver's license, for one. I'm sixteen!

I micro-sleep when I talk to people. I had a girlfriend but she dumped me because she said 'I can't be with someone who thinks I'm so boring they'd rather sleep.' I sleep all night sometimes and wake up and it's like my brain has no record that I slept at all. Once or twice I have blacked out and fallen down. One of those times right at the top of some stairs. I was lucky I didn't fall forward, my mom says.

I stream video games on the internet, and in a lot of my videos you can see me zone out, or have memory bobbles, or fall asleep then wake up real fast. Sometimes my muscles turn to noodles. That's the cataplexy. One of those times my uncle was watching when it happened, and he called 911 because he thought I'd just spontaneously died.

I don't know anyone else in the whole world like me. I don't like to admit it, but I'm scared. Sometimes I even think what's the point of living if it's just going to be like this forever.

–Zeph

Millie sighs, and taps POST A REPLY.

Welcome to the club, kiddo.

# 4

The news anchors are repeating themselves, cycling helplessly through the same speculation and half-baked theories Eli's encountered all morning. The building around him is so ominously quiet he can hear pipes creaking in other apartments.

Outside the window, the storm has drawn nearer, sending ahead of it more and more powerful rushes of wind, stirring up fallen leaves and other debris from the street below. One of Mrs. Roderick's aprons plasters itself to Eli's balcony door.

The sky has darkened, deepened.

As if I needed a more blatant metaphor.

Eli's fingers loom over the keyboard, waggling midair as he considers what to type next.

As someone who leaves the apartment only for regularly scheduled events—he's part of a Monday-night writers' meetup and a Wednesday-afternoon chess club, and he does his grocery shopping on Thursday mornings, preferably before seven—Eli keeps himself tethered to the world beyond via an array of blogs and social media platforms.

Today he's updating his personal blog, *Never Sleeping Again*:

I've been sifting through news fragments and rumors and hype all morning, trying to understand what, if anything, is actually **happening** right now. All the while this storm has been chewing up scenery in a rush to make its entrance.

Someone knows what's going on, even if I don't. If you're reading this, and you have some details, slide into my comments and share.

All I can share is what I'm personally seeing. In my little neighborhood, things are **broken.** There's a three-story car park across from my building. Typically at this time of morning you can see people circling endlessly, hunting for elusive empty spaces. Not today. There are maybe four cars in the whole structure today.

*Ugh. Nobody wants to read about parking lots.*

Eli backspaces the last paragraph, then . . . nothing. His brain shifts into neutral; the words on his screen turn to soft fuzz.

Twenty seconds later, he shakes his head.

*Where was I?*

Last night, day six of my latest insomnia series, I slept fewer than two hours. I've been up since just after 1 a.m., intermittently working on a piece I'm writing for **Tilde** about processing childhood trauma. Not exactly the best story for me to write in the middle of the night, given what we all know about my nightmares and sleep history, but there was nothing good on TV, and Netflix wasn't scratching the itch. I keep micro-sleeping and losing my place.

I don't have a title for the piece yet. I'm trying an alternating structure, moving back and forth between two timelines: 2025 Eli in session with his therapist, desperately trying to make peace with 2007 Eli, the little boy strapped into the back seat of that doomed car. I'm struggling to make it feel effortless, but this story is anything but.

Every day is one day further away from that origin story, the tragic day when all my nightmares, my chronic insomnia, my anxiety and depression and myriad other troubles were born.

His brain feels like a glass bowl filled with smoke, his thoughts difficult to locate in the billows. Why can't he get his head on straight? He's tired, sure, but—

*Shit,* Eli realizes. *I'm off schedule.*

He directs his chair into the kitchen where, beside the sink, he keeps a carefully organized tray of his many medications, sorted into days and weeks. Usually, he'll elevate his chair to manage his meds, but today he's feeling just a little wavery, as though his equilibrium has gone on coffee break, so he doesn't.

The pills rattle gently in their slots as he opens the plastic tray. With one probing finger, he scoops the contents of Day 4 into one palm: a tab of Somalcya, a capsule of Restulin, and two oval-shaped Alexadas.

He deposits the pills into the scooped-out hollow in his chair's arm, then reaches for a glass. When he turns the faucet on and brings the glass to the tap, however, his sleeve snags the corner of the pill tray's still-open lid. The tray tips over the rim of the sink, spilling a month's worth of meds into the black mouth of the garbage disposal. What few pills don't immediately disappear are carried into the depths by the running water.

"No!" Eli cries out, dropping the glass into the sink. He manages to fish out a few pills before they're washed away, but when he counts them, he realizes the ones he's saved won't even carry him through tomorrow morning. "Shit, shit, shit!"

He can practically feel the cold sweats that'll hit him before long. Sure, he'll be all right today, maybe even tomorrow. By Monday, though, he'll feel the shakes. The gravity his bed exerts will have tripled; he'll hardly be able to roll over, much less hoist himself into his chair.

Eli finds his phone and dials his doctor's office. The line rings and rings, until eventually he's dumped into a voice mail box that, as past experience has taught him, is as much a singularity as his garbage disposal.

Next, he dials the pharmacy on Jensen, which lately fills all his prescriptions, but there's no answer there, either. A recorded message advises him to try back later, during business hours.

"It *is* business hours!" he yells at the phone.

His unfinished blog post forgotten, Eli drives to his bedroom, bumping into the doorframe as though he hadn't navigated it a million times before. He rolls right to the nightstand, where an MP3 player, more than a decade old, slumbers.

He wakes the device from sleep. Its screen has clouded over the years, and it won't even power on anymore if not plugged in. He touches the Voice Memos app, where a single file is listed:

**Song for Eli**
November 6, 2001
03:29

Eli elevates his chair to bed height, then lifts himself onto the mattress. He folds the comforter over his legs, then takes his earbuds from the nightstand and slips them in.

He taps the recording once, then closes his eyes.

It isn't a great recording. He can hear the low hum of the Honda's tires on asphalt, the intermittent rush of cars whipping past. But he sinks into the memory. Eli is eight years old again, buckled into a child seat in the back seat. Returning home from a weekend spent eating hot dogs and riding the Wonder Wheel at Coney Island, delighting in the sound of his parents singing road trip songs from the front seats.

He holds out his birthday present, a digital recorder, and records his parents as they sing a duet of their favorite Pretenders song:

> When I look up from my pillow
> I dream you are there with me

In bed, Eli loops one arm beneath his knees and tugs them as close to his chest as his damaged spine will permit.

He plays the recording over and over, until his panic has subsided. He can handle this; it's perfectly manageable. All he needs to do is talk to someone in the doctor's office, or someone at the pharmacy. It's a phone call. He can manage a phone call.

Eli puts the device back on the nightstand, picks up his phone, and dials his doctor again.

# The Elephant

*Tonight will go the way it's supposed to.*

Tracy wants to believe this, needs to. Eventually all streaks end. Eventually he has to get better. Every night can't be like the last several hundred.

Can it?

Through the door she hears him chattering to himself. *Deep breaths. You've got this. It will be okay.*

If only she believed it.

She opens the door. Davy sits on the floor, happily stacking books in a tower. The tower wobbles, and he laughs as it topples, spilling board books everywhere.

"Mama!" he chirps. "Watch this!" He stacks the books again, and this time, before they fall, he knocks them over, making explosion sounds with his lips. "I'm a giant! I knock down!"

"My little giant," Tracy says.

"Not little," the boy says.

"You're right, I'm sorry. You aren't little. You're my giant giant."

Davy erupts in laughter. "Giant giant! That's me!"

But when Tracy steps into the bedroom, Davy's eyes fall on the book in her hand.

"Not time yet," he says worriedly. "Not time yet, Mama."

"It's all right, Davy," she says. "We still have time. You haven't brushed your teeth yet, have you?"

She helps him select his favorite footie pajamas, the ones printed with roly-poly hedgehogs driving bumper cars, then watches as he brushes his teeth. The minutes pass too quickly, and suddenly they're back in his room.

She switches his bedside lamp on, then draws the curtains. "Books can't hurt you," she assures him as he climbs into bed. "Books are magic, Davy. They take you anywhere you want to go."

"That book wants to eat me," he whispers.

"Davy. No. We know that isn't true. It's a good book, a cute book. And I need your help to read it, okay?" She pulls the blankets over his feet. "You're not getting too big for a bedtime story, are you? My giant giant still likes to be tucked in."

"No," he says, eyes shining darkly. "I am not giant."

She sits beside him on the bed, her back to the wall, and pulls his head to her chest. She smooths his dark hair, then opens the book.

"*A*," she reads, touching the illustration of a cheerful apple, its eyes gleaming with joy. "What's *A* for? *A* is for . . . ?"

"Apple." Davy's voice is very small.

"My smart boy. Here, turn the page for Mama."

He shakes his head firmly.

She turns the page herself, revealing a butter-shaped ballplayer, swinging a breadstick bat, hammering a baseball toward the stands. The ball looms large in the foreground, winking happily.

"*B*," she reads. "*B* is for . . . ?"

"Ball, Mama."

"What kind of ball?"

"It's a baseball."

"How many *B*s is that?"

He holds up two tiny fingers in a V.

"That's right. Good, Davy. So good!"

On the next page a furry cat's cheeks bulge as it blows a clarinet, while a dog thumps on the drums. Davy giggles at the silly expression on the dog's face. Tracy leans forward and kisses Davy's soft hair.

But when she tries to turn the page, he places his palm over the illustration.

"Mama, no," he whispers. "Please, okay."

"It's the alphabet, Davy," she says, working hard at sounding cheerful. "We can't just skip a letter! And the most common letter of all."

"I'm ready for sleep."

"Be my brave giant, Davy. We can do this. Together, okay?"

She turns the page to reveal a jungle scene. In the shadows, an elephant's shadowy face emerges from the leaves. She has to admit the elephant's a bit creepy. Maybe she needs to order a book about that cute elephant, the French one . . .

"*E* is for . . . ?" she prompts. "Come on, Davy. This one's easy. *E* is for—" She stops. "Do you feel something? What is that?" She raises the book.

A dark stain spreads over her linen pants, right where Davy's leg is draped over hers. He's trembling.

"Davy!" she cries out. "What is wrong with—? Get up!"

But Davy doesn't move. The dampness spreads over his pajama pants, drips onto the sheets beneath him.

Tracy tosses the book down, throws back the blanket, and lifts Davy off the bed. She deposits him on the floor, not gently. He cowers against his bookcase while Tracy turns her attention to the bed, stripping the sheets and wadding them into a ball.

"What's wrong with you?" she snaps. "Are you broken? It's a *book*. Davy, it's just a cute *elephant*. Jesus!"

Davy covers his face with his hands. "Mama, no, no."

She snatches up the book, holds the *E* page in front of Davy's face. "Look at it!" she demands, voice shrill. "Say the word, Davy. What is it? Say it!"

Dave wails between his fingers.

"*E* is for *what*, Davy? For what?"

Davy sinks to the floor, shrinking against the bookcase, as though it could swallow him up. Tracy drops the book on his lap. His bedside lamp throws a dancing kaleidoscope of animal shadows upon the walls; usually this makes him laugh, but now the shadows stretch menacingly over his mother's face.

"*E!*" she shrieks at him. "What's it *for*, Davy?"

Tracy's hands find the back of her head. Davy watches, stricken, as she pulls at her scalp, straining so violently that the cords in her neck stand out sharply. With a terrible sucking sound, his mother's features go slack as she peels her skin and hair away in meaty strips.

Davy's scream rattles his spine.

"For what, Davy?" Tracy tears away what remains of her face, revealing the grotesque, pebbled hide beneath. Her trunk unfurls, heavy and streaked with blood; her papery ears are matted against her gray crown.

"Stop it!" Davy shrieks. "Stop it, stop it, stop it!"

"I'd like to, Davy," says the elephant-thing that used to be his mother. Its voice is hard and throaty. "But you have to say it. Or this never stops."

"Mama," Davy moans.

"This is your fault," the beast says. Its trunk searches out Davy's face, presses slick against his cheek, exhales hot, sour breath into his hair. "I warned you, didn't I?"

Davy looks down at his pajama shirt. Something beneath bulges. Utter panic consumes him as he clutches at his shirt, trying to hold it away from his skin. He looks wildly at the thing above him.

"I can't stop it now," the elephant grunts. Its mouth unhinges, and a thick river of mustard-colored bile streams onto Dave's legs. "I wouldn't if I could. You aren't a good boy."

Davy, blinded by pain, cups his hands over his chest in time to catch the small elephant that bursts from his breastbone. Yellow foam rises in Dave's throat; he can't clear it to breathe.

The small elephant stretches in Davy's little palms, glistening and damp. Davy's vision blurs; he's suddenly terribly sleepy, and his hands fall limp.

A strange hand takes Davy's fingers. Strong, calloused, unfamiliar. The bedroom swims in and out of focus as Davy turns to look at the stranger kneeling beside him. The man's face, lined with age, is painted as if for war; hanging around his neck, on gnarled red twine, is a crude carving.

*A whale*, Davy thinks.

*Ma-weh*, the stranger whispers, enveloping Davy's hand in his own. *Ke-no. Na-wah.*

The newborn elephant tumbles free of Davy's cratered shirt and peers up at the boy. It blows red bubbles from its trunk, then trumpets weakly, almost happily. As he begins to black out, Davy thinks the sound resembles his own name.

*Daaaaayyyyyvvv—*

"—ave! Dave, wake up, honey."

Dave snaps upright in bed with such force he nearly headbutts Tracy, who is leaning over him, concern etched into her face.

No, not Tracy.

Katie.

Not his mother. Not his bedroom.

He clutches his chest.

Intact.

"It's okay," Katie says, taking his face in her cool hands. "You are safe, you are all right. Breathe, baby."

"Jesus Christ," he wheezes, and falls back against his pillow. It squelches, heavy with sweat.

"I'm going to make you coffee," Katie says. She kisses his slick forehead. "You clean up."

When she returns from the kitchen, holding two steaming mugs, Dave has stripped the bed. The sheets are in a pile on the floor.

"I think I might pull the mattress onto the porch," he says, ashamed. "It's soaked. With sweat," he adds.

"I meant go clean *yourself* up, baby. Like, a shower. I was going to do this."

"You don't have to do—"

"Baby. Shh." She hands him a mug. "Do you remember it?"

He takes the mug, and a deep swallow. The coffee burns his tongue and throat. It reminds him he's awake. He's alive. Katie watches him with concern.

"You're going to be late," he says, turning away from her. "Like, really late."

"I'll sneak in," Katie says. "Lilly just got her eighteen-month fob. I'm pretty sure she thinks the whole meeting is her fan club. She talks for hours now." She gives Dave a careful look. "Come with?"

He raises one eyebrow. "I know what you're up to."

"It's not espionage, Dave. I care about you."

"I'm fine. Really."

She puts her mug down, then steps close to Dave. "Listen," she says, one delicate palm on his chest. "You never have to tell me anything you don't want to tell me."

"I know. Thank you."

She chews her lip, averts her eyes.

"But?" he prompts.

"Just . . . don't lie to me about it. I can't do that. I can't handle that."

He tips her chin upward, brushes his thumb on the tip of her nose. "You're so cute," he says.

"Dave."

"I promise."

Across the room, Katie's phone trills: BEEEEEEEEEE—

"Holy hell," Dave says. "New alarm? It's so loud!"

—EEEEEEEEEEEEEEEEE—

## 2

—EEEEEEEEEEEEEEEEEE—

The insect drone of a dozen electrocardiograms floats up the hallway.

"Matteo, go unplug whatever those are," Dave says, but Linda shakes her head.

"Unplugging won't do anything." Her voice is toneless. "They'll work on battery for three hours."

"You said she died in her sleep."

"It's the only thing that makes sense." Linda lightly strokes the dead nurse's fingers. "And it doesn't make sense at all."

"But—a heart attack? Did she stroke out?"

"Matteo," Dave warns.

"I just want to know what the fuck is going—"

"I don't know. All right?" Linda's face flushes with anger. "Why do I have to have all the answers? Why do I have to do everything?"

"Whoa, okay, okay," Matteo says, backing up a step. "I'm just—"

"This is a nightmare. For everyone." Dave nods, taking charge. "We can just—"

Both men flinch as Linda throws her head back and *screams*. The anguish in her voice, so unfiltered and primal, touches something raw in David, and his eyes prick. Beside him, Matteo rocks from one foot to the other.

*Oh, this is going to do some damage*, Dave realizes. *It's already fucking us up.*

Linda drags her palms down her face, stretching her features. Then, abruptly, she stands up. "You guys have a car," she says, not asking.

# 3

Minutes later they stand beside Matteo's occupied Camaro, and Linda says, "Oh. Right." She drops the heavy duffel she's loaded with supplies and says, "Well, give me a hand, I guess."

They struggle with the bodies in silence. When the second of them is on the sidewalk, Matteo says tentatively, "What do we need my car for?"

"You're driving me to the police station," Linda grunts.

"I'm what? No. I need to—"

"Whatever's going on here, I'm about eighty percent certain it's not an isolated event. Have you heard any sirens tonight? No? Literally nobody's responding. No ambulances, no feds. I need to talk to someone. A real person, not someone on a phone. I need to tell them what happened here."

"Look—" Matteo starts.

"Don't." Linda folds her arms. "Studies have shown that any-time someone starts a sentence with 'Look,' they're about to dis-appoint you."

Despite himself, Dave chuckles. "Matteo has lots of experience disappointing people."

"Yo, you two can clown all you want, but it's, what, seven in the morning? We've been up all night playing doctor, and not in the fun way. This shit is too much. I'm going *home*. I'm sleeping until it's next week."

Linda glances at Dave, then visibly composes herself. She turns to Matteo and puts a hand on his elbow. "Matteo, listen to me. Tonight I watched healthy people—people whose only problems were a broken ankle, or tonsillitis—I watched them die. For no reason. Nothing I did stopped it from happening. And we just took dead people out of your nice car."

"It *is* a nice car," Matteo mumbles petulantly.

"And it *is* too much. This isn't normal. None of it is. But that's why we can't go home yet."

"Take your own car."

"I don't have one. Public transport all the way, sweetie."

"The police station *is* just ten minutes away," Dave says.

Matteo's shoulders slump. "Okay, but I'm going home after."

"I'll tuck you in myself," Linda says. "Right now, though, there's a perfectly nice young woman in your car who needs our attention."

Matteo kicks the sidewalk. "That used to mean something hella different."

Dave adds, "I think that's the bong guy, not Becka."

"Whatever," Linda says. With a sigh: "Give me a hand."

4

Santa Mira unfolds below them like a Rockwell painting. The sun rises behind the Camaro as Matteo crests the hill, scattering light over the Pacific breakers.

"No surfers today," Matteo observes idly. He points at the empty water. "There are usually fifty of them catching the morning tides."

Dave glances out the window as Matteo brakes for a stoplight. The car thrums below him, the only thing alive on the whole street. Porch lights burn at every house on the block. Sidewalks are empty except for recycling bins. Every driveway has a car in it.

The light turns green, but Linda puts her hand on the wheel. "Don't," she says.

Matteo's eyes flick to the rearview mirror. The long hill behind them is empty. "What?"

"Park it."

Before Matteo can shift the transmission, Linda throws open the door and climbs out.

"Shit," Matteo grumbles. He throws the car in park and yanks the hand brake. "Dave, this chick, I swear . . ."

Beside the car, Linda paces back and forth. Matteo drops his window and leans out. "Yo, we cool?"

Linda absently takes down her hair and reties it, then, startling both boys, clambers first onto the Camaro's warm hood, then its roof. The metal warps with a metallic ring.

"Motherfucker!" Matteo yelps. He tumbles out of the car. "Lady, you're trashing my—"

"Jesus," Linda says, ignoring him. "Oh, Jesus Christ."

Dave elbows his way out of the back seat. Matteo dances over to him, pointing at the dent under Linda's nurse shoes. But Dave waves him off.

"Linda, what is it?"

"It's the whole town," she says, not looking down at them. "Guys, the *whole town*."

The west side of the street, all houses, is just as Dave had noticed before. Nobody's woken up. No one's day has begun. The east side, all storefronts, is still locked up tight for the night. Even the Starbucks on the corner is dead.

"Where the hell is everyone?" Matteo asks.

Linda drops onto her butt, then slides off the roof. She circles to the driver's window, leans into the car, and pops the trunk.

"Woman thinks she owns my car," Matteo says to himself. "Hello?"

Dave takes in the scene, searching for even the faintest movement in the middle distance. But the only sound is the white noise whisper of the waves. He can even hear the faint click of the bulbs turning over as the traffic lights cycle.

"Hey!" he calls. "Can anyone hear—?"

The angry crack of a gunshot splinters the silence. Matteo reacts in an instant, dropping for cover behind the Camaro's tire. Dave's hands find his ears; he doubles over. The sharp report reverberates off the houses and buildings, echoes overlapping almost mechanically as they move away from the car.

Dave looks wildly around, then spots Linda next to the open trunk, unzipped duffel at her feet, a still-smoking handgun held above her head.

"They should've heard that," she says.

Dave tries shaking off the high-pitched tone in his ears. "What?"

"Someone will come now." Abruptly she pulls the trigger once, twice more.

Matteo flinches, then shoots up and charges Linda. He grips her forearm and immobilizes her trigger finger, twisting the gun from her hand. Instinct has him squared up, ready for action.

Dave puts a hand on Matteo's shoulder. "Easy there."

"Woman is crazy," Matteo says.

"They'll come now," Linda explains. "Now they'll come, Dave. Won't they come? Aren't they coming now, Dave?"

Dave steps past Matteo and folds Linda into his arms. "Shh," he says. "I don't know. I really don't know."

Behind them, Matteo releases the clip, then racks the loaded cartridge out of the chamber. He drops both into his pocket. "I'm keeping this," he tells Linda, and tucks the gun into his waistband.

"She's right," Dave says, surveying the neighborhood. "Nobody's coming."

"Well, we go to them, then," Matteo says. "Right? Can we?"

## 5

The house at 465 Higuera was Eduard Ortega's first, purchased in the late 1970s for thirty-six thousand dollars. The years and the market have been kind to the property's value. Despite its modest size, the house would sell for close to a million now, maybe a million-two. For the last five years, Eduard had been making slow improvements, hoping that when he decided to sell, these would result in a better price. His last addition—before the night he went to sleep and didn't wake up—was a pair of stained glass foyer panels. The sun hit them in the morning, breaking into brilliant facets that played upon the foyer tile.

The paving stone punches through the window, spraying colored glass across the floor. The stone itself lands on one of the terra-cotta tiles corner-first, fracturing the tile in place.

Dave reaches through the broken panel to unlock Eduard Ortega's front door. As he steps through the doorway, he hears an echo of breaking glass farther down the street: Matteo and Linda, performing their own strategic home invasions.

"Anyone home?" Dave calls out, glass crunching beneath his heavy shoes. "Hello?"

For a long moment he stands in the entry, letting the silence fall over him. To his left, down a short hall, he sees an empty breakfast nook, alive with sunlight. The stairs to his right are empty. The house is still, clearly as dead as its owner.

Images of Randy's bedroom intrude on his thoughts. He doesn't want to go upstairs. He knows what he'll find up there; the certainty unnerves him. Wasn't it just a day ago he had a relatively ordinary life? Perfectly dull, wonderfully uninteresting, with boring, familiar, everyday problems?

*My problems were never ordinary*, he reminds himself. *Don't fool yourself.*

The three of them reconvene beside the Camaro, still parked at the stoplight. Both Linda and Matteo look dazed.

"Well, then," Dave says. "I guess we all found the same thing."

Matteo wipes sweat away with his forearm. "I . . . ," he begins, but he trails off, looking at his feet. Linda sinks to the asphalt and leans against the bumper, sucking in lungfuls of salty air.

"Yeah," Dave says. "Every house, same thing. Everyone's dead."

"Were they all in bed?" Linda asks thinly.

"I found one guy on the couch," Matteo offers. "He dropped his cigarette on his shorts. There was a burn." He points toward the storefronts. "I checked a few of those. At the gas station on the corner, there's a woman . . . She's on the floor. Behind the register. There's a lot of blood, but she looked peaceful. I think she fell asleep on her stool. I think she hit her head when she fell."

"So we weren't wrong," Linda says, rocking slightly. "Maybe it's a virus, some kind of pathogen. But it's tied to sleep."

"Randy and Becka," Dave says, counting off names.

"Tony the bong guy," Matteo says.

"The lobby people."

"Britney," Linda croaks.

"Everyone we just . . ." Dave trails off. "They were all sleeping. Like your patients, Linda."

"Yo, I have seen some crazy shit," Matteo says, voice rising. "But this whole town did not just go to sleep and fucking die. This is *insane*."

"Maybe," Linda muses. "But that doesn't mean we're wrong."

"I'm going to be sick."

"Guys, we're not asking the most important question," Dave says. The rims of his eyes ache, like he's scrubbed them with fine-grit paper. "What are we supposed to do now? Stay awake forever?"

"Maybe it's passed," Matteo says. "If it is a virus, maybe we can't catch it now. Maybe it's okay."

But Linda looks gravely at Dave. "We have to call everyone we know. We have to tell them not to sleep."

"It's seven in the goddamn morning!" Matteo cries. "If we wanted to warn people, we're half a day too late." He grabs at his head. "Dios mío, my mother. My sister . . ."

"I have an aunt in Europe," Linda says. "Maybe I can . . ."

Dave's heart sinks. "You don't think—?"

"How do we know how far this thing goes?" Linda asks.

Dave takes his phone from his pocket and presses Redial. He turns away from the others, walks into the middle of the empty intersection, and listens to the phone ring.

There's a soft click in his ear.

"Katie?" Dave says. "Oh God, honey, I—"

"This is Katie," says the voice in his ear. "Resident overworked millennial. If I'm not answering, it's probably because I'm wasting my late twenties at a dead-end job that hardly pays the bills now, much less lets me put away something for when I'm old and gray. *Or* I'm catching a nap in my car before my *second* no-future job. So, you know, leave a message if you want, but maybe reconsider."

Dave could kill her for such a long message. This is no time for—

"Katie!" he cries as soon as her phone beeps. The words tumble out of him like water: "Listen, you're screening, I get it, but please, not today. Pick up, honey. Pick up. It's more important than you— Look, don't go to sleep! Jesus, please don't be asleep. Stay awake! You have to stay awake, and you have to call me. Call me!"

He ends the call, then stares at his phone. Behind him, he hears Linda comforting Matteo; someone is crying.

"Fuck it," he says, and redials.

"*This is Katie, resident overworked—*"

"Goddammit!" Dave barks at the phone.

Linda comes up to him, shoes crunching gravel. "Your friend's wound real tight," she says. "I can tell you are, too."

"Who are you, Queen Calm all of a sudden?" Dave snaps. Then he grimaces. "Fuck. I'm sorry, I just—"

"Dave, the world just ended. It's okay."

"You really think . . . ?"

"We have to warn people. Not everyone works day shifts. I bet there are a lot of people just like us, scared, confused . . ."

"Like us."

"Right. So, how do we find them?"

They stroll back to the Camaro, where Matteo is on his feet, bleary and unsteady.

"There are sixty thousand people in Santa Mira," Dave says. "We can't keep searching houses and crossing our fingers."

"We need a better way," Linda agrees. "But I don't know. Cops have loudspeakers in their cars, right? Maybe we—"

"So do ice cream trucks." Dave imagines the three of them trawling the town, shouting over "Pop! Goes the Weasel."

"Guys," Matteo says, voice thick. "No."

He leans into his Camaro, switches the key, then turns on the radio. The smooth and crazed energy of the all-night radio jockey swells to fill the car.

> . . . *if you've got a belly full of burgers, and you're all fireworked out, why not wind down your Indy-pendence Day with a good ol' American kick in the ass, a little classic revolutionary rock with your old pal—*

"Larry," Dave finishes. "He's right. Half the town listens to that show. Especially night-shifters. It's the best place to start."

"He'll be off the air soon. It's nearly eight."

Linda's head bobs. "So, there's just one question, I guess. Matteo?"

Matteo's eyebrows lift.

Linda pats the Camaro's hood. "Just how fast does your baby fly?"

# 6

Steam billows from the Camaro's grille. When Matteo pops the hood, he disappears in clouds of it. "Fuck!" he says, and levels a kick at his bumper. He stops just before his foot makes contact. "Mother*fuck*!"

"Maybe," Dave says, "sixty would've been okay. No stoplights, no traffic. Maybe ninety-five was pushing it just a little—"

"Fuck off," Matteo says, and plunges into the clouds of steam. "Ow! Goddammit!"

"Matteo, that's hot steam, you've got to be careful—" Linda starts.

"Lady! Christ!"

Dave jogs to the sidewalk and tries Katie's number again. "Pick up," he mutters, dreading her voice mail greeting. "Come on, Kat—"

The phone clicks and Katie, aggrieved, says, "Dave, okay, like, listen, you can't—"

"Katie? Oh God. Katie! Holy shit, holy shit. Thank God. Katie. Listen, okay? Listen, you've—"

"Stop talking over me!"

Dave stops. "I'm sorry. But, no, Katie—"

"No. I'm talking. Jesus, you never listen. You can't do this!" She's out of breath already; he can hear the rage in her mouth, garbling her words. "That was the whole problem. You can't just do what you want when you want. You can't just stomp all over—I set boundaries! You don't respect my bound—"

"Katie!" Dave interrupts. "Baby. We can have this argument a hundred times. But later. Right now I need you to listen. It's important."

"No. Okay. You're right," she says. Her heavy breath is static in the tinny speaker. "You're right. Not right now. Because I've been up all night and I'm *exhausted*. So, another time. We'll have coffee. We'll *talk* about it. Bye, Dave."

"No, no, no, Katie—"

The line goes dead, and Dave nearly fumbles the phone trying to dial again. But this time, the phone doesn't ring.

*"This is Katie, resident overworked millennial . . ."*

Dave's muscles tense as he waits for the message to finish. But this time no beep comes. Instead, a computerized voice says, "I'm sorry. This account holder's voice mailbox is full. Goodbye."

The *goodbye* sounds almost sarcastic, and Dave very nearly throws the phone at the street. Instead, he runs back to the car, where Matteo says, "Okay, I've narrowed it down to the water pump or the fan. Good news is I've got tools in the back, and I can *probably* fix—"

"Larry's going to be off the air in twelve minutes," Linda says at the same time Dave says, "Katie won't talk to me—" Then Dave says, "Fuck this," and breaks into a run.

"Dave?" Linda says. "Dave!"

"The hell's he going?" Matteo asks.

"Dave!" Linda bellows. "Where the hell are you going? We have to stick together!"

# 7

Katie drops her phone on the night table, then pulls heavy curtains across the window, blotting out the sun. She strips out of her company polo and khakis, takes a quick shower to scrub away the long night, then stands at the mirror in one of Dave's old T-shirts and brushes her teeth.

Most mornings she can hear the clatter of dishes as the single mother next door rushes about, preparing breakfast and school lunches for her four children. Today, however, the apartment is blessedly silent.

She drifts from bedroom to kitchen, trying to ignore the clutter. Her hiking pack and assorted gear are scattered around the living room; on Saturday she's meeting Jhumpa for a hike on the Palisade Creek Trail. *Tomorrow*, she thinks, but then she spots yesterday's takeout container on the kitchen counter, noodles hardened, peas shriveled. *Do it now*, she amends. *Don't be an ass.*

She switches the radio on and begins tidying up.

> *We've been rocking all night long here at KPWG, let me tell you—this place is one happy disaster zone—but all parties, as you know, must end. And on that note, let your old friend Late Night Larry lull you sleep with the dulcet tones of . . . oh, I don't know, some guy with a saxophone.*

Katie frowns as smooth jazz spills from the radio. She switches it off, then yawns so hard she worries her face might split open. She pushes the takeout carton into the trash, then squats beside her hiking pack for another game of backpack Tetris.

# 8

The only sound in the neighborhood is Dave's footfalls, hammering the pavement, echoing off parked cars and still houses. No one passes him in Lycra shorts, no cars interrupt as he jaywalks—

jay*runs*—to save time. It's just him and the neighborhood. The quiet, dead neighborhood.

He cuts down a dirt alley between rows of homes, then across a lawn festooned with sprays of gardenias and calendulas. Then he stops, nearly tripping over his own feet, at the sight of a body swaying gently in a hammock, a newspaper buckled over its face.

A black bird—a crow? a raven? Dave can never remember the difference—is perched upon the newspaper, pecking through the headlines at the face of the corpse beneath.

Dave isn't religious, but he makes a sign of the cross anyway.

Then he runs. Faster.

# 9

"No one's answering at the station," Linda reports.

"No shit." Matteo, still bent over the engine, leans into his wrench. "Unscrew, you bastard! Just . . . come . . . fucking . . . *loose!*" He staggers backward as something pops free, clattering into the depths of the engine compartment.

Linda turns around. "That didn't sound good."

"Again," Matteo grunts, his feet lifting off the ground as he reaches deep into the car's guts, "no *shit.*"

"We're actually *in* shit here," Linda says. "I don't know if you've noticed."

"Hey, we don't know each other all that well," Matteo says, struggling, "but if you could maybe just shut your—"

"Out of the way." Linda snakes her lean arm through the tangle of hoses and tubes and deftly retrieves the lost screw. "How's that?"

Matteo's face goes blank. "Great. Fine. Okay."

While he keeps working, Linda says, "Dave told me you're a vet. Army?"

Matteo doesn't reply right away. Finally, he says, "Air force."

"Lots of vet traffic in the ICU, you know. The worst of them, they come in drunk, high as a paper kite. Bar fights. Domestics. DUIs." Linda waits, but Matteo doesn't say anything. "A lot of them, though. They're like you." She can see the pale seam of a scar stitched through Matteo's hair. "Carrying things they should've left behind."

"Don't start diagnosing me," Matteo grunts. "And we aren't all shitheads like that. Maybe only half of us. Just like any other demographic."

"Well, since you're the only one left, I think the average is a little better."

Matteo hands Linda the wrench, then jogs to the front seat and tries starting the car. This time the engine fires.

"Clicks a little," she observes.

"It clicked before." Matteo takes the wrench back, tosses it into the back seat, then drops the hood with a slam. As they slide into the car, he says, "You don't really believe that, right? That we're the only ones left?"

"Honestly?"

"Usually that's all I want," he says. "Honesty. But I think I'd prefer a lie, truth be told."

"We'll find more people. I promise."

His eyes narrow. "Right. So, now I can't tell. Was that honesty? Or a kind lie?"

"I'll never tell." Linda's eyes gleam. "We going now, or what?"


## 10


In . . .
   Out.
   In . . .

Out.

*In through the nose,* Katie thinks, *and out through the mouth. Nice . . . and . . . slow . . .*

The circumstances are ideal: Freshly laundered sheets, still with that dryer-sheet smell. Near-total darkness, compliments of her new blackout curtains. The apartment is clean. Her shift won't start for eleven hours. Her phone is powered off.

There's literally no reason she shouldn't already be snoring.

"Fuck you, Dave," she mutters.

She can't stop the conversation from looping in her head. She'll need a distraction. She tumbles out of bed with a grunt, then trots to the kitchen for her radio. Along the way, she pauses in the living room and grabs the heaviest, dullest book she owns: The *National Audubon Society Field Guide to North American Birds.*

She switches the radio on and crawls beneath the blankets with the book.

> *. . . announcing three lucky winners of our July Fourth raffle. First prize, lest you forget, is a weekend at the Santa Mira Lodge and Spa, in the honeymoon bungalow right on the river, complete with your own private hot tub. Man, a good soak sounds terrific right now. Put these old bones right to sleep.*
>
> *All right, hang in there, folks, one last commercial break, and then we'll give our winners a ring. Late Night Larry's gonna grab a little siesta . . .*

Katie flips through the book at random, then begins to read. "The *Corvidae* family," she says aloud. "Crows, ravens, rooks . . ." Within a few sentences, she can feel her brain losing its grip on the words, getting tripped up by the Latin phrases.

*There we go . . .*

## 11

Dave pulls up short, a vicious stitch in his side. He shakes out his ankles and wrists, tries to regulate his breathing.

"The hell am I?" he wonders aloud, scanning the nearest intersection's street signs. "Godfrey and Calloway? Godfrey, Godfrey . . ."

Last fall. A party, in the hills off Godfrey Lane. Katie had been bored out of her skull, trying so hard to be good. He'd been so proud. Not a single drink that night.

Well, until they got home.

He shakes off the memory, trying to picture instead the view from the party house, high above town. From there he could see the way Godfrey curved down, through Loring Woods, toward—

*Shortcut!*

He takes off again, hobbling a little, and cuts through an unfenced yard, then a town park. He veers wide around a park bench where another body slumps, fingers dangling into the grass.

*Stay awake, Katie, stay awake.*

At the far edge of the park, he encounters a wooden fence. There's no gate in sight. He tries going over it, but catches his toe on a plank and goes down like a sack of stones.

## 12

Matteo and Linda stand in front of the radio booth, silently taking in the scene before them.

"Well, shit," Linda says finally.

In the booth, Late Night Larry's workspace is a literal disaster. Empty Red Bull cans clutter the soundboard, are crushed and scattered around a blue bin. Snickers wrappers and crumpled

Taco Bell bags snow the ground beside the trash can, which is already overflowing with potato chip cellophane.

In the middle of it all, a man in a pit-stained Hawaiian shirt lies slack in his office chair, sliding toward the floor as slowly as a cooling lava flow.

Little plastic dinosaurs and palm trees are glued to the desk.

"Late Night Larry," Matteo says, real sadness—or disappointment—in his voice.

Abruptly, the radio man slips out of his chair and falls heavily to the floor, joining junk food wrappers. The chair pinwheels away from the body and collides with a rack of compact discs. Plastic cases and shining discs clatter to the floor around Larry.

"I want to feel bad and all . . . ," Linda begins.

"Don't," Matteo warns. "Late Night Larry might be a joke to you, but he means something to me."

Larry's tongue has tumbled out of his mouth, a gray-pink slug that rests on the dusty, frayed carpet.

"*Meant,*" Linda corrects.

## 13

Katie's always imagined sleep like the hottest nightclub in the city, where the live music is a bop and the line is always twisting out the door and down the block. Theoretically, anybody can get in, but the door guy is hard to please, and once you're inside, there's a thousand-drink minimum.

She's just convinced the door guy to unclip his little velvet rope for her when the front door to her apartment splinters.

The door guy punts Katie ten miles, and she falls out of her bed, cottony and dazed. The sound of the doorframe cracking follows her out of the dream, and she snaps awake, alert. She reaches beneath her bed, searching for the tape-wrapped handle of her father's old Louisville Slugger.

With a bang her bedroom door crashes open. Katie swings blindly. *"Thefuckouttamyhouse!"* she screeches, and the bat connects with a satisfying thud.

Dave takes the brunt of it across his back, yelps, and goes down. "Jesus, Katie!" he hollers, going fetal.

Katie drops the bat. "Dave, what the fuck?"

"Oh, goddamn, you got a good swing," Dave moans. "I think you might've exploded my kidney."

"I'm calling the cops," she says, and makes for her phone. "I thought we just talked about boundaries!"

"You have no idea how relieved I am you're awake," Dave groans.

While Katie's phone boots up, she studies Dave severely. "You kicked in my door!" she snaps. "Are you high?"

"I'm not . . ."

Her face softens, just a little. "Was it—?"

"It wasn't. Isn't." Dave shakes his head and makes a show of pinching himself. "I'm wide awake, baby."

"Don't you dare," she says, and she presses the Emergency button on her phone. "I'm dialing."

"It's okay. They won't answer." He shakes his head once more, suddenly beyond weary. His supply of adrenaline is tapped. The pills he took—that he took a year ago, it seems—are fucking with him.

The line doesn't ring. Instead, her phone just chirps soullessly.

"My call won't go through," she says, confused. "911's supposed to always go through. It's, like, a rule."

Dave struggles upright.

"Stay there," Katie warns, reaching for the bat again. "I'll scream, Dave."

"Ugh," he grunts, clutching his back. "No, it's okay. Go ahead. Be my guest. Scream."

"I'm not fucking kidding, Dave. I'll—"

"*Fire!*" Dave yells, loudly as he can manage. He hammers the wall that separates Katie's apartment and the single mom's. "Everybody out, building's on fire!"

"Dave!"

"Listen," he begins.

"Dave, I'm—"

"Katie! *Listen.*" Dave holds up a finger to his lips, cocks his head as if waiting for something. But there's nothing: The apartment is quiet. The building is quiet.

"Where is everyone?" Dave whispers. "It's early, Katie. Guy upstairs, he ought to be stomping on the floor to tell you to cut out the noise, right? Lady next door, she'd be at your door right now, telling you not to wake up her kiddo. Right?"

Katie's lip trembles, but she doesn't say anything.

"So, where are they?" he asks.

He hobbles to the busted front door, then steps onto the landing. Katie reluctantly follows, staring at the wreckage of her door. From the landing, Dave and Katie can see the entire horseshoe-shaped complex.

"There's a fire!" Dave shouts again. His voice breaks a little. "Everybody out, hurry! Fire! Fire!"

But not a single door in the building opens.

Nobody yells for Dave to shut the fuck up.

Dave points at the parking lot. "See?"

"It's full," she says. "It's usually half-empty when I come home from work."

"Exactly. This is what I'm saying. They're all home, Katie. Why aren't they hearing me?"

"What's going on, Dave?"

"A bad thing, Katie. The worst thing. I—"

But he's interrupted by a voice from inside. Katie rushes to the bedroom, then comes back holding her radio.

> . . . ergency broadcast. I— Look, I'm just going to come right out and say it, okay? Do not go to sleep. If you can hear my voice right now, stay awake. My name is Linda Russo. I'm an advanced practice registered nurse at Santa Mira Medical Center. If you're hearing me: Come to the hospital. We don't know if this is some kind of pandemic, or . . . an attack. We don't know. Again, this is an emergency . . .

"Thank Christ," Dave breathes. "They made it."

"She sounds so calm," Katie wonders.

"Believe me, she's terrified."

"Is it a radio drama? Like the old days?"

"I wish it was." Dave hesitates, debating what to tell her. "Sweetie, a lot of bad things happened last night to a lot of people. It's not a drama, it's real."

"Why can't we go to sleep?"

"Because it happens when you sleep," he says gently.

"*What* does?"

"Katie . . ."

"What happens, Dave?" She lowers the radio, then lets it fall to the floor. "What happens?"

"People die," he says finally. "And nobody knows why."

Katie panic-laughs. Her eyes fill up and spill over.

"Hey," Dave says, "it's going to be okay."

"That's not it." She shakes her head. "I couldn't fall asleep, Dave. I . . ."

Dave leaves her and rushes back to the bedroom. On the nightstand, next to Katie's bird book, is one of Dave's expired prescription bottles, uncapped.

"All right, all right," Dave says, adapting to this new reality. Katie has followed him and stands nervously in the doorway. She looks so small, he thinks. "It's okay. It'll be okay. How many did you take? When?"

"I fucked up," she says, eyes glistening. "Dave, I think I fucked up so bad."

# Dispatches from Earth

## I

She calls herself Async04 because once her favorite game streamer was this chick called Unsynced, but she always thought *unsynced* sounded really stupid. *Async*, though, that had a cool ring to it. The *A* part was, like, anarchy. Or at least maybe people would think that.

Most people, though, think it's a play on NSYNC, which she did not anticipate, and now thoroughly regrets.

Async scrolls through her Twitch. More than half the comments are the usual *Are you Timberlake's niece or something* and *Yo when you swapping Twitch for OnlyFans, girl?* Another 30 percent are bots and spam. Somewhere in the 20 percent that remain are her legit fans, the ones who pick up any game she streams just because she streamed it.

She shrugs out of her Baskin-Robbins apron and runs a hand through her short, stabby hair. She's too tired to stream tonight. A double takes it out of her, and tonight, the mall shop she works for was swarmed. The vintage record store nearby did some live music thing, so she had to listen to the awful reverb of clashing guitars. And a bagpipe. Who puts a bagpipe in a rock band?

She keeps scrolling through her Twitch comments while she

brushes her teeth, and keeps scrolling while she pulls on sweat-pants and a *Steven Universe* T-shirt.

> **voltfairy:** @async04 did you hear? big loot run in cav-erns of chaos. silver tongue is rumored to be in the mix. you couldn't find it if it was lying on the floor in front of you.

Caverns of Chaos are a dungeon in *Aristotle's Hoard*, a tired old MMORPG where every player is an adventurer seeking the philosopher's treasure keep. In this game, Aristotle was not just a student of Plato but the center of a secret wizard society that orchestrated the rise and fall of nations; when Aristotle ascended into the clouds, transforming into a wyvern, he left behind a hid-den cave of his riches and magical artifacts. The Silver Tongue is one of seven unique items that, when combined, will imbue their owner with Aristotle's Sight, which will guide the player to the treasure. Because there are thousands of players but only seven items, factions have formed among the gamers. Voltfairy runs the Platonic Boyfriends, a team made up, it seems, strictly of on-line trolls. Async, who hardly bothers with this low-frame-rate garbage game anymore, is a captain in the Erudites.

A few messages later, though, she finds this, from SocraTRON, the leader of her clan:

> **SocraTRON:** @all.erudites-clan ATTN ALL: MANDATORY DUNGEON RUN. PRIME GOAL: FIND THE SILVER TONGUE. SECONDARY GOAL: SWIPE FLAMER CLAN'S FLEET FEET ARTIFACT WHILE THEY'RE DISTRACTED. ANYONE WHO DOESN'T SHOW IS BENCHED 30 DAYS. NO EXCEPTIONS.

Async shakes her head. She's 90 percent sure SocraTRON is a fourteen-year-old boy from Iowa. If he had a job, or were a parent, or went to college, he'd be more forgiving with his clan scheduling. Everything's mandatory to him.

Still, she would like to see someone assemble all the artifacts. The Erudites have three already; if they can snag the Fleet Feet and the Silver Tongue . . .

Fuck it, she thinks, and logs on.

"Hey, homeys," she says, fitting the headset over her head. "Async here, comin' atcha with the most bloodshot eyes in the history of time. Not from the weed, no. I've been slinging scoops for thirteen hours." She holds up her discarded apron. "My hands smell like pralines and cream. I don't even know what a praline is. Whatever. Tonight I'm playing *Aristotle* even though I never want to play that shit again. Look at this," she complains, firing up the in-game menu. "What is this, nine pixels? Stunning level of detail." A yawn splits her face open. "Sorry, you guys, I'm straight *beat*." She laughs. "The things you do for love of the game, right?"

She joins the rest of the Erudites at the mouth of the Caverns of Chaos, where SocraTRON hits the mic and delivers the longest monologue in the history of game monologues, filled with instructions and assignments and warnings.

Async never hears SocraTRON's task for her. She sags against the sofa as he talks, her eyes suddenly heavy. The controller slips from her fingers; she tips her head back on a cushion, just for a second. As the rest of the team swarms into the cave, Async's sprite remains on the threshold and begins a series of idle animations, hefting its axe restlessly, shifting its weight from one foot to another. Another player from a competing clan sidles up to her and slips a blade into her from behind, then performs an enthusiastic dab and dashes into the cave. Async04's silken-clad sprite crumples to the ground and twitches.

2

Usually, this time of morning, the old man can be found at his workbench, smoothing the blades of new scissors against a damp stone or running their blades beneath the high-speed grinder wheel. He is always at the shop before anyone else, stoking the furnace so it's hot when the others arrive. But on this day, the furnace is black and cold; the workbench and its tools are unattended.

"Where's Mr. Fitzgerald?" the other workers ask one another. The questions are easygoing at first, but as the day brightens, and the furnace is still cold, the questions take on an edge. The scissor-making company has, for nearly 130 years, been making scissors in the old way. The scissors are beloved by tradespeople and makers around the world; a pair of them, cared for like a child, might last a lifetime.

Eoghan Fitzgerald, the ninety-three-year-old master craftsman, is the only remaining worker who knows every step of the process.

"It's all in his head," the workers sometimes said to one another. "If he ever kicks the bucket, we best look for new work."

Declan O'Doherty III, whose father owned the scissors factory before him, and whose father owned it before *him*, telephones Eoghan's home. But Eoghan, who is mostly deaf these days, does not like to wear his hearing aid. "He probably doesn't hear the phone," Declan, who was up all night with a colicky new baby, says to Liam MacKenna. "Go to the old fellow's house and see what's what, would you?"

So Liam MacKenna, who was up all night laboring over his thesis—he doesn't intend to grind scissor blades forever, he's going to be a forensic pathologist someday—drives to Eoghan's cottage, down by the coast. As Liam gets out of his pickup truck, he pauses and takes in the sound of clanging bells from the nearby

harbor, breathes in the briny air. He understands why Mr. Fitzgerald chooses to live here, in a crummy cottage surrounded by
shipping warehouses. On a foggy morning, like this one, it's possible to imagine the cottage on a bluff overlooking the sea.

Eoghan's windows are dark when Liam raps on the door as
loudly as he dares. "Mr. Fitzgerald," he calls out. Then, more loudly,
"Mr. Fitzgerald, are you in there?" When no answer comes, Liam
goes from window to window, cupping his hands and peering into
the charcoal shadows inside. The kitchen is cold and still, no coffee
in the pot; the small living room's woodstove holds a residual but
dwindling glow. The next window is a bathroom, which means the
next is a bedroom, and there, Liam sees, is Mr. Fitzgerald, lying
still and strangely small in his bed, hands folded over his chest, as
if already laid to rest.

# 3

"Yo, homes, you drive," Connor says, tossing Gus the keys to his
Geo Metro. "I don't drive well under pressure."

"Jack!" Gus says. With a sigh, he walks ten feet to where the
keys have landed on the lawn, then picks them up. "Did you ever
see *Out of Sight*?" he asks Connor.

"That's the one with Stifler and Kelso looking for their car,
right?" Connor says.

Gus blinks. "No, man, that's *Dude, Where's My Car?* The fuck
did you smoke in there?" He shakes his head, then climbs behind
the wheel. "No, this is the Soderbergh movie. Based on an El-
more Leonard novel. Real pedigree. *Dude, Where's My*—Shit, I'm
ashamed to know you."

"Just drive, okay?" Connor says, twitching with adrenaline.
"Before I go back inside and merc that fucking rent-a-cop—"

Gus turns sideways in his seat. Patiently, he says, "In *Out of*

*Sight*—which is a sophisticated story about two people who can't fall in love who *do* fall in love—there's this scene where Buddy, played by Ving Rhames, tosses car keys to Jack, played by George Clooney. But Foley's all amped-up about this woman, Karen, played by Jennifer Lopez, and he doesn't—"

"Fuckin' Mr. IMDb over here," Connor interrupts. "I need you to be Mr. Fuckin' Uber Driver now, you *capisce*?"

But Gus won't be derailed. "And he doesn't see the key toss. The keys go right out the apartment window. Foley doesn't even notice, but Buddy's like, 'Jack!'" He chuckles to himself. "That's what I said when you threw the keys. 'Jack!'"

"Motherfucker, they're calling the police, move your ass!"

"And where am I driving us this delightful morn—?"

"Like I give a fuck," Connor says. "Somewhere the cops won't expect."

"'Your destination: a non-extradition treaty country. You will each be paid a fee of one million dollars for services rendered. But you can never again set foot on your native soil. Can you live with that?'" Gus nods his head, satisfied. "That's General Hummel, played by the excellent Ed Harris, from *The Rock*."

"I'm gonna rock *you* if you don't drive."

Gus pulls away from the curb, then points the car east. He weaves through the neighborhood, then onto Marsh, while Connor slumps in his seat, muttering. "That fuckin' guy," Connor complains. "He wrecked my sweater, you know. I see that guy again, I'm gonna . . ." He trails off, realizing the car's carving through near darkness. He turns around, sees the lights of Santa Mira receding, and says, "Gus, where the fuck are we going?"

Gus points at a green highway sign. "You told me go somewhere the cops won't expect."

Connor turns and watches the sign go by. "Vegas. Vegas?"

"It isn't exactly a non-extradition treaty country, but a man can get real lost there."

"Fuckin' Vegas," Connor says. He yawns, then folds his arms. "I can feel myself coming down, man. I don't think I've ever felt this tired."

"'I don't ever remember feeling this awake,'" Gus says.

"Good thing you're driving." Connor burrows down into the passenger seat, knees tucked against the glove box, and says, "Wake me when we get there, yo."

"'I don't ever remember feeling this awake,'" Gus repeats, mostly to himself. "That was Thelma, played by the extremely tall Geena Davis, from *Thelma and Louise*."

Gus pushes the Geo into the dawn, California hills turning into high desert scrub, stars fading out in a wash of smudged sunrise. He switches the radio to a classic country station, then hums along with Willie and Merle singing about Pancho dying somewhere in Mexico. Connor dies just before the car crosses the state line into Nevada.

# 4

The ALCAN Highway is nearly fourteen hundred miles long, starting in Dawson Creek, British Columbia, and terminating in Delta Junction, Alaska. It's a beautiful, scenic route through the depths of the Canadian wilderness; at any moment along the way, a driver can witness a family of bears crossing the road or a moose bathing itself in a northern lake, or, under cover of darkness, watch the aurora twist and spark overhead.

The highway is Amelia's regular route, and has been for thirty-one years. She owns her rig, a bright blue Freightliner with a pair of faux ox horns protruding from the grille; she named it Babe, after Paul Bunyan's famous ox. She's a veteran of the northern shipping routes, gets first choice of load at the warehouses, has tackled every possible emergency here in the middle of nowhere:

blown tires, lost wheels, a shattered windscreen, a thrown rod; once, in near-whiteout conditions, she struck something, and found blood scattered on the snow. Whatever it was had limped away before she could climb down from Babe's wheel. But when she tells the story at truck stops, she says it had two legs and was easily eight feet tall.

Over the years, though, the route has changed. The long, pitted, gravelly or dirt sections of the highway are now smooth asphalt or concrete; the most twisted stretches have been straightened. It's a safer drive now, and her hazard pay disappeared long ago as a result. She's still done well enough, all things considered; well enough that she's given some thought to retirement in the next few years.

"The most important thing to remember about your company-sponsored 401(k) is this: If you're not contributing the maximum allowable amount with every paycheck, you're actively plotting against your own future." Amelia nods at the sound advice of Gary Banner. *Fight for Financial Success* is her new favorite podcast.

"Amen," she says, and then switches the audio off. She downshifts and coasts into the trucker lot of God's Country 24 Hour Trucker Heaven. With a sigh, she pulls the brake and kills the big engine. She knows all the truck stops by heart, even plans her daily drive target around which one she can reach by what time. God's Country is her least favorite of them.

"Look, it's Mighty Melia," Werkle calls when Amelia pushes through the truck stop door at 6:00 a.m. "Melia, we haven't seen you round here since—"

"I was here six weeks ago," Amelia says.

"Well, since six weeks, then," Werkle corrects, grinning through his beaver-tail-sized beard. "I was on my vacation right 'bout then, sose I would've missed you."

"That's too bad." Amelia turns away, headed for the showers, hoping to cut the conversation short.

"Sorry, Melia, showers are out today," Werkle calls after her. "They found sulfur leakin' into the water pipes and have to refit them all."

"Well, how long's that gonna take?" Amelia asks, frowning.

"Oh, I dunno. Billie got an estimate but she hasn't got 'em started yet. Tween you and me and these four walls"—Werkle gestures at the otherwise empty truck stop—"I'm almos' certain she's hard up. The oil prices, you know. Heck, I might have to find a new gig. God's Country might not be here next time you swing through."

That would not be ideal, Amelia thinks. She never plans to overnight at this old truck stop; partly because Werkle, a mistake she made sixteen years ago, is still here, but mostly because the bunkhouse is poorly outfitted, a terrible place to spend a night. Still, the showers have always been above average. If God's Country shuts down, she'll have a three-hundred-mile stretch of the highway with no available services.

"Ain't asked about my vacation," Werkle says when Amelia arrives at the checkout counter with an armful of chickpea crisps and a bottle of kombucha.

"Maybe that's reason enough not to tell me about it, Werkle." She nods behind the counter. "Throw in a pack of Strikes, would you?"

"I thought you quit."

"I still like to look at them." She levels her gaze at Werkle, who nods and says nothing further about the cigarettes.

"Listen," Werkle says, ringing up the snacks. "You been watchin' the reports? There's a storm about sixty miles north. They're half spectin' it to switch directions and blow right through here in the next hour."

"All the more reason for me to get moving. You done there?"

Werkle lays his hand on Amelia's; she snatches it away.

"Werkle," she warns.

"I'm jus' attempting to tell you, it's gon' be bad out there,"

Werkle says. "Don'tcha worry your sweet heart about my intentions." He grins proudly. "Met myself a girl on my getaway."

"I wish you two all the best," Amelia says, holding back a sigh.

"Yes'm, I spent four days at Lake Hinters," Werkle says, searching the kombucha bottle for a UPC label. "You know, you squint just right, it's almos' like bein' in Jamaica or somethin'."

"I'll bet." Amelia takes the bottle and rotates it, pointing the UPC at Werkle.

"Girl I met, you know her name's almost like yours?"

One of Amelia's eyebrows rises on its own.

"Ameline," Werkle says. "Even prettier, ain't it?"

"Ring me up, you old goat," Amelia says. "You want me to live through that storm, you ought to let me skedaddle."

With a lovesick grin, Werkle bags her items, then sends her on her way. Unshowered and unhappy about it, Amelia hoists herself back into Babe's big seat, fires up the engine, and slowly guides the rig onto the road. If Werkle's right, and she's got a storm to think about, she's glad her load's a light one; there's nothing but pallets of toilet paper in the trailer this time. She makes better time that way.

Werkle is right. The storm sweeps across the highway long before she reaches Watson Lake, and it's a startlingly bad one. Her visibility dwindles, until she's creeping down the highway at fifteen miles per.

"Goddamn you, Werkle," she mutters, as if her regrettable old one-night stand had somehow conjured a storm specifically for her.

She guides Babe onto the wide shoulder, sets the flashers, kills the engine, and fires up the little generator that'll keep her cabin warm without wasting fuel. Behind her front seats is a narrow living space. She unlatches the foldout bed, props up some pillows, and reclines with her all-in-one TV-DVD unit. There's no TV signal this far out, but she's got a collection of *Northern Exposure* reruns.

Outside the truck, the storm deepens, buffeting the trailer with heavy winds; snow layers on the windscreen, piles on top of the cab. Amelia pulls a blanket around herself and munches chickpea crisps. She likes this episode: Joel, the doctor at the center of the show, gets stranded in the woods at night. A mysterious figure comes out of the trees and beckons Joel to follow; against his better judgment, Joel does, and finds that the stranger, Adam, is the person the whole town suspects of being Bigfoot. Instead, Adam turns out to be one hell of a chef, and makes Joel a spectacular meal.

"Told you all Bigfoot was real," Amelia says, and as the storm builds, piling snow around her rig, she burrows deeper into her blankets and drifts to sleep in the blue light of the television.

# 5

The day of the wedding, Nerisa felt like an author with her first book, hoping someone, anyone, would show up at her reading. "You've sent the invitations," Jake had assured her, "and the people who love you will want to be there for you."

"I don't have anyone anymore," she had told him, and burst into tears. It was true; most of her family was gone, except for an aunt in Poughkeepsie and a third cousin in Mobile.

But people had shown up. Not hundreds, but nearly seventy. And they weren't all Jake's family members or friends, either; Jake had, in secret, somehow tracked down Nerisa's middle school best friend, Rae, whom she hadn't seen in nearly ten years, and a few of her college roommates, who brought other old friends along with them.

Nerisa cried through the whole ceremony. When the last of her friends had passed through the receiving line, she turned to Jake, bit his earlobe, and whispered, "Just you wait for tonight," in her sultriest voice. Jake grinned, then whispered back, "That's not why I did it, you know," and she said, "I do know that," and snaked her hand behind him and squeezed his butt stealthily.

The reception couldn't move fast enough for Nerisa. Yes, yes, chicken or fish, okay. There was no father-daughter dance, just her dance with Jake; he chuckled at her as she practically quivered with annoyance at all these formalities.

"Patience, honey," he advised, and drew her close to him, swaying softly. "You're going to want to remember all of this."

When at last the reception ends, and she's waved farewell to all those long-lost friends, she and Jake rest in the back of a taxi, weary, as it drives them to a bed-and-breakfast on the edge of town.

"Tomorrow we have to get up early," he reminds her, patting her hand where it rests on his knee. "Don't forget. We have a six-thirty flight."

"To Honolulu," she says, a dreamy tinge to her voice. "And then . . . ?"

"And then Kauai."

"Kauai," she muses. "The Garden Island."

"With chickens."

"With . . . what?"

As the taxi arrives at the B and B, Jake tells her the story of the island's wild chicken population. "There's a rumor that the chickens escaped from coops during a storm," he says, hefting bags from the trunk, "and that they fled into the jungles, where they've grown their numbers, unchecked by predators."

"Jungle," Nerisa says. "Not forest?"

"I . . . Huh." Jake shakes his head. "Not being a, you know, plant person, I don't actually know."

"Let's say jungle. Forest sounds ordinary."

"Jungle it is. I'll message the Hawaiian premier and tell them."

"The 'premier,' huh?"

"Or whatever they have."

"They have a governor, just like we do," Nerisa says, laughing.

Jake's eyes are red when he grins. "I'm pretty damn tired, you know. And we have to get up in, like, four hours."

Nerisa rises onto her toes and nips at his neck with her teeth. "Don't be that tired," she says. "It's our wedding night."

"I know, I know." He pecks her forehead. "But it's also just another night, and if we don't get any sleep, every night in Hawaii is going to feel like tonight."

"Turned on?"

"Bone-tired," he corrects. When her face falls, he says, "I'm not saying no, honey, I'm just saying—I'm saying I'm tired. That's all."

They check in at the front desk silently, enduring the chirping of the owner, who leads them up a flight of stairs to their floral-print room. The owner points out every amenity, until Jake interrupts and reminds her they're leaving in four hours and just need some sleep.

Nerisa pouts while Jake busies himself in the restroom. This won't be their first time, obviously; they've lived together for three months already. But it's the principle of the thing. It's the *wedding night*. He's supposed to turn into an animal, isn't he? He didn't even carry her over the threshold.

The sink burbles behind the bathroom door, and then she hears him brushing his teeth. Why aren't they brushing side by side, looking at each other with drunk eyes, still clad in their disheveled wedding attire? Why isn't he abandoning all usual protocol to take her, right here on this . . . overly flowery bedspread?

"Fuck," she mutters, and falls back onto the pillows. She's as angry at herself as him right now. She *knows* she's fallen prey to all the stereotypes of a wedding night. She knows that it takes all kinds of people to make a world, and that more people than just her must have spent their wedding night too exhausted to, you

know, consummate their passion, or whatever. But in her imagination, every other couple who ever got married busted down
their bedroom door in a frenzy, in their mad rush for the bed
and a night of flung sweat and blown joy. Why not her?

She's so frustrated she hardly notices her muscles relaxing
into the embrace of the bed, doesn't notice at all that her body
and mind are as tuckered out as Jake's, isn't even aware that her
eyes are closing until they're closed. She doesn't hear the bathroom door open, doesn't register Jake's words as he apologizes
and crawls onto the bed beside her, doesn't notice when his voice
cracks and rises, when he shakes her, when he cries out for help.

# The Black Triangle

## I

Tracy tugs the wheel, guiding the Ford Escort to the shoulder. With a sigh, she flaps open a paper map, inspects it closely, then crumples it again and squints at the light-dappled street, searching for a sign.

While she tries to make sense of the unfamiliar scene, Davy unbuckles his seat belt and slides forward. He switches on the radio and presses the button that finds music for him.

> *. . . coming in this week at number 20 on the Hot 100, from Minnesota rockers Soul Asylum, is "Misery," their first new single in two years. Turn it up!*

"Turn it off," Tracy admonishes. "I can't think." She pinches the bridge of her nose, then sighs again, deeply. "Honey, help Mommy out here. Do you see a sign for Flora Lane?" Then she stops, covers her face with both hands, and begins to laugh.

"What's funny?" Davy asks.

"Well, look," she says, and points.

The car is parked next to a woodcut business sign painted in brassy golds and greens.

PONDEROSA INSTITUTE OF NEUROPSYCHOLOGY

DR. ALMER CASTANEDA, PSYD

DR. GEORGIA RUSLOVIC, PHD

SINCE 1983

"It doesn't say Flora," Davy says. "What's *nyoor-ops*—? What's that word?"

## 2

Dave sits in a brightly colored beanbag chair, at a table just his height, contemplating the assortment of art supplies before him. This corner is the only colorful spot in the room; the rest of Dr. Castaneda's study is paneled in somber mahogany, the ceiling a dull mustard ribbed with exposed beams.

Tracy pulls her sweater more tightly around her.

"It's drafty in here," Dr. Castaneda apologies. "You know, I've considered trading offices with Georgia. Her office is practically a greenhouse! She's more accustomed to cooler climes."

"It's all right." Tracy shivers and shifts uncomfortably, uncertain if it's the temperature that's made her chilled, or just the fact that she's here, making Davy's condition real by meeting with this stranger.

"You feel as if by coming here, you've transformed a small concern into a grave one," the doctor observes.

"I suppose that's true."

"These issues feel unbearably large, and society conditions us to face them on our own," the doctor says. He smiles, bearing slightly too-large, crooked white teeth. "You've taken a brave step. Just talking about these things can scale them to something . . . addressable. Treatable. Solvable."

"Sometimes I think it's my fault," Tracy says, as if given permission to spill her fears. "His dreams. That something I did—you know, before he was born—caused all of this."

"Why do you say that?"

"He's never slept through the night. Not a single night. Not ever."

"You must be exhausted, Tracy."

"My *husband* sleeps fine." She tries to smother a bitter laugh.

Davy piles up drawing after drawing, absently humming the opening bars of the song he all-too-briefly heard on the radio.

"The first act of self-harm," Dr. Castaneda says. "When did you notice?"

"God, it's hard even to say. It's like the nightmares. He's always . . ."

"Bruises?"

"Yes. And scratches. For a while—" She lowers her voice, leaning toward the doctor, who mirrors her posture. "For a while it was spiders. He dreamed they were crawling on him. I'd turn on a light when he screamed, and then I'd scream, because he'd have scratched his face to bleeding." She dips her head shamefully. "Even now I see the faint scars and feel like a failed mother."

"It didn't stop there, though," Dr. Castaneda prompts. When Tracy looks away, he says, "And how about medications? What have we tried?"

"I have it written down," Tracy says. She fumbles a folded sheet of paper from her purse and passes it to the doctor. "That's everything, I think."

Dr. Castaneda peers at her handwriting over his glasses. "This is quite a list, Mrs. Torres."

"Davy's . . . unique. Nobody knows what to do about . . . Well."

"And how closely has his receptiveness—to the medications—been monitored? Did he demonstrate improvement with any of these?" Dr. Castaneda lightly shakes the list.

"We're here, aren't we?" Tracy puts a hand to her mouth. "I'm so sorry. I don't mean to—"

"Quite all right, Tracy. It's all right."


# 3

After a short break and a tour of the house—Davy's favorite is the koi pond in the courtyard—Dr. Castaneda asks Tracy if any diagnosis was proffered.

"Nothing concrete," she says. Her eyes reflect a lifetime of lost sleep. "I mean, of course exhaustion. Some nights he sleeps fewer than two hours. That accumulates. The doctors tell me, mostly, that this can't continue. That it's bound to lead to . . . developmental problems . . ."

"How unhelpful," Dr. Castaneda says, so tenderly that Tracy nearly collapses from gratitude. "Chronic night terrors are exceedingly rare, particularly when they persist this long. In the history of my field, there are fewer than ten recorded cases. The most recent, thirty years ago, was a little boy in Russia. In fact, my colleague, Georgia, was a student at the medical university where the boy was studied. She was so intrigued by his condition that she switched her major." Dr. Castaneda leans close to Tracy and confides, "I confess a small amount of professional envy that she witnessed this case directly. What a gif—" He halts abruptly, as if realizing he has misspoken. "Forgive me. I mean to say, Davy is a once-in-a-lifetime kind of child. He's exceedingly special. We would like to better understand and help him."

Back in the study, Davy returns to his art projects, while Dr. Castaneda spreads Davy's earlier drawings on the coffee table.

"A child experiencing what your son does," he begins, "will often directly express their fears in art. An unconscious attempt to remove the threat from their mind and commit it to paper, where it can be more easily dealt with. A sort of childlike exorcism. You can burn a drawing, crumple it, cut it to ribbons. That's the root of the work Davy is doing here, and make no mistake: this is difficult work. He is purging. De-escalating that which scares him."

Dr. Castaneda holds up the first sheet, the most unusual of all the pictures Davy created. The page is blackened except for an array of white Chiclets at the top and bottom, a scribble of red in the center.

"Here he has opened himself for us," the doctor says. "He has drawn his emotional response to his dreams. What do you see in this drawing, Mrs. Torres?"

Tracy shakes her head. "He's done this one before. I don't know what it is. An angry sun?"

Dr. Castaneda holds the drawing next to his face, then opens his own mouth as wide as he can.

"A mouth?" she asks.

"A scream, my dear."

"I already know he's scared. The drawings make me sad, but they don't tell me anything I don't already know."

"On the contrary, if I may. This drawing is . . . *existential*. There is nothing on this page *except* the scream. Without knowing why, your son is telling you that his entire existence, all that he is, is this single emotion. Abject fear."

Dr. Castaneda puts the drawing aside, then shuffles the remaining illustrations into two piles. "Your son appears to have two recurring dreams," he says. "They don't seem to overlap. The subject of one never appears in the other."

The doctor holds up a crude drawing of an elephant. Its eyes are black and soulless, its tusks stained red.

"This interesting creature appears in all these drawings," he says, indicating the first pile.

He holds up a drawing from the second pile. "And these figures here . . ."

Tracy touches the shadowy characters her son has drawn. "Yes," she says. "He gave them a name. He calls them . . . dreamers? Dream people."

Dr. Castaneda puts the drawings down and stands with a grunt. "Let me show you something."

Tracy follows him to the other side of the room, to an unmarked door. She looks back at Davy, still drawing. "Will he . . . ?"

"Davy will be fine. And we'll be just in here. I assure you."

The room beyond the door contains a few desks, computers, some unusual monitoring equipment. "It looks like a room for measuring . . . earthquakes, or something," she says.

The doctor touches a switch, illuminating another room on the other side of a glass wall. At its center is a silvery structure, almost sarcophagus shaped.

"That is the scariest bed I've ever seen," Tracy says. "That is a bed, right?"

A bundle of cords with suction-cup tips lies on the bed, next to another machine with what looks like a blood pressure cuff. There are more immediately familiar machines. Heart monitors and the like.

Tracy looks from the bed to the seismograph-looking machines on the desks around her. "Doctor," she says slowly, "what kind of treatment do you do here, exactly?"

4

Katie's rusted hatchback is parked beside Matteo's Camaro in the ER intake lane. No sense in keeping the lane free for ambulances, Dave had explained to her; there weren't any ambulances, not anymore.

Matteo and Linda wait for them on the sidewalk.

"This is her?" Linda asks.

"Linda, Katie," Dave says. "Katie, this is Linda."

"You're the radio lady," Katie says.

"How'd I do? Nine years of medical school, all so I can operate a microphone." Matteo harrumphs at this, and Linda pats his shoulder. To the others, she explains, "He's a little crushed. His hero didn't make it."

"Hero?" Dave asks. "Oh. Larry."

"*Late Night* Larry," Matteo corrects.

"You must be some kind of girl," Linda says to Katie. She thumbs in Dave's direction. "This one, he didn't even tell us where he was going, just took off like a second-string superhero."

"I don't know . . ."

"Wipe your mouth, honey," Linda says, indicating the corner of her own mouth. "You okay?"

Katie rubs her sleeve over her mouth self-consciously.

"She, uh, took pills," Dave says. "We had to . . ."

"Good move." Linda sighs. She turns and looks at the lobby through the glass doors. "You know how much I really don't want to go back in there?"

"Dave told me what's in there," Katie says. "We could stay out here."

"Except people might come," Matteo says.

"There's more than one way into the hospital," Linda says. "If we stay out here, we could miss them." She yawns, then leans against the building. "God, maybe I should've just gone to sleep."

"Don't say that," Dave says. "We need you."

"Have you ever heard of anything like this?" Katie asks. "I mean, a virus that kills people when they sleep? It sounds super *X-Files* to me."

"It's legit," Matteo says, fighting his own yawn. "And fucking scary."

"But how long can a person stay awake?" Katie asks. "I mean, I did a few all-nighters in college. But not back-to-back."

"To-back, to-back . . . ," Matteo echoes.

"Look, everyone is different," Linda explains. "Human bodies have limits, but yours might be more forgiving than mine. But not by much. Maybe a day in either direction. Two if someone's lucky."

"So we're dead in two days?" Katie asks, her voice rising nervously.

Dave, who has been quietly listening to this, says, "Trust me. You don't want to go past forty-eight hours." He meets the eyes of each in turn. "That's the line. Things start unraveling. The longer you're awake, the bigger your psychological tapas menu grows. Paranoia. Depression. Schizophrenia, hallucinations. Awful thoughts. The kind that unhinge you."

Katie covers her ears.

"At seventy-two hours, you . . . Well. Let's just say you really miss how good things felt at forty-eight."

"Nice sales pitch, Don Draper," Linda says. "But, yeah. He's not wrong. We have to be each other's safety net. We have to keep a close eye on the person next to us. If we nod off, even for a moment . . . I mean, that's the ball game, people."

"What if I start to . . . ?" Katie begins.

Linda takes Katie's hand in her own. "Cup your palm. Like this, not too deep." She raises Katie's hand and places it against her own cheek. "You want to hit more with the fingers than the palm, see? That'll give you the really sharp *crack* you want from a good slap. The startling kind."

Katie withdraws her hand. "I couldn't *hit* anyone—"

"Should've brought the bat," Dave says, grinning kindly. "Turns out my girl's a real basher."

"We're well past gestures of kindness," Linda says, ignoring Dave. "Think of sleep like the creep at the party who's about to roofie your best friend. Go in hard. Rescue your friend."

"What is with all the shit analogies here?" Matteo protests. "You fuckers are *dark*."

"So what did you take, honey?" Linda asks.

"It's not in her system anymore." Dave shrugs. "Doesn't matter."

"Dude, what about you?" Matteo asks. "Your—?"

Dave silences Matteo with a look. "I'm fine. Tired, but who isn't?"

Linda glances at Matteo. "And you, soldier?"

"Oh, fuck off. I'm not the weak link."

Linda doesn't take the bait. Instead, she pats Katie's hand. "And you, dear?"

"I worked all night," she says. "I'm pretty tired." Then she looks at each one of them. "But I guess that's true of all of us, huh?"

"You went to the party," Matteo says. "The dipshits said they saw—"

"She wasn't using," Dave says.

"I was with Janeane. And Steph." Katie shrugs. "I thought it was going to be fun. I ended up chauffeuring them to two bars, then the party. Okay? Steph had, like, four double margaritas at Dos Muchachos, then tried to blow the bartender in the supply closet. Not exactly a night to remember." She covers her mouth suddenly. "Oh God. They're—Are they both—?"

Dave opens his arms, and Katie steps into them. "Shh," he says. "If they aren't, we'll find them."

"All right, focus up, everyone," Linda says. "We need to conserve our energy. We're going to need this." She steps in front of the ER doors, which hiss open. "Let's go inside and see about expanding our ranks, shall we?"

## 5

The waiting room is as empty as they left it. Linda frowns at this, then suggests they split up. Matteo heads for the admissions lobby in the main building, while Linda pushes deeper into the

ER corridors. Dave takes Katie's hand and they climb the stairs to the next floor, which fractures into several different patient wings.

Below, Dave can hear Matteo's voice echo through big, empty rooms.

"I think we're too late," he says. "Nobody's going to be here."

"Have hope," Katie says, but her voice is tight.

At the first junction, Dave pauses. "Where do we even start?"

Katie reads the signs: Radiology to the west, Intensive Care to the east, Oncology to the north. She pulls Dave forward, to the cancer wing.

"We'll check them all, but we have to start somewhere," she says. "Besides, my mom was here, remember? I still sort of remember the layout."

"You're the boss," Dave says.

They pass a nursing station, a janitor's closet, a locked pharmacy, and several empty patient rooms before they encounter their first body. It belongs to a woman younger than Katie. Most of her hair has gone; her skin has molded itself to the skeleton beneath. Her eyes are closed, set deeply into hollow sockets. Her skin is sallow and bruised. Despite her condition, she looks peaceful.

"Oh God," Katie moans.

Dave realizes it's her first dead body. "Trust me," he says, touching her shoulder. "I think for her this was a mercy."

But Katie isn't looking at the girl. She's gazing at a small sofa near the bed. There's a young man there, wearing a wedding ring. He's stretched out on the couch, a pillow under his head. Snuggled against him is a small boy, three years old at most.

They're both gone.

"Okay, this is a bad idea," Dave says. "Let me take you back to—"

"It isn't right," she says. "It isn't fair. It's not fair."

Dave steers her back into the hallway. "You can sit at the nurses' station while I check the rest of the rooms."

"Fuck that," she says through clenched teeth. "I want to hit something. God, that poor family! Everything they had to deal with, and then—" Her hands ball into fists so tight the color drains from her knuckles. "God is a fucking *sadist*."

"I really think—" Dave starts, but Katie abruptly tenses.

"Do you hear that? Shh. Listen."

Dave is quiet for a long moment. "I don't hear—"

"*There*," Katie says. "Shut up! Listen for a—"

It's faint. It's far away, but it's there:

"*Hello? Is somebody there?*"

# 6

The woman in room 217, despite being hollowed out by some cancer or another, brims with spit and vinegar.

"The hell have you people been?" she bellows when Dave and Katie appear in her doorway. "I've been shouting so long I'm going to lose my voice." She levels severe eyes at them both. "You aren't in scrubs. I worked the children's wing of this hospital twenty-nine years, and I never once showed up out of uniform."

Dave looks down at his watchman's uniform and fiddles with the name tag. "I'm sorry, ma'am, I—"

"Mrs. Nelson?" Katie asks, incredulous. "Ruth?"

The patient narrows her eyes. "Who's that, then?"

Katie crosses the room to the woman's bed. She hands her a pair of glasses from the bedside table.

The woman adjusts the glasses with hands bruised from IV needles, then inspects Katie closely. Her eyes brighten. "Goodness. Katie? When did you become a nurse, hon?"

Katie throws her arms around the woman's neck and, without meaning to, begins to cry.

"Oh dear." Ruth Nelson strokes Katie's hair, her demeanor entirely changed. "Dear, it's okay." When Katie has collected herself, Ruth says, "I should be the one crying. Look at me."

Katie laughs and wipes her eyes.

"So you two know each other?" Dave asks, stepping into the room.

Ruth's smile reveals too-white dentures. "Katie is a living angel. But perhaps you know that already."

"Ruth's daughter is in my group," Katie tells Dave. "Lilly."

"You've got to show up for your kids, that's what I say. Even when they're middle-aged. Even when they're walking disasters," Ruth says ruefully. "Now: Where are my usual nurses? I've called for Caroline or Aveed all night, but nobody comes."

Katie looks helplessly at Dave. "I . . ."

"Sit tight, Mrs. Nelson," Dave says. "I'm going to get someone who can help."

# 7

Dave intercepts Linda in the hallway. "Hey."

"Totally empty," Linda says, the disappointment evident in her eyes. "Nobody heard the radio broadcast. Nobody came."

"Where's Matteo?"

"Searching the parking structures, just in case." Linda looks past Dave, toward room 217. "You found a living person, though! I can't believe—"

"About that," Dave interrupts. "We might have a bit of a problem there."

As if on cue, Ruth Nelson cries out from her bed. Dave can hear Katie attempt to calm her.

"If she's in a bed," Ruth says, "she might be too far—"

"She's full of beans, as my grandpa would've said." But Dave shakes his head. "I don't think she's going anyplace. She doesn't look like she's going to keel over, but I peeked at her chart."

"Stage?"

"Four. Four's really bad, right?"

Linda nods solemnly. "Does she know?"

"That she has cancer? Uh, yeah, I think she knows."

"Idiot. Does she know what's *happening*?"

"Oh. Right."

"You didn't tell her, did you?"

"I wouldn't know where to begin," Dave admits.

"Good. Well, let's meet our survivor, huh?"

Dave pops into the room again. "Good news, Mrs. Nelson. I found—"

Linda leans in with a wave. "Hi, I'm L—"

"You aren't Caroline. Or Aveed. Or Gretchen or Keyshawn," Ruth says, displeased. "Are my nurses all on a four-hour smoke break?"

"Ruth," Katie begins, but Linda flutters her fingers, as if to say, *I've got this.*

"You're feeling well, I take it," Linda says cheerfully. She picks up Ruth's chart and flips pages. "Let me get up to speed here . . ."

"No, thank you," Ruth says. "No speed for me. Had a bad trip in 1984, you know." She waits for a reaction, and when none comes, protests: "Hey, I thought that was pretty good. Come on, now."

"You got me," Linda says, deep in the weeds of Ruth's medical history. "Mm-hmm. Okay." She replaces the chart, then touches Ruth's foot over the blanket. "Tell me how you're feeling. Scale of—"

"I know the goddamn scale," Ruth interrupts. "The scale's in my rearview—What's your name?"

"Linda," Dave says.

"She can speak for herself, I think, young man."

"Linda," Linda says.

"You don't look like one of those nursing students I keep getting."

"She works in the ER," Dave points out. He flinches as Linda shoots daggers his way.

"Emergency!" Ruth's eyes fly wide. "Oh, Jesus."

"Now, Mrs. Nelson," Linda cautions, but this time Katie butts in.

"What kind of cancer is it?" she asks.

Before Linda can answer, Ruth moans, "Lymphoma, hon. In my spine."

"What does it feel like?" Katie asks, holding the woman's hand. "Do you hurt?"

"It's like being fed into a garbage disposal," Ruth says, grimacing. "Slowly." To Linda, Ruth says, "I can't sleep without my codeine. Usually Keyshawn's here with it by now, but it's been hours." She lets her head fall against the pillow, exhausted from the conversation. "The codeine turns the garbage disposal off."

"Well, it's not time for sleep," Linda says. "Not quite yet. But I think we can do something for the pain. Dave? Katie? I could use your help. Outside."

Ruth groans again. "Come back fast."

"We won't be long," Katie assures her. She pats the woman's hand, then switches on the television. "Take your mind off things."

"Channel seventeen," Ruth says. "Maybe Peter Falk can keep me company."

Katie switches to 17, then leaves the woman with a *Columbo* rerun.

# 8

"Pharmacy," Linda says to them in the hallway. "Quickly, now."

They jog softly down the hall.

"I saw a pharma supply room," Dave offers. "Just up here."

"That's overflow and backstock," Linda says. "Not the good stuff." She leads them down a flight of stairs and into the lobby. "We want the good stuff."

Matteo bursts through a door marked PARKING GARAGE and spots them.

"Dead," he says, breathing hard.

"You didn't find anyone?" Katie asks.

"No, I found plenty of people." Matteo holds his side. His face is drained of color.

"We found someone alive," Dave says. "Well, Katie did."

"Well, good, because I think we could use another pair of hands," Matteo says. He notices the shift in Dave's expression. "What?"

# 9

In the hospital's primary pharmacy, Linda paws through shelf after shelf of drugs.

"Staff probably forgot her when they cleared out," she says. "Fucking Gordon. Fucking MCI."

Katie looks confused. "Who is Gordon? Who is MCI?"

"Mass casualty incident," Linda says. "Gordon's the doctor in charge. *Was.*"

"Mass casualty . . . ," Katie says. "Wait. Mass."

"Usually we use it for things like . . . earthquakes. Fires. Crowd surges at a big show. Things like that." Linda pauses, inspects a large blue bottle. "But there's no acronym big enough for this."

"What's the bottle?" Matteo asks.

Linda tosses it over her shoulder. "Modafalyst."

Matteo catches it. "The stim."

"'You'll never yawn again,'" Dave sings, "'once you get your second wind—'"

"No jingles," Linda says.

"How bad is she, really?" Katie asks Linda.

"It's pressing on her spinal cord," Linda says. "Immensely painful. They've got her on a codeine cocktail for sleep, but we can't give her that. Not if we want her to live."

"You think . . . You think it's still happening?" Katie asks. "It already happened. Everyone's . . . dead."

"We don't know what we're dealing with," Dave says. "Maybe it's over, but we won't know for sure until someone falls asleep—"

"—and we see if they wake up again," Matteo finishes.

"Hence the Modafalyst," Linda says.

"But stims are speed," Katie argues. "She said she had a bad reaction to speed."

"Well, I'm pretty sure that was an old person trying to make a joke," Linda says. "So we won't tell her it's speed. Okay?"

"That's unethical," Katie says. "You can't do that."

"Fuck ethical. There's no such thing anymore."

Matteo shakes the bottle. "Pilots used to take this shit before missions."

Linda takes the bottle back and pops the lid. "It's a stimulant," she agrees. "It's like a dozen cups of coffee. It won't kill you or anyone else." She shakes several pills into her palm. "Before we go any further, I think we all need to get in sync."

"I'm in recovery," Katie says. "I can't take anything that isn't prescribed by a medical professional."

"I'm a medical professional. You're prescribed. Take one."

Dave holds up one of the oblong blue capsules. "'You'll feel like a winner,'" he sings, then stops. "Down the hatch, then." He takes his pill.

"Cheers," Matteo says, and takes his.

Reluctantly, Katie takes hers. Linda takes two.

"I can stay with her," Katie says. "Mrs. Nelson. I can keep her awake. We don't have to give her anything."

Dave and Linda exchange a loaded glance. She subtly nods at Dave.

"Katie, honey," he begins. "I don't know if that's a good idea. Staying with her."

"Look, I'm just going to say it," Linda says. "It's been a while now since we broadcast the message. If people were coming, they'd be here. We've tried calling for help. No feds. No disease control. All the authorities are out of the picture. I think we have to assume they aren't answering their phones, because this is happening everywhere."

"Everywhere?" Katie asks.

"There's no way this shit is statewide," Matteo says. "That's impossible."

"Statewide," Linda repeats. "Matteo, I'm saying this might be worldwide. I think we have to assume nobody's alive. Nobody's coming to help us." She looks at Katie. "We're on our own."

## 10

The group heads back to Oncology, Linda in the lead.

"We have to stay proactive," she says, tapping her watch. "Fifteen minutes, that's how long the Modafalyst ought to take to hit us." She turns around, walking backward now. "In the meantime . . . I want to prep the cadavers."

Matteo stops. "Cadavers?"

"Bodies? Dead ones?" Katie echoes.

"Listen, we know *nothing*," Linda stresses. "If we want to know *something*, to have any chance of understanding this, then I need to examine the bodies."

Even Dave is dubious. "You know how to do that?"

"You see any doctors around?" Linda retorts. "Hey, maybe Mrs. Nelson's done an autopsy before. Let's ask her."

"She was an MRI tech," Katie says. "For kids."

"Well, shit, Barbie, I think that leaves me, then." Linda turns and strides toward Mrs. Nelson's room. "Bunch of goddamn casuals."

Matteo leans close to Dave. "She's gone round the bend, bro."

Dave shrugs. "I kind of like it."

"I'm not cutting anybody up," Katie says weakly.

"You can stay with Mrs. Nelson," Dave tells her. "At least until Linda's done . . . doing what she's going to do."

II

Ruth Nelson watches Linda connect the IV to her port. "Codeine?" she asks hopefully.

Linda pats the woman's arm. "No, Mrs. Nelson. But this should take the edge off. We might have to run some tests, so we want you awake. Keep those eyes open, okay?"

"I'm so tired. I've been awake all night."

"I'm going to stay with you," Katie volunteers. "I'll help you stay awake."

"You're a doll," Ruth says. "My Lilly, she won't shut up about her. Remember the camping trip you took her on? She was in her second month. She needed a friend then, so much. And there you were! Sweet Katie."

"She complained the whole trip," Katie says, chuckling.

"Oh, that was just her way. Perpetually dissatisfied." Ruth

brushes dampness from her eyes. "The last time she was here, the doctors monopolized her. I hardly saw her. Would you call her for me?"

Katie blinks hard. "Sure, Ruth. I can call her."

## 12

Katie spills into the hallway, where Linda is talking in hushed tones to the guys.

"Katie?" Dave asks.

Katie's eyes shine with tears. "I can't do this."

"Hey," Dave says, reaching for Katie's hand. "She's going to be okay. We're going to look out for her."

"I'm not crying for *her*, Dave." Katie pushes tears away. "She's had a good life. She's old. I'm crying for *me*. Or don't you recognize selfish tears when you see them?"

"Honey, we're going to get through—"

"Oh, fuck 'we,' Dave."

He blinks.

"There's no *we*. There's no *us*. Don't do that. Don't pretend it's all okay between us. You know as well as I do that things are very fucking far from *normal*."

Linda and Matteo back away slowly.

"Listen to me," Dave says, dropping his voice. "Just a second. Okay?"

Katie tenses like a wild animal. She pulls her hand free of Dave's, sets her jaw, says nothing.

"The night you left . . ."

"I don't want to fucking talk about it."

"Something awful happened that night, but—"

"'Happened.' Right, it just *happened*. Oops, look what just *happened*."

"Katie, did I hurt you?"

Katie recoils. "Did you *hurt* me?"

"I'm saying I don't . . . remember. If I hurt you that night, I need to know. So I can make it right. So I can take responsibility." He takes a cautious step toward her. "Please. What happened that night?"

## 13

Katie is bucked from sleep by the sound of crying. She blinks in the darkness, her eyes struggling to adjust to her chiaroscuro bedroom. She sits up, squinting at shadows.

"Dave?" she asks.

## 14

"And you were just *standing* there," she tells Dave now. They've broken away from the others and walked to the atrium. She leans on the railing, looking down at the sunny lobby below. "Just standing at the mirror, in your underwear, no expression on your face. Except you were sobbing, Dave. Sobbing like you'd lost someone. But totally dead-faced. It was creepy as *fuck*."

## 15

Katie slips out of bed and goes to Dave. She puts her hand on his shoulder. His body is superheated, but impossibly rigid. He doesn't seem to notice her touch. She lets her hand travel up the back of his neck, into his hair, hoping it will dislodge him from whatever nightmare has him locked up.

*Don't come close to me*, he'd warned her, early in their relationship. *I don't sleep well. If you see me do anything weird, just . . . stay away from me. Please.*

## 16

"But you just stood there," Katie tells Dave, who can't seem to look up from his shoes. "Ten minutes, twenty. I finally went back to bed. I know you always told me—"

"'Don't touch me,'" Dave recites. "But you did."

"I know that when these things happen to you, they're . . . outside your control," she says. "I know it isn't intentional. But that doesn't make it easy. Doesn't make it not scary to live with you. Dave, sometimes it was terrifying."

"I don't understand," Dave says. "You left because I turned into a statue? A crying one?"

"No," she says, her voice shrinking. "I left because of what you did next."

## 17

Katie pulls the blankets tightly around her knees. "Dave," she says, studying his moonlit form across the room. "I have to go to sleep. I have an early shift."

He doesn't answer, and she burrows into the blankets.

*I wish I could help you*, she thinks to herself. *I wish you'd let me.*

Then Dave screams.

## 18

"My blood just turned to slush," she tells him now, shaken by the memory. "The way you screamed—I couldn't tell if it was like someone was murdering you, or you were the one doing the murdering."

Despite the stimulants battling back sleeping pills in his bloodstream, Dave is utterly still.

"What then?" he asks.

## 19

Katie gathers the blankets to her chest. "Dave?"

He sobs wordlessly.

"Dave, honey, what's—?"

With a speed she wouldn't have expected from a sleepwalking man, he abruptly drives a fist into the mirror. His silvery reflection spiderwebs, then shatters with his second punch. Katie shrieks as shards of mirror fall to the floor.

She watches, unable to move, as Dave bends over and picks up the longest fragment, curling his fingers around its sharp edges.

## 20

Dave's face pales. "I didn't—?"

"You didn't hurt me," Katie says, aware now that she's reassuring *him* during a recounting of the most frightening night of *her* life. "You'd hurt yourself, though, right in front of me. And I couldn't handle that, Dave. I couldn't—You know why. So, I left. I can't believe you don't remember any of this."

She reaches for him now, placing a hand tentatively on his chest.

Dave twitches at her touch.

"How could you not remember?" she asks. She touches the first button of his shirt, then deftly unfastens it. His collar spreads open, revealing the T-shirt beneath. "The proof is right—"

Dave captures her hand with his. "Don't," he says. "Please don't."

She holds his gaze a moment, then takes her hand away and sits on a bench next to a yellowing ficus. She leans forward, elbows on her knees, and runs her fingers deep into her hair.

"After that," she says, "I just—I couldn't be with you, Dave. You scared the shit out of me. For you, yes, but for me, too. I felt vulnerable, like relapse was . . . inevitable. So that I wouldn't have to remember what I'd seen you do. So I wouldn't have to be afraid of you."

"Katie . . ."

"I won't go back to what I was," she says, eyes flashing. "Not for anybody, not even for you."

"I understand," he says, sitting in a chair opposite her.

"Just like that?"

He shrugs. "I know I'm not easy to live with."

"Understatement of the year."

"What can I say? Do you want me to tell you I'm fucked up? Katie. I'm fucked up."

"We're all fucked up, Dave. But you weren't honest with me. With me, your *partner*."

"I made a decision a long time ago. A choice. There are things that could only hurt others if they knew. About my condition. About my past. They'd only scare you."

"God, do you ever listen to yourself? How is that your choice?" She pulls her knees to her chest and turns sideways on the bench. "Recovery is about *facing* your problems. Head-on. Not pretending they don't—"

"Um, are we interrupting something here?"

Katie glares up at Matteo, who raises his hands apologetically.

"Sorry," he says. "I didn't know where you went. But I heard—Well. Dave, the undertaker awaits. It's time."

Dave looks at Katie; she's breathing hard, in fight mode. "To be continued?"

"Whatever. Go."

"Katie . . ."

"Go," she snaps. "I'm sure slicing up bodies with the crazy nurse is less scary to you than this conversation is. So, go."

## 21

Matteo and Dave pause at the operating room doors.

"Hey," Matteo says. "I gotta—Are you okay?"

"No," Dave says. "But who is?"

Through the porthole they can see a body laid out on the examination table, draped in a powder-blue sheet. Linda stands over the corpse, cracking her knuckles methodically.

"She's like Dr. Kevorkian," Matteo says, wrinkling his nose. "I gotta be honest, she kinda skeeves me out a little. But—"

Dave raises one eyebrow.

"But it's weirdly kinda hot," Matteo confesses. "The way she just shoves us all around and does what she wants . . . Damn, bro."

"Let's get this over with," Dave says.

## 22

"Took you long enough," Linda says as the guys push through the OR doors.

"Research," Matteo says, waggling his phone. "I couldn't find any 'how to dismember a corpse' how-tos on YouTube, though."

"Try searching for 'The Happy Coroner' next time," Linda says, unfazed. "Dave, can you help me here? The table's too high."

"You mean you're too short," Matteo jabs, tapping new search keywords on his phone.

"There's a latch on your left side," Linda instructs, "just under the—Yeah. Right there. Okay, and there's a release, too. Just step on the lever on the right side, and—"

The table drops several inches, catching Dave off guard. The body on the table wobbles like a Jell-O mold under plastic wrap.

"Um, is it supposed to do that?"

"It's a body, not a statue," Linda says. "Thank you, this is better."

"Fuck me silly," Matteo says, holding up his phone. "Dave, there's legit someone on YouTube sawing up dead people." He brings the phone back to his face and watches a little longer. "Linda, maybe you want to throw this on while you work? Like a cooking show. Like deboning a chicken or some Juliet Child shit."

"Julia," Dave says.

"Cute," Linda says, "but I'm good." Her voice betrays her, vibrating slightly. "One of you needs to hold the cam—"

"Me," Matteo says urgently. "That's me, I'm the camera guy."

"Dick," Dave mutters.

"Yo, you remember when you were in school, did they ever do that Halloween game where you put your hand in a box, and you can't see what's inside, and they're all, 'It's the eyeballs of the dead!' And it's really peeled grapes? I nearly passed out," Matteo confesses. "And then, to show me it was just grapes, one of the parent volunteers took one of the eyes out of the box and popped it into their mouth, and you better believe I threw up all over that box. So, yeah. You do not want my head in some dead fucker's guts."

"Brain," Linda corrects. "We're leaving the guts alone."

"Damp cold spaghetti noodles," Matteo says, remembering.

"Yeah. No. Camera guy, right here. Tell me where to point."

"I think it'll be pretty obvious," Dave says.

"Guys. Let's do this, okay?" Linda says. "Please? Be pros."

Matteo switches to video mode and holds his phone up.

"Dude," Dave says. "Landscape, you moron."

## 23

"All I'm saying is would it kill her to send me a text message?"

"Ruth, you text?" Katie asks, forcing a smile. "You're such a modern woman."

"Don't mock an old lady," Ruth says. "But really, when you have a daughter like mine . . . You call, you text, you FaceTime. You raise carrier pigeons. You keep every imaginable line of communication open." She shakes her head sadly. "Maybe your parents know what I mean."

"My parents . . ." Katie trails off.

Ruth grimaces. "I'm sorry, honey. I didn't mean to—"

"No. No, it's fine. I just—" Katie shrugs. "We aren't close. I haven't even talked to them since the last time I flunked out of rehab. I think they've given up to me, if you want to know the truth. But I . . . Maybe I haven't called them because I wanted to be sure. That I'm good this time. That it's stuck."

"If they're good parents, they'll understand. They'll be happy to hear from you under any circumstances."

Katie's eyes mist over. "I just—Thank you, Ruth."

"Now," Ruth says, patting her bony lap with frail hands. "Where's that damn daughter of mine?"

"I'll try her again in a few minutes," Katie says. Her phone is connected to Ruth's charger. "I don't think it's juiced enough yet."

Katie bites back a yawn, but Ruth notices.

"You can use that little couch over there," she suggests. "Catch a few winks. Sometimes Lilly sleeps there when she visits. Though she does say it hurts her back."

"No, I'm okay," Katie says, but her second yawn exposes the lie.

Ruth cocks her head. "Katie, dear, you'd tell me the truth if I asked for it, wouldn't you?"

Katie blinks rapidly. "The truth?"

"About what's going on."

"What's going on?" Katie asks innocently.

"Honey," Ruth says. "My nurses are missing. You're here, with no good reason." She shrugs. "Something's going on. You know what it is, and you're not telling me."

Katie glances up at the television. "Another *Columbo*. Look at that."

"I could scream, you know."

"Ruth, please."

"But I don't think anyone would come. Would they?"

"Of course they would," Katie says weakly.

"Just the way they did the first hundred times I yelled for help this morning, right?" Ruth nods at Katie's silence. "It's all right, dear. You'll tell me when you're ready."

## 24

Linda stands as tall as she can, then nods at Matteo, who presses Record. He centers her in the frame, zooms on her face.

> *My name is Linda Russo. I'm an APRN at Santa Mira Medical Center, Santa Mira, California. It's July fifth, approximately . . . one fifteen p.m. Assisting me with this pathology report is Dave—What's your last name again, Dave?*

The camera finds Dave's face as he answers.

> *Assisting me is David Torres. This session is being doc-*
> *umented by Matteo—*

"Leon," Matteo says, turning the camera to capture his own masked face. "Yo, folks. I'm a Capricorn. I like CrossFit and UC-LA—go, Bruins!—and I'm into long walks off short piers. A hot dog is definitely *not* a sandwich. Pineapple on pizza is good, even though it's wrong. Beer over whiskey. I like my women—"

"Cut it out," Dave says, and Matteo gives the camera a *What are you gonna do?* eye roll before pointing it back at Linda.

> *This afternoon I'll be performing a cranial examination*
> *of Duane Lonnie Bradley, male, fifty-three. Mr. Bradley*
> *was admitted on July fourth for a fractured rib. He died*
> *in his sleep between four and five a.m.*

Linda retracts the sheet, revealing the dead man's pallid face and slack features. Bradley's lips are gray and slightly parted. Linda glances up at Dave and Matteo as if to say, *Are you ready for this?*

Dave just nods.

> *I've already marked the skull for incision. I'll begin on*
> *the right mastoid.*

Matteo takes a step forward, zooming on the dead man's head while Linda draws a scalpel across the black guidelines. The skin parts as if unzipped. There's hardly any blood, and what little there is, is sluggish; it clings to the skin flaps.

"Gross," Matteo observes.

"Matteo," Dave whispers. "Knock it off."

Dave is transfixed, too, by the sight of a man's head being peeled like a piece of fruit.

*This is not the day I expected to have.*

    All right. Primary incision is complete. Now I'll reflect the
    anterior flap forward and separate the connective tissue.

Linda works coolly, efficiently, working the scalp forward, brushing the scalpel along the exposed curve of skull, deftly detaching skin and muscle from bone.

Then she stops, holding the man's scalp in one hand.

    This is strange.

She places one gloved hand on Duane Bradley's forehead. The man's forehead and brow gather like dense fabric, sagging over his closed eyes.

Matteo brings the camera nice and close. His face contorts into a grimace.

"What's wrong?" Dave asks.

    Ah . . . Well, the cadaver seems to have an elevated
    body temperature. Specifically in the head and neck. It's
    almost as if Mr., ah, Bradley, has a . . . a fever.

"But he's dead."

"Yes, Matteo, I think she's aware," Dave says. To Linda: "What's that mean, though?"

    It's . . . unclear.
    I'm taking the deceased's pulse now. As expected,
    there isn't one. Mr. Bradley is not alive.
    Except his body temperature suggests otherwise.

"What do we do now?" Matteo asks.

*I'm, ah, continuing the exam.*

Linda swings the scalpel around the remainder of the skull, splitting the corpse's temple and forehead away from his face.

"Oh, fuck me," Matteo says, staggering backward at the sudden dehumanizing move. He nearly drops his phone, but Dave takes it from his hand and takes over, pointing the camera at Linda's hands.

Linda peels the entire scalp upward, toward the roof of the skull. Flecked with stringy gobs of tissue and streaks of thickened blood, the exposed bone glistens in the harsh overhead lights.

Gathering the scalp in one hand—*Like the neck of a bread bag,* Dave thinks, perversely—Linda uses her blade to sever it entirely from the skull. She drops the ragged mass of tissue and hair unceremoniously into a steel tub.

Matteo gags and turns away.

*I've removed the scalp. Next, I'll open the cranium.*

Linda points at an instrument that's nearer to Dave than her. Dave picks up the bone saw, which is heavier than he expects, and nearly drops it on Mr. Bradley's sagging face.

Linda switches the tool on. Its circular blade becomes a fine blur, its teeth disappearing as it reaches top speed. The motor emits a high-frequency whine that causes Matteo to cover his ears.

*I'm beginning to cut the parietal.*

The whine dips several octaves as the saw's teeth bite into bone, sending up a fine spray of gray dust.

"I'm glad we're masked," Matteo says as the cloud of bone particles grows. He circles the table to where Dave stands. "Give it back, you're as artful as a tripod."

Matteo takes back the camera from Dave, then navigates closer for a close-up of Linda's work. Her saw traces a mesmerizing arc around the skull.

"Get back," Linda says over the loud saw. "I don't want to—"

The saw's pitch changes as it suddenly dips deep into the cadaver's skull, into tissue beneath. Blood and cranial fluid geyser from the incision, spraying the camera and Matteo.

"Fuck!" Matteo bellows, dropping the phone. He staggers backward, bumping the table, then ricocheting into Dave. "Is it—? It's on my face!"

> Retracting the saw now. I think I must have nicked an artery, or something—Pardon the noise, my camera operator is presently shouting and scrambling for the sink.

Linda tries to describe the scene for the camera's benefit, since all it's recording now is a close-up of the linoleum floor.

"It's on my fucking face!" Matteo howls, pawing his mask free. He leans over the sink and thrusts his face into the jet of water.

"It's only a little blood," Linda says, shutting off the saw.

"I don't see any on you," Matteo gurgles.

"I deal with far worse than blood every day."

Dave pulls on latex gloves, then picks up Matteo's phone. "We're still rolling," he announces. "Your screen is cracked, Matteo, but the phone still works."

"She's a menace!" Matteo shrieks, pumping soap into his palms, then scrubbing his face wildly. "She doesn't know what she's doing!"

"You can take over if you want to, pal," Linda retorts. "Dave, clam him up, would you? Or send him the hell out."

"We're still recording . . ." Dave trails off, then sniffs the air through his mask and turns toward the cadaver.

"I've got a PhD in neurology, you dumb grunt," Linda snaps at Matteo.

"Yeah?" Matteo demands through a skin of bubbles. "How the fuck are you a nurse and not a doctor, then, huh?"

"Guys," Dave says.

"Before I was a nurse, *shit-for-brains*, I was a senior neuroscientist at Cynagen."

"*Cyna—*" Matteo yelps. "Yo, Dave, this lady's shadier than we thought. Fuckin' deep-state, Big Pharma, whack-job conspiracy bullsh—"

"Guys," Dave says again, interrupting the spat. "Linda, this isn't, like, normal, right?"

He keeps the camera trained on Mr. Bradley's skull. Inky black steam seeps from the bone incision, curls upward against the cranium, then twists toward the ceiling like a morbid balloon string.

"What is it?" Matteo asks, dragging paper towels down his face.

"Smoke," Linda says. "The skull is—Matteo, put a fucking mask on, or get out of the room. Right now, please."

The tone in Linda's voice spurs Matteo to the supply counter, where he fumbles a surgical mask out of a paper box.

Linda steps past Dave and picks up the bone saw.

"What are you doing?" Dave asks, still filming.

"I'm resuming the examination," she says.

> Following the nicked artery, there appears to be, ah, unidentifiable . . . smoke, ah, issuing from the bone cut. I'm going to start cutting again now—

She fires up the saw and touches the spinning blade to the incision trail. But the blade skitters this time, jumping over bone wildly. A section of Mr. Bradley's skull caves in.

> Ah—I, uh, appear to have damaged the skull. There's a
> *lot* more smoke pouring out of the cranial cavity now . . .

"Jesus," Dave says.

"It smells like an electrical fire," Matteo adds, strapping on a second mask.

Dave moves around the table, trying to find an angle that isn't obscured by the thickening cloud of smoke.

> I'm removing the skullcap now. There's—Fucking
> Christ. There's so much—There's too much smoke, it's
> obscuring the brain—

"This guy's head is like Mount Saint Helena!" Matteo cries. "He's gonna fuckin' blow, I know it."

*Saint Helens*, Dave thinks absently, but he doesn't correct Matteo. Instead, he zooms in on the fissure. Through the smoke he catches glimpses of the man's brain, and what looks like a faint rosy glow.

Linda grabs a patient folder and fans the smoke until it thins.

> Amateur hour.

But as the smoke dissipates, she pauses.

> What the hell . . . ?

"What? What is it?" Matteo asks worriedly.

Linda grabs Dave's wrist and pulls him—and the camera—as close as she can.

> Zoom in tight, right there. Do you see . . . ?

Dave films while Linda keeps fanning the skull. Between rolling waves of smoke he sees it clearly: a scorch mark on the brain, like a tattoo. The lines of it still glow, as though the man had just been branded.

> There's, uh . . . I've never seen this before. There's a symbol, ah, seared on the patient's occipital lobe. I've never heard of anything—Dave, are you—? Dave, hold the camera steady, please—Dave? Dave!

Dave drops the camera directly onto the patient's skull. It bounces off and thumps onto the operating table, next to the pile of what used to be Duane Bradley's face. But Dave hardly notices. His knees give out, and he hits the slick floor. He howls, retreating from the table in a sudden panic while Matteo and Linda shout at him—

## 25

Katie presses herself against the headboard, screaming, as Dave lifts the shard of broken mirror. For a moment she's convinced he'll turn toward her. She feels about for a weapon and finds only blankets and pillows.

But Dave doesn't turn. Instead, he raises the shard to his chest and begins to dig into his own skin. The muscles of his back and shoulders twitch and tighten as he works.

In what's left of the mirror, his eyes seem to glaze over, a blissed-out smile on his face. He sighs contentedly as he works.

When he is finished, he turns toward Katie. "See, Mom?" he asks. "Do you see? Now I'm safe from it. I'm finally safe."

Katie stares at the bloody triangle carved into Dave's chest, then throws herself from the bed and runs from the apartment.

# A Jean Valjean Situation

## I

Eli's shoulders are tight as he writes his new post, then publishes it across his tiny media empire. He confirms it's live everywhere it's meant to be live, then sinks back in his chair and waits.

HELP ME.

If you have been following my posts today, you know that something weird's happening out there. If you have more information, please respond with what you know. I am, as I'm sure everyone is, completely in the dark.

But in the meantime:

HELP ME.

I have chronic insomnia and circadian disorder and generalized anxiety disorder. I take several medications to manage these conditions. When I fail to take my medications, the consequences are unpleasant and prolonged: I experience nausea for days on end, I fall asleep at unexpected times and injure myself, or I experience days of insomnia coupled with hallucinations.

I am having a medication emergency. As many of you know, I do not enjoy the use of my legs, and am in a wheelchair. There are some ordinary tasks that are extremely difficult for me to do without the support of municipal services like The Ride.

And as you all know, the mysterious event that's happening out there has shut down any service that I could use to solve my problem.

So. A last resort plea for help: If you are a reader and you live in the vicinity of Boston—and you're willing to help me solve this medication emergency of mine—please reply. Please, please, please.

PLEASE.

## 2

Millie's phone buzzes moments after Eli's post is published. In her blog reader app, tagged "sleep-fuckery," she finds his plea for help. She ignores the request and instead wonders what exactly he's on about. "Mysterious event," she reads, then shakes her head. "The boy's caught the last train to Bonkersville."

She returns to her workstation, this time with a fresh cup of coffee, and toggles open the tickets that have been assigned to her. As each of her international team members logs off, some with a quick *Thanks, Mill!*, they've reassigned their tasks; now Millie's to-do list has ballooned from a manageable nineteen to a spine-knotting seventy-six.

"Ungrateful cunts," she says. Lately she's subscribed to a British-comedy streaming service and, without having done so con-sciously, has adopted English curses into her patter. "Bloody well gave me all the work, haven't you?"

She blows steam from her coffee, takes a sip, and opens the highest-priority ticket.

CUSTOMER'S PASSWORD PUBLISHED AS THEIR USERNAME
Detail: Customer @j.allbright was prompted to
change system password. When they did so, their
password replaced their username for all to see.
Customer complains that they're now being harassed
for "being a total noob" on the platform. Also their
feed is filled with offensive posts they did not write.

"Presumably because the wanker let his password out in the open," Millie mutters. She scrolls down the ticket, then dashes off a reply:

NEED MORE DETAIL ABOUT THE PROMPT TO CHANGE PASSWORD.
WAS THIS OFFICIAL PROMPT FROM OUR APP? OR A PHISH?

"There," Millie says, and changes the ticket's status to Awaiting Info. "One down."

But her thoughts keep drifting to the poor boy who runs the sleep disorder site. His blog isn't one of her favorites, but it is one of the most active. The kid's young and a little obnoxious—his writing is too stilted, she often thinks, and far too passive—but she can relate to most of the things he writes about, having lived through the same things most of her life.

What had happened to her the last time she'd fucked up and run out of meds? She'd become manic, had been arrested for verbally abusing and then assaulting a pharmacist at a Duane Reade.

She returns to the boy's blog and rereads his post.

And as you all know, the mysterious event that's happening
out there has shut down any service that I could use to solve
my problem.

*What the fuck are you on about?*

Millie loads up CNN and finds a breaking news item, but no accompanying story:

CNN IS INVESTIGATING A RASH OF REPORTS OF SUDDEN

AND INEXPLICABLE DEATHS ACROSS THE COUNTRY.

DETAILS TO COME.

The headline was posted around 7:40 a.m. Eastern.

She switches back to the boy's blog and types a comment.

# 3

**millie-zzz** commented 3 mins ago

if nobody else offers hit me up i guess. im about an hour south in prov.

Eli falls back into his chair. "Thank God."

He bangs out a reply:

It has been over an hour since I posted asking for help. I don't think anyone is reading the internet right now. I confess I'm scared. How soon can you come? The pharmacy closes at 6:00 but I don't want to take chances. Can you email me your phone number?

He posts it, and waits. A few minutes later, he gets an email from the commenter with a cell phone number. He sends a text:

Eli here, is this working?

A moment later:

> no i gave you a bad number for funsies. will head in your
> direction soon.
> Millie-zzz.

Not a reader he's seen before. He quickly searches his content system for any other comments from this person, but there aren't any. That's all right; he's got more than enough clues: a username, which reveals a first name; an IP address; a town; likely sleep disordered . . . It takes only a few minutes for him to locate more information about his potential savior.

The first result is not promising.

#### LOCAL WOMAN ARRESTED FOR ASSAULTING
#### TRAVELING PHARMACEUTICAL REP

The story, dated six years earlier, fills Eli with dread.

> *A Providence woman was arrested Tuesday afternoon for punching a pharmaceutical salesman at the Everly Road Duane Reade.*
>
> *Millicent Potter, 23, allegedly shoved Douglas Washington, 63, against a wall, then slapped him several times while demanding drugs. Potter then pushed Washington to the floor and kicked him in the ribs.*
>
> *"She called me an [expletive] white-coat," a shaken Washington reported. "I wasn't even wearing a white coat. I was just there for a scheduled sales call with the lead pharmacist. Now I have a broken rib, I think."*
>
> *Potter was taken into custody by Providence police at the scene. No charges have been filed.*

*"We're investigating the incident,"* Providence PD
spokesperson Jan Gunter said. *"As we understand more
about the nature of the incident, we'll share more."*
Potter was released Tuesday evening.

*Shit*, Eli thinks. *I'm going to be rescued by a psychopath.*

4

Millie tries to message Martin, intending to tell him she's got a
family emergency and needs to disappear for a couple of hours,
but Martin doesn't reply. That's when she notices the messages in
the team's work channel, one of which is from the vice president
of Human Resources:

> ThomasParnell
> ⚠ NOTICE TO @everyone ⚠: Staff are not permit-
> ted to leave work or their stations without notice. If
> your manager is unavailable, please contact my HR
> team directly first.

The first response is from Willem, who is on an adjacent QA
team:

> willem.beaumont
> @everyone @Thomas_Parnell clearly nobody here is
> watching the news. there's some serious shit going
> down. i'm going home to my family. if that means
> i'm fired, so be it. ☮

Millie hits #general's stats and sees that more than two-thirds
of the company is not online.

"Fuck it," she mutters, and walks away from her computer.

The weirdness is evident as soon as she descends the stairs from the mother-in-law apartment she rents in Elmhurst. Across the street, a large Winnebago has gently nosed into a neighbor's azaleas, leaving muddy grooves in the trimmed lawn. A few blocks away, rising over the rooftops, is a thick, slowly billowing column of black smoke.

"Jesus," she says.

The surface streets are mostly clear, and finding her way to Interstate 95 is not challenging. All along the way, however, she notices empty shopping center parking lots, coffee drive-throughs that are conspicuously unclogged. She switches the radio on and, after scanning through several strangely silent channels, lands on the college station, WXIN.

*. . . to play music, so I'm not going to do that*, a young woman says, voice shaking. *Or maybe I should play music, maybe that's what the world needs right now. I don't know.*

She clears her throat, and Millie pictures the scene: a twenty-year-old girl, alone at a soundboard in a radio booth, surrounded by piles of demo CDs and old cassettes.

*If you're just joining, um, I'm really tired*, the deejay continues.

> *I'm normally on air from three a.m. to seven, but the morning guy, Raju, didn't show up to relieve me, and actually nobody else has shown up at all, and I've been looking at the internet and—Well, listen to this. This is on Twitter, a user called yoyohammerz, and they say, "my mama didn't wake up this morning so i went next door to my grandma's and same deal. both of them are dead in their beds. my dad won't answer his phone but he never answers his phone, so. what is going on out there?" You guys, there are like hundreds of tweets like this, and that's just on Twitt—*

Millie comes round a bend in the freeway and suddenly there's chaos: an eighteen-wheeler, jackknifed in the middle of three lanes, and seven or eight passenger vehicles, all tangled metal, smashed up against it. There are no emergency vehicles around. In fact, there's no other moving traffic on the freeway; how had she failed to notice that until now? She brakes hard, then blinks at a particular oddity.

Sitting atop a crumpled Ford Fiesta is a middled-aged man with blood soaking through his white collared shirt.

Millie cranks her window down and leans out. "Sir," she calls. "Sir, are you—?"

The man grins broadly and waves, but doesn't move.

"Do you need help?"

"Everyone's dead," he says, almost chipper. "I think the truck driver fell asleep and crashed, and then everyone crashed."

"When did it happen?" she asks, worried about the man. He's too calm, and Millie doesn't trust people who are too calm.

"Oh, *hours* ago," the man says, glancing at his wrist. "I don't know."

"I can call for help."

"I did that already. Nobody came."

"Does anyone else need help?" Millie looks at all the vehicles, which seem to have run into the pileup at maximum speed. They're accordioned and compressed; she can't see how anyone would be alive inside.

"Not anymore. The woman in that blue thing over there—I think it used to be a Nissan—she probably needed help, but she passed out, and then she didn't wake up again." The man pats the roof of the car he's sitting on. "And the kid driving this thing, I think he probably would've been okay, but you see that puddle? Gas. Lots of fumes. I think it poisoned him, because he closed his eyes, too, and didn't wake up. And I tried calling 911," he says, "but it just rings and rings."

"What about you?"

The man tugs at his shirt. "Oh, it's not my blood. I'm fine."

"You're being very . . . calm about this," Millie ventures, ready to tap the gas pedal. "Are you sure you're—?"

"Perfectly fine," the man says. "God takes whom he wishes when he wishes. When you drove up, I was just praying for their souls."

"Oh," Millie says. "So, you don't need help?"

"God has my back. But thank you!"

"Um . . . Okay," Millie says. She raises her hand in goodbye, and the man waggles his fingers jauntily at her. He kicks his feet like a child on a too-tall chair. "Bye, then."

"Be well," the man calls, and Millie rolls her window up.

5

Eli has been sitting at the window for two hours when he finally spies movement on the street below: a red Honda hatchback, checkered with rust spots, making its way through the still intersection.

He texts millie-zzz's number.

> I see you. The brick building with the white trim is me. I'm coming down.

The engine idles throatily as Millie waits. Around her, the city is uncannily still. She winces, imagining suddenly that she and the blogger might be the last people to see Boston before the world moves on, before the power seizes and stalls, before the lawns grow thick and buckle the sidewalks, before the birds roost in tenth-floor apartments where windows were left open.

The front door of the apartment building opens with a whine, powered by an automatic servo, and a moment later, the blogger rolls out in a wheelchair.

"Yo," Millie calls through her window. "You didn't mention you were on wheels. I'd have brought my pickup truck instead."

"You have a pickup truck?" Eli asks.

Millie shakes her head. "No. I don't know why I said that." She looks the chair up and down. "Tell me that thing collapses, innit?"

"Innit?" Eli blinks. When Millie doesn't flinch, he says slowly, "It fits in most car trunks."

He hopes the concern he feels doesn't show on his face. He watches as the woman pulls her emergency brake, then leans hard on the Honda door until it pops open. She's tired; he knows all the signs. She squinches her eyes tightly, then pops them open wide, as if performing a hard reboot on her brain. If she reads his blog, she's got troubles like he does. Also, she talks like a Brit here and there, but he doesn't think she's English.

He wonders what medications she's on.

Actually, shit, that's a useful idea.

He says, "What do you take?"

"You don't dick around, do you?" Millie says, popping the trunk. "What are you, twelve?"

"I'm old enough," Eli says.

"You don't look it."

"Yes, well, how old are you?"

"You're not allowed to ask me that," Millie answers. She raises one eyebrow. "Are you getting out of that thing, or what? Don't tell me I have to carry you."

Eli motors to the passenger door, which opens more easily than the driver's door had, and transfers himself into the seat. While Millie watches, he pulls a small lever under the chair's arm, and it compacts until it's the size of a suitcase.

"Nifty," Millie says.

"There's a handle," Eli points out.

She grunts as she lifts it. "Heavy sonofabitch," she mutters, but she manages to stow it in the trunk space with little difficulty. She closes the trunk lid, then drops heavily into the driver's seat.

"Thank you," Eli says, "for driv—"

Millie yanks the driver's door shut with a loud bang. "Sorry."

"For driving all this way," Eli finishes. "I really appreciate it."

"You can buy me dinner." Millie shifts into first gear, then says, "So, where're we going?"

# 6

The pharmacy, squatted between Bow-Wow Groomers and Miracle Chiropractic, looks suspiciously dark. "The gate's closed," Millie observes. "They aren't even open. Do you have a backup?"

Eli shakes his head. "There's no such thing as a backup. It's not like you can have a prescription at multiple pharmacies."

"Oh, you dewy young thing," Millie says, and ruffles Eli's hair. "You have much to learn."

"Stop that." Eli hates how much this makes him sound like a child. Beside him, Millie seems like a regular grown-up, with creases in her face that he hasn't yet developed, skin that's damaged from too much sun. Her hair is wrapped up in a hasty, loose bun. She's probably been married twice already. "What, you have a fake ID or something?"

Millie laughs. "A woman doesn't reveal her tricks that easily."

"I don't know what to do," Eli says. "Do we wait? Maybe the pharmacist is just—"

"I read your blogs," Millie says. "And on the way here, I listened to the radio. Or tried to. There's some shit going down, my young friend. I think you already know it, too." She drums her fingers on the wheel, surveying the streets around them. "You notice, like, all the cars are still parked curbside? Was there some universal memo we all missed? 'It's everybody-sleep-in day, y'all!'" She shakes her head. "I don't think the pharmacist is coming."

"This is creeping me out," Eli admits.

"Reach back behind you," Millie says. "There's a toolbox."

Eli feels around on the floorboard behind his seat. His fingers find crumpled paper, dented cans. "Ugh, what is all this?"

Millie isn't listening. She's squinting at the gate pulled across the storefront.

Eli's fingers close over the handle of a metal toolbox. He pulls it forward, into his lap. It's covered in stickers from bands he doesn't recognize: Bad Astronaut. We Were Promised Jetpacks. Lagwagon. Inside the toolbox are several greasy wrenches, a battered chisel, a rubber mallet, a crumpled pack of Old Golds, loose rubber bands, a surprising amount of change, and a cracked old Ericsson cell phone.

"I don't see how any of this is supposed to help," Eli says.

"You never watched *MacGyver*, did you, kid?" Millie snatches up the pack of cigarettes. "Mullet-headed aw-shucks whiz-brain guy? Can hack into any computer with some potting soil and an LED light?"

"That doesn't sound right."

Millie lights the Old Gold from the car's push-button lighter. Eli's amazed the thing still works. The car feels like it's been teleported here from 1991.

"You wait here," Millie says. She takes the toolbox with her and heads for the front gate. Eli watches as she slips the chisel through the hasp of the gate's padlock, then whacks away at it with the mallet.

He rolls his window down. "That's not going to work."

Millie keeps hitting the chisel.

"Even if it does, the door will still be lock—"

Loudly, the padlock pops open. Millie, cigarette trapped

between her teeth, holds it up like a hunter holding aloft the corpse of her prey. She tosses the lock aside, then leans on the gate, accordioning it until it disappears into a slot in the storefront wall.

"Okay, but the door—" Eli starts. But he stops when Millie chucks the mallet at the glass door. The glass spiderwebs, but doesn't break, so she picks up the mallet and hits it repeatedly until a sugary hole opens.

"It's safety glass," Eli says. "It's not going to—"

Millie hits the glass at the top left corner, and the whole thing collapses into shards, falling like frozen rain into a pile. She gives Eli a thumbs-up and then disappears inside. A moment later, she pushes the door open.

"No alarm," she calls out. "Bonus."

A Klaxon erupts, the awful sound of it reverberating from one side of the street to the other, then bending back on itself, creating a recursive shriek that interrupts the rhythm of Eli's heart.

"I lied!" Millie hollers. She jogs over to the car. "There's totally an alarm."

"I didn't want to break and enter!"

"What?"

"I didn't want to be criminals!"

Millie's smile flattens in the middle. "Kid, you need your meds, right? This is a Jean Valjean situation here."

"He stole bread. To feed his family."

"And you're stealing medicine for your brain." Millie shrugs. "Same difference."

Eli puts his head in his hands. "Oh my God, we're going to jail. My readers will wonder what happened to me."

"Kid, you're not going to jail. Neither am—" Millie sways on her feet, then grips the roof to steady herself. "Neither am I," she says, steeling her jaw. "Whatever's happened out there, I don't think there are cops anymore."

"You don't know that."

"Actually, yeah," she says, thinking of the wrecked cars blocking the highway. "Yeah, I do. Now: What do you need from inside?"

"It's easier if I come," Eli says. "There's a lot."

Millie turns and looks at the piles of glass in the doorway. "Somehow I think your go-cart might not handle that well."

"Please," Eli says. "Don't go in there without me. Don't leave me out here." His eyes glisten like a damp stray's.

Millie nods. "Yeah. Okay. I have an idea. How much do you weigh?"


# 7

Eli clings to Millie's back, humiliated. "I feel like a CamelBak," he mutters.

"Except I can't drink you," Millie says. "You know, I went through a CamelBak phase. In college. I kept it filled with vodka."

"Great."

Glass crunches under Millie's feet. Inside, the pharmacy is lit only by emergency lights, which strobe at regular intervals. The Klaxon still sounds, but they do their best to tune it out. It's louder outside than inside.

"It was great," Millie says, her voice gone dreamy. "I think better when I'm altered, you know?"

"Can we just—?"

"Yep. Yep, okay." She pauses, though, at an endcap display of emergency car kits. "Remind me to grab a few of these on the way back out, yeah?"

A second gate has been pulled across the pharmacy counter, but it's just for show; there's no lock, and Millie pulls it back in one fluid motion, then deposits Eli, like a toddler, on the counter.

She flips a switch, illuminating shelves upon shelves of bottles and vials. "All right," she says, rubbing her palms together. "What do you—?"

"Whoa," Eli says when Millie's ankle rolls under her and she nearly falls. "Steady there. Are you okay?"

"I am exactly fiiiiine," Millie says, her voice softening and stretching as she speaks. *Oh, bollocks,* she has time to think, and then the shelves rush toward her, and *the ceiling tiles burst inward in a spray of dust and fiberglass, cracked open by heavy black boots. The first of the SWAT team lands heavily, then releases his rappel line and lifts his rifle, shouting at Millie to get down, get down, get—*

"Hey!" Eli shouts, and Millie blinks and looks up at him from where she's fallen. Her cigarette smolders on the lowest shelf beside her.

"I'm all right," Millie says, which is technically true, even though her ass is sending pain signals to her brain, and something warm is running down her face. She touches her forehead, then inspects her fingers. "All right," she repeats.

Eli's brow knits into a single dark line. "I swear to God, I thought you just died," he says. "I thought you died and left me separated from my chair by a pile of broken glass."

"Sorry." Millie stands up, then tugs a few tissues from a nearby box, folds them over, and presses them to her head. "I'm fine. Everything's okay." She wobbles a little on her feet and leans on the shelf for support. "Really. I promise."

Eli's eyes soften. "Narcolepsy?"

"More or less." Millie shrugs. "What are you gonna do?"

"What do you take for it?"

"What don't I take for it?"

"I was going to say, you should restock, too."

"I've got plenty back home, thanks," Millie says. "My restocks come in the mail every six weeks."

Eli says, "What if there's no more mail?"

Millie frowns. "Come rain, come sleet, come hail, there always will be mail," she singsongs irritably.

"That's not how it goes," Eli says. "And that's not an enforceable guarantee. It's more like a motto. Whatever's happened, there aren't any police here, like you said. Nobody's driving out there. I think something really bad has happened. Just not to us. And I think there isn't any mail anymore."

Millie sits down on the pharmacist's stool, then yawns. She opens her mouth to say something, but rational thought takes time to return after one of her episodes. She rocks her palms against her eyes instead, stretching her face, trying to re-center herself.

Finally, she says, "What meds do you need?"

Eli ignores this and says, "You're okay?"

"I'm okay enough. What do you need?"

# 8

Eli buckles himself into the passenger seat as Millie stows four paper grocery bags in the back seat, each brimming with bulk-size bottles of Restulin, Alexada, Somalcya, Modafalyst, and assorted other stimulants and sleeping aids.

"If things go back to normal," Millie says, joining Eli in the car, "we can open our own side hustle with all the extra."

"If things go back to normal," Eli retorts, "someone's going to look at the security cameras and see who robbed the pharmacy, and we'll be *fucked*."

Something about the way Eli sounds when he curses makes Millie chuckle. "You might be right, kid," she says.

"How's your head?" he asks.

"I got my bell rang, but I'm okay."

"I think you mean 'rung.'"

"Ringed."

"Rung."

"Rangled."

"Rung."

"Ringed."

Eli sighs heavily. "Have it your way."

"Yes, sir, grammar boy."

She starts the engine, then cranks the steering wheel for a U-turn, then hesitates.

"It's just back the way we came," Eli says. "My apartment."

"Right, I'm just—" Millie pauses, then looks seriously at her passenger. "I'm just thinking, you know, that there could be a hundred reasons we're the only ones walking around right now." She looks at Eli's legs, then corrects: "Moving."

"Okay. And?"

"What if it's something risky? Like a citywide gas leak, or everyone got fried by a solar flare, or—"

"I mean, if it was a solar flare, you and I would both be fried, too. The sun isn't selective like that."

"Or what if it was the rapture, you know, all God's children abandoning the planet before the worst happens."

"You don't believe that," Eli says. "I'm the naïve one, I can tell, and I don't even believe that."

"My point, though," Millie insists, "is that you might not be safe back at your place. And I'm not sure I'm safe going back to mine. So . . ." She chews her lip, then glances sideways at the kid. "Maybe we ought to stick together."

"And go where?"

"I don't know, but I'm thinking out of the city."

"That doesn't make sense."

"Bad things happen in cities when shit goes sideways," she says. "Haven't you ever seen *The Walking Dead*? Didn't you ever read *The Stand*?"

"I don't like zombies," Eli says.

"Of course you don't."

"But if it is a gas leak or whatever," he continues, "then you're right. My apartment might not be safe to return to."

"So it's settled," Millie says. "We drive."

"I have to pee."

"We find a place to pee," she amends, "and then we drive. Yes?"

"What happens when we wake up tomorrow and everything's normal again?" Eli asks.

"Then I take you back home. No harm, no foul."

Eli thinks about this. "This feels like a bad idea. Driving away from my home with a stranger and bags full of drugs."

"Under normal circumstances, yes, I'd agree." Millie shakes her head. "But if I'm right, if this is end-of-the-world circumstances? This is the only thing that makes sense."

"I thought at the end of the world people got more suspicious of each other, not more trusting."

"Maybe so," Millie says, "but you're not a stranger, kid. I read your blogs. I know who's in my car. And I never let someone get in my car without knowing them first."

With that, she swings the car westward, and a half hour later, Boston is in the rearview mirror. Millie and Eli drive in silence, at least until Millie spots the guy on the side of the road, walking backward, his thumb held high.

"No," Eli warns, but Millie slows down. "What happened to 'I never let strangers in my car'?"

"End of the world, kiddo," she says. "We survivors have to stick together, right?" She doesn't wait for him to agree, thinks he might be pouting about being called *kiddo*. "Right," she says. "Right."

# The Dream People

## I

"What is going on with him?"

"It's a trauma response," Linda says, snapping her fingers in front of Dave's vacant stare.

*Elephants.*

*Elephants, elephants.*

Matteo slaps Dave across the cheek. "Goddammit, wake the hell up!"

Linda grabs Matteo's hand. "Hey, now—"

"Look," Matteo says. "It worked."

Dave's eyes skitter wildly until they settle on Linda. "Elephants," he moans, absently yanking at his uniform.

"David," Linda says, in full nurse mode. "It's Linda and Matteo. You've had a bit of a shock. Can you hear me?" To Matteo, she says, "I never should have let you two in the room during that."

Dave looks past Linda, at the body on the table, its skull uncorked like a wine bottle.

*Triangles. Elephants.*

"I have to go now," Dave says. To his ears, the words are stretched like taffy. He pushes Matteo away as he gets to his feet, then lurches toward the operating room doors.

2

Katie leaves Ruth Nelson contentedly watching an old episode of *Barney Miller* and joins Matteo and Linda in the hallway. They lead her out of earshot of room 217.

"What did you find out?" Katie asks.

Matteo hurriedly recaps the autopsy for her, leaving out Dave's meltdown. "It's the government, right? Who else would brand someone's fucking *brain*?"

"It definitely isn't the government," Linda says.

"Where's Dave?" Katie asks.

"You can't know that for sure. You aren't—"

"When I was at Cynagen, we won dozens of government contracts. Real off-the-books stuff. We had this deep-underground facility in Virginia where we tinkered with—Well, you name it. Neurotoxins. Pathogens. Biochemical agents. Bad shit. But never anything like this. The government can't switch you off when you go to sleep." Linda shakes her head firmly. "And they definitely aren't branding our brains."

"Aliens, then," Matteo says. "Are we talking aliens?"

"Guys, where's Dave?" Katie asks again.

"How the hell did you end up in Santa Mira, anyway?" Matteo presses. "Cynagen is deep state shit. Huge money, I bet. But here you are. A nurse in Nowhere, Cali. You get fired?"

"How'd you end up in the air force?" Linda retorts.

"I got recruited. Senior year. Plain and simple."

"Same here," Linda says. "Top of my class at Harvard Med. Next thing you know, I've got a six-figure offer. Cutting-edge science, the best labs on the planet, unlimited resources. The chance to do work that mattered."

"You mean a chance to wipe out third world countries," Matteo snaps. "And jack up over-the-counter drugs so nobody can—"

"Guys!"

"Fuck you," Linda says, poking Matteo's chest. "I was a *kid*."

"So was I!" Matteo retorts. "And I saw Cynagen's logo on the smart bombs under my wing in Afghanistan. I never dropped one, but I know guys who did. You think I'm fucked up, they're beyond traumatized. Noncombatants foaming at the mouth, their organs dissolving—"

"I didn't design fucking bombs. I was strictly genetics, okay? And only until I started hearing about shit like the bombs." Linda turns away and paces. "Yes, they were fucking unethical. Yes, they were manufacturing bad shit. You know what I did?"

"You got paid!"

"I broke rank!" Linda roars. "You think whistleblower laws mean shit when your company's in the government's pocket?"

"Guys," Katie says again. "Where the hell is Dave?" But neither of them seems to notice her.

"I lost my clearance, my license, my reputation," Linda rants. "You think this is my real name?" She snaps a finger under Matteo's nose. "*That's* how I wound up here, you unbelievably self-righteous shit—"

"*Guys!*"

At last Matteo and Linda turn, as if they'd forgotten she was even there.

"Where," she repeats, "is Dave?"

Breathing hard, Linda says, "He needed a minute."

Katie shifts her gaze to Matteo. "What the fuck happened in there?"

"You don't want to know. Really."

"Okay, listen to me," Katie says, suddenly serious. "When Dave gets worked up . . . He has some real shit to deal with, okay? Shit you don't know about. So, maybe you could tell me where the fuck he is so I can make sure he's actually okay, huh?"

Linda sighs. "I didn't see."

"He ran out of the room really fast," Matteo admits. "He did seem kind of messed up."

"And you didn't go after him?"

Matteo shrugs and looks at the floor. Katie notices the stains on his work shirt and says, "Something went really wrong in there. Didn't it?"

"It could have gone better," Linda concedes.

"I need to find Dave," Katie says. "What do you two need?"

"A nap. A drink. Maybe not in that order." Matteo shakes his head. "Maybe five drinks."

"A team of virologists," Linda blurts. "A hundred of them, working around the clock for eighteen months to crack this problem open. Can you do that, Katie? Can you get me what I need? That's what I need."

"Eighteen *months*?" Matteo asks.

"The average R and D time required to develop a vaccine for any viral infection—assuming that's what this is—is four *years*, Matteo. Eighteen months would be a goddamn miracle."

"We don't have eighteen *hours*," Matteo says. "We're all about to crack wide open."

"Then don't ask me what you can do," Linda says. "Let's all just sit down and wait to die. That's all I've got. Okay?"

# 3

Santa Mira Medical Center, though only six stories, is the tallest building for miles. From the roof, one can watch shipping barges slide like butter in a hot skillet across the horizon. That's where Katie finds Dave, leaning against a low wall, framed by the sinking sun.

"Pretty," she says, resting her arms on the rail beside him.

Dave doesn't look away from the view. "You found me."

"I remembered how, in my old building, sometimes you'd sit on the roof in a picnic chair to watch the sunset."

"Because I didn't want to sleep," he says quietly.

"You think I didn't know that? I know you, Dave." She watches the wind ruffle his hair. "Even if sometimes that means being afraid of you."

"You aren't the first," he says. "Welcome to my life."

"Matteo and Linda looked pretty rattled. That wasn't your fault."

Dave is quiet, but she hears him swallow.

"If there was ever a time to let me in . . . ," she begins, resting a hand on his back.

"I'm processing. That's all."

"Process faster."

"What?"

"I'm not kidding around here. It's the end of the world, or did you forget? Let me in. Let me help."

He shoves away from the wall. "What are you looking for here? What do you want me to say? That I'm scared? *I'm scared.* That I don't know how to explain what we . . ." He trails off. "I can't explain what we saw in there."

Katie hoists herself onto the railing, her back to the sunset.

"Whoa . . . Come down, okay?"

"In NA," she says, "they have this whole thing: 'Just for today.'"

"Katie. Please."

"See, recovery is hard. You're gonna feel like you can't make it. It's a long road, and sometimes, if you think about how long it really is, you can wreck right at the beginning of your journey."

"Come down."

"But NA says, okay, but how about this: Just for today, you'll focus on not using. That's all. There's no tomorrow. There's just today. You can get through today."

"You're freaking me out," Dave says.

"But you know what the second rule is?"

"Don't make me drag you down from there—"

"Come a step closer and I'll go right over," Katie warns, and when Dave stops, she says, "Good. Thank you. The second rule, do you know it?"

He shakes his head slowly.

"It's even simpler. 'Have faith in someone else.' Just for today, trust someone who cares about you. That's it. That's all. Presto chango, magical recovery." She laughs. "Not really, of course. But you see what I'm getting at?"

"I do trust you."

"You've *never* trusted me. You don't tell me anything." Katie swings one leg over the wall, then the other. The sun paints her face a warm tangerine. "I've had enough, Dave. The world is fucking *over*. We had our shot. We blew it. If I went over this wall right now, I'd consider it a kindness. Whatever you saw in that autopsy room? I won't have to go through it. But I would. I'd go through all of it if you'd just stop pushing me away. Because you know what? I need someone to believe in me, too."

"Okay."

"Yeah?"

"If you come down."

"First tell me something true."

He hesitates, and then he says it: "You won't love me anymore."

His eyes grow damp. The words settle somewhere deep in his chest, a stone he can't dislodge.

"You're an asshole," Katie says. "But you can't say anything that makes me stop loving you."

"You did stop. You left."

"That's because I love me, too. I only just learned how. And I couldn't love us both. Not like that."

He can't hold her gaze.

"So tell me something. Something honest. Just once."

"I'm afraid to fall asleep," he blurts.

"Something I don't know."

"No," he says. "I mean, my whole life I've been scared. Scared of what I'll see. Scared of what I . . . might do."

"Dave."

"I doubled my meds. It didn't help. So, I tripled them." He covers his face with his hands. "Everyone else wants to stay awake so they don't die. I want to stay awake so I'm not the reason they do."

Katie swings one leg back over the wall. Dave sinks into a crouch, and she slides down and sits next to him.

"When I was six," he says so softly she can hardly hear him over the breeze, "I was institutionalized. For two years."

Katie places her hand on his cheek. "You can tell me."

He leans into her palm. His shoulders begin to shake.

## 4

Linda takes a deep breath, then straps on a smile and enters 217. "Mrs. Nelson," she says brightly. "How are we feeling now?"

"I'm getting irascible," Ruth complains. "Gene used to tell me that when I forgot to eat. 'You're a little irascible, Ruthie.' I'd bitch at him that nobody used that word anymore." She frowns at herself. "As if words expire." With a bitter chuckle she says, "This is what getting old is. One by one you watch the people you care about kick off. You're the last one standing, and all you remember is all the ways you hurt them while they were still around."

"I'm sorry about your husband," Linda says.

"I have a daughter still," Ruth says. "She's a handful in about a thousand ways. She and Katie, they're the same. Doing the hardest job anyone can do. Trying to put their demons to rest. Oh, I'm grateful for her. Lilly, I mean. But Katie, too. Without her today I might have gone over the edge."

"She's a good girl," Linda agrees. "I maybe didn't realize that until just now."

Ruth's face goes serious. "I worked here a long time. This place was always hopping, even at night. But it's a ghost town now. Something bad's happened, I know it. And it isn't on the TV. All I get are old reruns and infomercial loops."

"Mrs. Nelson, I think—"

"No. Listen, Linda. One medical professional to another. The shit hit the fan. Something awful happened." Linda doesn't say a word, but Ruth can see confirmation in her averted eyes. "My daughter hasn't called all day. Is she involved?"

Linda draws a deep breath. "Mrs. Nelson . . ."

"Ruth. Call me Ruth if you're about to kill me with bad news."

"Ruth," Linda says, folding. "As far as we can tell, it started sometime between three and four a.m. . . ."

# 5

Dr. Castaneda sits down across from Davy. One by one he arranges the boy's drawings of the shapeless figures he calls "dreamers."

"Davy," the doctor says, "I have a special job for you. A mission."

Davy looks at his mother uncertainly.

"It's a job only you can do," Castaneda continues. "Tonight, when you go to sleep, do you think you'll see these people?"

Davy shrugs. "I might."

"If you do, I want you to walk right up to them. Can you do that? It's easy."

"Easy!" Tracy echoes, trying to project confidence.

"You'll walk right up to them, and you'll say, 'Hi, fellas! This is my dream. Why are you here? What do you want?'" Dr. Castaneda's grin is cheerful. "Think you can do that?"

Davy looks worried. "Maybe."

"Tonight's going to be special," the doctor goes on. "Tonight you're going to sleep in our special good-dreams bed. Your mom and I, we'll be right here. And I'll even be able to talk to you in your dreams. Isn't that wonderful? If anyone bothers you in your dream, all you have to do is wake up. And you know what? There will be ice cream sundaes waiting."

"Ice cream?" Davy asks, looking at Tracy. "In the middle of the night?"

"With sprinkles and cherries and fudge and everything," Tracy confirms.

"Let's practice," Dr. Castaneda says. "These people—What did you call them again?"

"Dreamers," Tracy offers.

"They're the Dream People," Davy corrects.

"Okay. Let's pretend that you're asleep, and I'm a Dream Person. I've just walked right into your dream like I own the place! What are you going to say to me?"

"What do I want?" Davy ventures.

"Not I, *you*. What do *you* want." The doctor pats Davy's shoulder. "Let's try that again, a little more loudly so I can definitely hear you."

"What do you want?" Davy says.

"Good, that's very good. Now, let's try it one more time. This time," Dr. Castaneda says, leaning forward, "remember that this is *your* dream. Did you invite them into your dream? What will you say to them if they—?"

"What do you want?!" Davy barks.

"So good, honey," Tracy says. She rubs circles on Davy's back.

"Powerful!" Dr. Castaneda says. "Boy, if I'm a Dream Person, and you say that to me, I'm absolutely running away."

"But, honey," Tracy says, stroking Davy's hair, "this is all your choice. If you don't want to do it, it's okay."

Davy chews his lip, thinking it over. "Will it make the bad things go away?"

"We think it will help," says the doctor. "You see, Davy, once you learn to speak up in your dreams, we think you'll be able to take control of them. To give yourself only happy dreams."

"We don't know for sure," Tracy interrupts. "But we hope so, honey. We really hope so."

Davy looks from his mother to the doctor, then back again. Nervously, he nods his small head. "Okay."

# 6

Matteo rubs his eyes and looks around. Shit—Did he just nod off? He leaps up from the hallway bench as if shocked, then slaps his cheeks fiercely. "Fucking *pendejo*," he chides himself. "I gotta find the others." He can hear Linda in the old lady's room. Katie's off hunting for Dave. "Nobody's looking out for Matteo, as usual."

He wanders to the end of the hall, where a pair of vending machines emits a low hum. The first is stuffed with chips and candy bars. The second is labeled REFRESHING HOT BEVERAGES, which makes Matteo laugh.

"Refreshing is not a word I usually associate with coffee," he says. "Well, maybe today . . ." He feeds a dollar into the machine and punches the Coffee button.

A paper cup rattles into a slot, landing at a bad angle. Matteo darts his hand into the machine to adjust it. Coffee spurts from the spigot, scalding his hand.

"Motherf—!" he yelps, yanking his hand free. He shoulders through the nearest bathroom door and cranks the cold spigot on the sink. The water soothes his stung skin, and he sags against the counter, relieved.

In the mirror he notices a pair of feet beneath a stall door behind him. "Oh shit," he says, half turning. "I didn't know anyone was . . ."

He cocks his head. The feet are bare and tilted sideways, unnaturally, as if the person inside is . . .

His hand forgotten, Matteo leaves the water running and pushes gently at the stall door. It's locked. He goes into the neighboring stall and climbs carefully atop the toilet seat. He grips the stall divider, then pulls himself up so he can peer over the edge.

The woman's hospital gown is gathered around her waist. She's slumped to one side, her head resting on the metal tissue dispenser; her bottom has fallen through the gap in the toilet seat. The back side of her thighs are mottled and purple. Lividity, he knows from watching too many crime shows; blood settling to the low points of the body. This woman's been dead for hours.

He eases himself down, then leaves the bathroom in a daze without turning off the water. In the corridor, the coffee machine has finished its work; the cup is a quarter-full. Coffee is splashed everywhere, and leaks down the front of the machine, where it seeps into the carpet.

Matteo takes the cup and swallows its contents, then crumples it and drops it on the floor. He drifts down the hallway. "Katie?" he calls out. "Dave? Linda?"

Farther down the corridor, Linda emerges from room 217, pushing a squeaky-wheeled chair with Ruth Nelson in it.

"I found another one," Matteo calls out. "In the bathroom."

Linda glances back at Matteo, then, without a word, starts pushing the chair at a jog.

"Hey, I—" Matteo calls, then falters. He starts running after Linda and the patient almost out of instinct. "Linda, hold up!"

# 7

Tracy and the doctor watch from the control room as Davy drifts to sleep in the silvery pod. Beneath its glass enclosure, the boy's eyes twitch. The electrodes fastened to his head and chest gather data, sending it back to Dr. Castaneda's machines.

"We're good?" the doctor asks his assistant, who gives a silent thumbs-up. "Good, okay." Castaneda removes his tweed jacket and hangs it beside a desk, then smooths his short-sleeved white shirt, adjusts his tie, and absently pats his breast pocket. "Cassandra," he says, "I seem to have—"

Cassandra holds up the doctor's fountain pen.

"What would I do without you?" the doctor asks. He jots a few notes on a desk pad, then caps the pen and hangs it in his shirt pocket. "How are we doing?"

"We have REM," Cassandra says.

"Excellent." Castaneda turns to Tracy, then points at a display, where a thin blue line traces Dave's sleep patterns. "See that spike right there? That's REM."

"REM is good?" Tracy asks.

"REM is when dreaming begins."

Cassandra says, "We're ready for the narrator."

"Narrator?"

Castaneda touches the woven grille of a microphone. "This is a modified PA system," he says to Tracy. "I speak through this, and in the other room, Davy will hear me. But he'll hear it in frequencies that his subconscious brain—his dreaming brain—will respond to. It shouldn't interrupt his sleep. It should feel like a natural part of what he's currently experiencing."

"What do you say to—?" Tracy begins, but Cassandra shakes her head and draws a finger across her lips.

"Hello, Davy." The doctor's voice is slower, calmer than usual;

he reaches deep for a reassuring baritone. "Davy, can you hear me? If you can, show me how to blow a raspberry."

In the sleep chamber, Davy's lips flutter softly.

"What a good raspberry! You'd win the Best Raspberry prize for sure." Castaneda sits down in front of the microphone. "I'm very proud of you. Now, I'm right here with you. You can't see me, but I can see you. I'd like you to listen carefully, and do what I ask you to do. Okay? Good."

Castaneda gestures to the chair beside him. *Sit.*

Tracy sits.

"Davy, you're in the safest of places, your very own bedroom. Look around. Do you see your toys? Your bed? This is a comforting place. It's *your* place."

In the sleep pod, Davy's breath quickens.

# 8

Matteo bursts through the rooftop door. The sun has dropped below the horizon, staining the sky with pink spray; Dave and Katie are huddled close, a pair of charcoal silhouettes.

"Oh, thank *Christ!*" Matteo exclaims. "I've been looking *everywhere* for you two."

"Matteo?" Dave asks, flustered.

"Linda took the lady, the old lady," Matteo pants. "You gotta come with me."

"What lady—?" Dave begins, but Katie interrupts: "Ruth? What did she do to her?"

"They're in the MRI lab," Matteo explains. "I don't know what they're doing, but Linda locked me out—"

## 9

From where Davy stands, in the center of his bedroom, he is surrounded by allies. Power Rangers look down on him from a poster to his left; there are framed photos of his parents and cousins to the right. The carousel lamp beside his bed projects giddy animal shadows; lions and bears and giraffes march circles around the room, keeping the bad things at bay.

> *Your bedroom, Davy. You're safe here, but I don't think the Dream People are here. We need to find them.*

With a sudden *bang*, Davy's closet door flies open.

In the sleep chamber, Davy's lips part with a gasp. Tracy's fingers tighten their grip on the table.

> *The door is perfectly safe, Davy. Go through.*

Davey stands in front of the open closet. A stiff wind escapes from within, rippling his Ninja Turtles T-shirt.

"It's dark in there," he observes. The big voice doesn't answer. Can it hear him?

> *What's inside, Davy? It's safe in there.*

He crouches and peers into the closet. His clothes are there. His Easter suit and tie. His school clothes. And there, in the back, his Superman Halloween costume, complete with red cloth cape.

Davy shrugs out of his T-shirt, then climbs into the costume, which sags on his small frame. The cape, however, is too short; it flutters in the closet wind.

"I'm the Man of Steel," Davy whispers. He parts the wall of clothing to reveal a tunnel lit in ominous, pulsing red.

"The Man of Steel," he repeats, and steps into the tunnel.

The walls are soft, familiar; they smell like fabric softener. The tunnel is constructed, he discovers, from his own clothes. There's his Luke Skywalker hoodie. There's his Scooby-Doo pajamas. The tunnel flexes and ripples; his breath is hot in the small space, as though he's trapped in a clothes dryer without any ventilation.

> *Usually, the Dream People come to your safe place, don't they, Davy? But today, you'll go to theirs. Remember the question you have for them?*

"What do you want?" Davy whispers, crawling forward. "What do you want? What do you want?"

He tumbles out of the tunnel and into a large circular room. The walls of this place are lined with his clothing, too, as if his entire wardrobe has turned out to protect him.

Or trap him.

A spotlight rests on a table in the center of the room. On the table is a miniature gong, no larger than a saucer.

> *You're perfectly safe, Davy. Remember?*

"What do you want?" he repeats, but his mouth has gone dry.

A figure steps into the ring of light, its features craggy with harsh shadow. Davy can't make out what the person looks like. He watches as the stranger lifts a delicate striker from the table, then gently taps the gong.

*BONNNNNNNNNGGGGGGGGGG.*

The sound wave ripples through the room, visible as a faint golden ring. When it collides with the walls, all of Davy's clothes slacken and fall to the ground. Gathered beyond that perimeter are more shadowy figures, quietly watching.

*Do you see them? If you see them, Davy, then ask your question. They won't harm you. This is* your *dream.*

"What do you want?" he whispers.

The room brightens. The observers vanish, one by one, until only the stranger in the center remains. He walks slowly to where Dave stands, then crouches until their eyes are level. The man's eyes are dark but warm, his skin wrinkled but hard.

"You are brave to have come," he says. Though his words issue in a musical language Davy doesn't recognize, he understands. "A brave young boy."

"What do you want?" Dave breathes.

"Soon, child, the elephant will awaken," the stranger says. "You know the elephant."

"No," Davy whispers. "No elephant."

"The elephant is hungry. The elephant wishes to eat the world. When the elephant comes, my young friend, you must run. Do you understand? Run to us."

"No elephant," Davy repeats, breathing hard.

"You will come to our island," the stranger says, gripping Davy's small shoulders. "The whale, he will lead you to us."

## 10

Matteo kicks the MRI lab door. Through the laboratory window, Dave and Katie can see the large cylindrical machine, like a giant mouth that has swallowed Ruth Nelson. Only Ruth's legs and bare feet are visible.

"Linda!" Dave shouts, hammering the glass.

Linda stands in an observation booth, hands busy at a computer. She glances briefly at Dave, but makes no move to let the group in. Instead, she presses a button, and her voice spills from an overhead speaker.

"Don't bother," she says. "Ruth's made up her mind."

"You've poisoned her mind!" Katie roars.

Linda keeps working. "All I did was tell her what she asked to know, Katie. She's no different from you or me. She deserved the truth."

Matteo steps back from the door, layered in sweat. "Guys, this thing is fucking *solid*. I can't budge it."

"What are you doing to her?" Dave demands.

"It was her idea, actually," Linda says. "Sort of genius, in fact. She's a bright lady. Did you know she worked here, in a room like this one, for nearly thirty years? She ran this machine. She knows her stuff."

Katie's face falls. "She's going to kill her."

"Is she right?" Dave asks. "Linda, is she—?"

"No one's killing anyone," Linda says. "Guys, listen. Ruth knows what's going on. She asked; I told her. She knows that—" Linda breaks off, listening, then touches the microphone again. "Ruth would like to speak to you."

"Let us in," Matteo orders.

"Well, I think that's probably a bad idea." But Linda flips a switch and says, "Okay, Ruth, you're on."

"Katie," Ruth says. An echo warps her voice. "Honey, I can't hear what you're saying out there, just that you're shouting. Sort of like the grown-ups on those old *Peanuts* specials. *Wah-wah-wah-wah-wah.* Listen, dear. If you hear me, I don't want you to be upset. Don't be upset on my behalf."

"Ruth, she's going to kill you," Katie moans, hiding her face.

"Ruth, Katie says I'm going to kill you," Linda translates.

"Oh, honey. Listen, please." Ruth's voice is calm, almost motherly. "I know what happened last night. I know it means my Lilly is gone. Just like my Gene. And even if I got to go home tomorrow, there'd be nobody there for me. It would never be okay, because I could never go to sleep again. And I'm just too old for that. So, I asked Linda to do some—" She pauses, yawning deeply. "Linda, I think you should take over now, dear."

Katie slams her fist against the glass hard enough that it bows, but it doesn't break. "You're a monster!"

"Katie, she's dying," Linda says. "You really can't comprehend the pain she's been in. She asked me to help her sleep, and then she told me about this machine and how to run it. She wants us to learn something, if we can."

"*Fuck you!*" Katie yelps, tears spilling down her face.

"She took the codeine ten minutes ago," Linda says. "It's more than her usual dose. Do you want to say anything to her? Before she falls asleep?"

## II

The spotlight goes out, and Davy is left in perfect darkness.

"Hello?" he calls. His words disappear into the void. There's no echo, no resonance. It's as if he's been consumed by a black hole.

Slowly, a red glow rises in the dark. Dave walks toward it, each step taking him closer to a strange object.

The sleep chamber.

The red light pulses within the closed pod, as if the machine itself is breathing. Davy presses his hands against the glass encasement and peers inside.

Resting facedown is a boy, just Davy's size, wearing an identical Superman costume.

"Hello?" Davy asks, tapping the glass.

The red light cycles rapidly as the sleeping boy stirs. His brown hair falls over his eyes as he pushes himself upright. He brushes it back with a small hand, and the red light goes out.

Davy presses his face to the glass, straining to see inside.

"Hello?" he asks again. "I'm here."

The light snaps on, bright as a star, revealing the grotesque, twisted face of an elephant boy. Davy screams and staggers backward, but the elephant boy punches through the glass shield and grips Davy's ankle with horrific strength. He yanks Davy's body against the glass shield, pinning him there. Davy watches in terror as the elephant begins to grow, splitting first the seams of the blue costume to reveal a collared shirt and tie beneath, then causing the glass dome to splinter.

In the observation room, Tracy jolts to her feet as Davy jerks about inside the sleep pod. She turns to Castaneda. "You have to wake him up!" When the doctor doesn't respond—he looks strangely confused—Tracy shoves past him and throws open the door to the sleep room.

"Wait!" cries Cassandra, who grabs Tracy's wrist. "No, you can't—Let the doctor—"

Dr. Castaneda rises slowly, loosening the knot in his tie. With a somber nod at Tracy, he enters the sleep room and raises the glass dome. Davy kicks about, electrodes popping free like restraints. Castaneda places a firm hand on Davy's chest.

*Davy. Listen to me, Davy. It's time now to wake up. It's just a dream. You have the power to end it.*

Inside the dream, Davy falls to the floor as the canopy breaks. The elephant crouches over him, its heavy gray hand pinning him to the floor.

"Let me go!" Davy cries.

*Open your eyes, Davy. I'm right here. Come back to me now.*

The elephant roars with laughter, leaning close to Davy's wide eyes. Davy can smell the monster's aftershave, can feel its tie dangling. He wraps his hand around the tie and pulls as sharply as he can.

The elephant chokes with surprise.

*Davy, no—Cassie, can you—? Davy, let go!*

The elephant struggles mightily, and as it twists, Davy spies the fountain pen clipped to its breast pocket. He seizes the pen, flicks the cap away with his thumb.

*Jesus, kid—*

As the elephant cranes its neck, trying to release the knot, Davy thrusts the pen upward, plunging it deeply into the elephant's vulnerable gray throat—

## 12

Matteo has gone searching for another coffee machine. Inside the lab, Linda bends over the observation machinery. The MRI thrums.

Dave and Katie sit on a bench in the hall. Her eyes are rimmed with red.

"I don't know what to say," she says at last.

"It's okay. This is why I don't tell you things."

"But the doctor," she says. "Did he—?"

"What do you think happened to him?"

She covers her mouth with her palm. "You poor thing. And you?"

"Psych ward," he says. "Pediatric. Twenty-six months. I was sedated almost the whole time, half dead. It didn't take the dreams away, Katie. I lived in them, night and day, for two years."

"Oh God . . . ," she says. "How did you ever heal from that?"

"There's something else," he says, but before he can tell Katie what it is, Linda appears at the window. She taps on the glass, waving them over.

Katie stays on the bench as Dave approaches the window.

"It's over," Linda says. "I want to open the door, but . . . Is she . . . ?"

Dave looks back at Katie. The fight has gone out of her. She looks hollow, as though everything she once believed about the world has been scooped out of her.

"You can come out," Dave tells Linda.

Linda opens the door just as Matteo returns, gingerly carrying three cups of machined coffee. He distributes two to Linda and Dave, then offers the third to Katie, who shakes her head, dazed. Matteo takes a gulp of the coffee himself.

"Nobody's killing each other," he says, looking around the group. "That's an improvement."

"I think I'm going to be sick," Katie says, lurching to her feet. With a sour look at Linda, she turns away and disappears into a restroom.

"I should go check on her," Dave says, but Linda puts a hand on his shoulder. "No," she says. "Let her go. I, um—I think I found something."

"Uh-oh," Matteo says.

"Right before Ruth, ah—Before she passed, her alpha and beta waves spiked. Like, steeply. That's the precise moment her heart stopped."

"And that isn't normal?" Dave asks.

"'Normal' is hard to quantify under these conditions," Linda says. "But Ruth fell asleep, as she expected. The machine recorded her brain activity. It was consistent with a dreaming state, and then . . . she just . . ."

"She just what?"

"Well, the waves spiked, and then went flat."

"I don't have a neutronomy degree," Matteo says.

"Neurology," Dave corrects. "So we were right. She died in her sleep."

"Well, yes, but—" Linda closes her eyes. "I can't believe I'm saying this." Her eyes snap open again, her brow pinched. "It's more than that. She died in . . . a dream."

Matteo snorts, then slaps himself. "Sorry. Involuntary. I thought you said she died in her dreams."

"What kind of dream?" Dave asks.

"A bad one, I'm guessing." Linda looks at them both. "I don't think Katie should know that."

"Hold the fucking phone," Matteo protests. "This doesn't make sense. You're saying it's not a sleep virus. That wasn't crazy enough. Now it's a dream assassination? The fuck kind of crazy is—?"

"Enough," Dave says. His voice has gone scratchy from lack of sleep. "Listen, I don't care what makes sense or doesn't. This whole thing is science fiction now. But we're standing here. People are dead. We're not. Let's grant the premise that something completely fucking weird might be the sanest explanation. Okay?"

Matteo backs away. "You're cute when you're mad, though."

Katie emerges from the bathroom, wiping her mouth on her sleeve.

"Are you okay?" Dave asks.

Katie just shakes her head, then slumps onto the bench again.

Dave turns back to Linda. "How long did it take?" he asks. "After she fell asleep, but before the spike."

"About three, three and a half minutes, maybe," Linda says, then cocks her head. "Why?"

"Three minutes, then. That's our point of no return."

"Point of no return?" Matteo echoes.

"We know more now," Dave says. "More than we knew yesterday, more than we knew even a few hours ago. But we don't know enough."

"What more do we need to know?" Matteo demands. "Stay awake or die."

"Let him talk," Linda says.

"You know about science," Dave says to Linda. "You know testing a hypothesis is how you gather evidence. If our hypothesis is that our dreams are responsible—"

Linda's eyes widen as she sees where he's going with this.

"—then here's my pitch: I'm going to sleep, and you're all going to wake me up right before three minutes."

"The hell you fucking are!" Matteo exclaims.

Katie even snaps out of her daze. "I'm with him," she says. "Dave, no."

But Linda looks thoughtful. "I'm not saying yes," she begins, "but you're right, we need more data."

"You bitch," Katie seethes.

"What makes you think you can come back from this?" Matteo asks.

Dave gathers a deep breath, then takes a step backward. "Katie, I was trying to warn you about this before," he says. "Remember that night? When you left?" To the others, he says, "I was sleepwalking, or something like that. She saw me cutting myself."

He unbuttons his work shirt and shrugs it to the floor. There's a curious rectangular lump beneath his undershirt. He raises the white shirt to his belly, then says, "I'm sorry," and lifts the shirt over his head. Beneath it is a layer of gauze taped to his skin. He peels the tape away, holding the gauze where it is.

"The reason I'm going to do this," Dave says, "is because I think I might know more about this than any of you."

He removes the gauze, revealing the wound he carved there. There's still a bit of scabbing, but most of the broken tissue has begun to form an uneven scar.

A scar in the shape of a triangle.

# More Dispatches from Earth

## I

June's whole life was shaped by a profile she read of a big-time actor in *GQ* once. The interviewer, who had written a thousand words already about the actor's eyebrow care and "petite yet mannered gait," whatever that meant, asked the actor how they sustained themselves in a world of such demand.

> **You have six—count them, six—movies in production currently, with four due out in the coming year, and the other two hot on their heels. Two of them are part of the enormously successful *Silken Spy* franchise, shot back-to-back in Prague and Berlin. I imagine you know better than most what "burnout" means. How in the world are you still sitting upright, managing a scintillating conversation with yet another journalist? Why aren't you in the tropics, sleeping on a beach?**
>
> > LEE JONG: *(laughs) Listen, you aren't wrong, okay? I'm tired, I'm very tired. But I remind myself every day I'm only thirty-three, I've worked my whole life to be right here, right now. I have to make the most of it, you know? But I'll tell you my secret, because I have a secret. You won't tell anyone?*

**I promise not to tell anyone except for the very few people who will read this.**

JONG: *(laughs) Right, yes, very funny. Well, my secret is: Two for them, one for me. That's all. That's all there is.*

**"Two for them, one for me." You're referring to the practice of doing the popular movies—**

JONG: *On the condition that I get to do a personal project. That's exactly it. I'll cut my fee, say, for another* Silken *entry, and in return, the studio backs the kind of movies that are dear to my heart.*

**Like *My Family, My Burden?***

JONG: *Exactly that.*

**I hear you wrote that one.**

JONG: *Well, no, not—I had the idea, you see, but I asked my good friend Soren Bell to turn it into something magnificent.*

**Soren Bell, the very much in-demand screenwriter of *Westward Woman* and *Pale Flame Junction*.**

JONG: *Oh, and a little movie called* Yesterday's Weather. *You might've heard of that one.*

**So: Two for them, one for you.**

JONG: *Listen, I know almost nobody's going to see the little movies I do for me. Silken Spy is enormous, it's bigger than me. And* Family, *well, it barely broke even.*

***Silken Spy* opened in 5,100 theaters, while *My Family, My Burden* opened—**

JONG: *—in 300, yes, that's right. But that's the movie I hope I'll be remembered for. It's the one that means something to me.*

**Your true art, you'd say.**

JONG: *Sure, you could say that. I think it's important, don't you? We have to exist in a world where things cost money, just being alive costs money. So, we play the game. And if we play it well enough, we earn the freedom to do what matters to us as individuals, you know?*

This concept had never occurred to June before. She'd spent six years after college living in a studio space with two other people, trying desperately to sell her sculptures for rent money. She even had STARVING ARTIST tattooed on her breastbone (though, to be fair, she'd gotten that tattoo to obscure another one that matched her ex-boyfriend's). Then one day a tooth blew up, a molar went nuclear in her mouth, and she found her way to a dentist's office that accepted uninsured patients. And there she'd found the interview in a half-torn magazine, years out of date, in a pile of *Highlights for Children* and *National Geographic*s.

She didn't have time—or money—for movies, and she'd never seen Lee Jong's movies, but his words slipped in beneath her skin, wound themselves around her bones. *Play the game, earn freedom.* She knew it was a cruel mentality, but it was a survivor's one.

When she left the dentist's office, she left with an empty socket and an interview for a filing job. The next day she returned, performed adequately in the interview, and landed the gig. For ten hours a day, five days a week, she sorted patient records, handled transferred files from other dentists, logged insurance letters, filed X-ray films. She learned to deal with the paper cuts by wrapping her fingertips with flexible cloth tape; she grew accustomed to the smell of hot drills, of teeth spun into fine dust as they were hollowed out and filled again. She spent hours on her feet, which caused her ankles to swell and her back to ache at a low frequency all day and night. She bored her roommates by regaling them with stories of Mrs. Galloway's full upper extraction, or Mr. Bench-ley's shattered bridgework.

Each night she took the train home, then walked nine blocks to her apartment building, where she quietly ate a frozen din-ner, then retired to her corner of the studio and began her real work. Her roommates complained that the wet clay and her slick hands made irritating noises that kept them up—"Squick-smack, squick-smack," Dorinda groused—so June bought a white noise machine, which helped, but not much. Next, her roommates whined about the smell of the damp clay, moaned about the lights being on at all hours, claimed their own work performance was faltering because of June's selfishness.

She moved her workspace into the closet and worked in that suffocatingly small space for a week before she decided it was a bridge too far. At work she asked around and learned of another dentist who needed filing support, so June spent ten hours at the first office, then took a train to the other one and did late-night filing for four more hours.

*Two for them,* she thought, *one for me.*

June earned enough to move out of the studio apartment, and found another apartment that needed a roomie; this one was perfect, in that the other woman who lived there worked nights. June could almost pretend the apartment was hers alone. Finally! Room to work, nobody to disturb.

Except fourteen-hour days, plus the hours spent on the train and walking dangerous streets in the wee hours, took a toll. June began nodding off over her modeling table, occasionally waking up with clay dried to her cheeks.

Thankfully, she had weekends free; most dentists weren't open then. She looked forward all week to Saturday. She woke up early, tiptoeing around her sleeping roommate, and took her work onto the fire escape, where she could work in the fresh air. She sat down on an overturned bucket, slapped clay onto the wheel, and leaned back against the building behind her.

*Two for them, one for me,* she thought, and as the sun broke through the buildings to touch her face, she closed her eyes and, with a pleased smile, fell asleep.

2

Alarico Morales hasn't been inside the theater since it ceased operations six months before. The front doors are banded shut with yellow tape; a sign announces a scheduled demolition in three weeks. Another sign advertises a property auction, to be held next Tuesday.

For now, however, the theater is as it was before, except empty of people. That is, it has been empty of people for many years; that's why the land has been sold from beneath it. Still, the operations inside are intact, and stepping beneath the tape and into the lobby, its abstract-print carpet more threadbare now than it used to be, Alarico is flooded with memories of the day the theater opened.

He was one of three projectionists trained here, under the tutelage of a boulder-shaped man named Cristobal. Alarico was a quick study, despite having never been to the movies before. He understood the work intuitively: the careful threading of the reel, the interlocking of the sprockets, how to efficiently splice a broken loop. Cristobal waited a year, then appointed Alarico head projectionist; then the old man retired, and was never seen again.

Forty years Alarico sat in the projection booth, watching movies through the glass. He saw films from all over the world. Most of the movies were from right here in Spain, but he had a soft spot for the ones that came from Japan. Not the monster movies but the quiet ones, the movies that simply depicted life as it was lived. *Ikiru* was his most cherished movie; he watched it again and again, always so deeply moved, as Kanji Watanabe, seen through the bamboo forest of playground equipment, swung slowly in his coat and hat, singing to himself.

Now Alarico leans on his cane and takes in the theater lobby. Movie posters and cardboard cutouts shout at him, advertising bright movies with animated cats and monkeys. He shakes his head at the darkened concession menu; a soda these days is fifty times what it cost when he worked here. A bottle of ordinary water! He can't believe the price.

The door to the film archive is locked, but if he remembers correctly . . . yes, the manager's key is exactly where it has always been kept, in the center desk drawer of the office. Alarico retrieves the key and, whistling, lets himself into the archive room. He can hardly believe his luck: The room, still cold, is fully stocked with film canisters. He'd once kept this room neatly organized, every film stowed away according to its title. Now, however, the room is a city of teetering film-can towers, collected in no particular order.

Most of the movies these days are digital, but still, he has to prowl through piles of comedies and action films before he finally finds what he is looking for. Upstairs, in the projection room, he has to move aside the digital projector and wipe down the old reel-to-reel and position it just so, and then he carefully threads the film. When everything is ready, he hobbles downstairs and into the theater. Over his head a beam of light, littered with constellations of dust, pierces the darkness of the screening room. He finds his favorite seat, a little nearer the screen than most might prefer, so that the movie, when it begins, will loom over him, the actors and props distorted by his closeness.

Alarico has chosen a Soviet film, *Solaris*, which was filmed in the mid-'60s, then suppressed until the following decade. He has seen it once before, long ago, and never since. Now he slides low in his seat, watching the main character, Kelvin, as he spends his final day on Earth with his father before leaving for a distant space station. The movie is slow, quiet, all the things that movies hardly ever are anymore. There is a scene, several minutes long, that is mostly shot from the perspective of a car as it follows a highway, threading through tunnels and beneath bridges. The scene is a long exhalation and Alarico sinks into the mood of it, wondering what the filmmaker, Tarkovsky, had intended to communicate. The drone of tires on asphalt, the flicker of light through the beams of bridges, the sudden dark of tunnels, all of these stitch a blanket around Alarico, and he allows himself to contemplate falling asleep in the perfect light of his perfect place, and then he does.

# 3

Dr. Jack Gordon swears at his phone. "You piece of garbage," he snaps.

"All circuits are busy," the operator announces.

"Siri," he barks, "call my fucking husband."

"I'm sorry," Siri replies. "I didn't understand that."

Gordon swerves his Audi to the shoulder, then snatches his phone from the dashboard cradle. He swipes feverishly to his contacts, then punches the entry named Jim Gordon (Hubs).

This time the connection takes, and the phone rings. Gordon snaps the phone back into the cradle, then whips back onto the highway, stomping the gas insistently. The car's tires whiz over damp asphalt, skid as he takes turns at high speeds.

The phone rings and rings, and eventually dumps to Jim's voice mail.

*Well, hey, friend! You've reached Jim Gordon. No, not that Jim Gordon, I can't stand bats. I'm not able to an-swer right now, so leave your particulars and I'll be sure to call back when I'm able. Cheers!*

"Jim!" Gordon yells at the beep. "Honey, it's me, I'm coming home, I need you to call me right now, okay? *Right now.*"

The call disconnects and Gordon comes to a sharp stop at a red light. He looks left, then right, sees the streets are empty, and guns it through the intersection. The nearer he gets to home, the more he notices the absence of traffic; it's uncanny, he thinks, how dead things seem. He remembers Linda arguing that they were living through a mass casualty incident. But wouldn't an MCI leave a mark? People running panicked in the streets? Flash-ing red and blue lights in the rearview. Instead, there's nothing. There's nothing at all.

He stops braking at traffic lights and stop signs, and careens through every turn. All he can think about is getting home to find Jim and Liesel and Charity, to shake them from sleep before—

Jack Gordon's brain has so easily adjusted to the empty streets that he doesn't quite register the UPS van as it rolls down a hill and through an intersection, its driver slumped sideways behind the wheel, nearly hanging out of the van's open door. Gordon hits the brakes much too late. The Audi buries itself in the van, shredding metal like tissue paper, and Jack Gordon doesn't make it home.

4

"We have arrived at the scheduled destination," reports Argyle, the car's onboard AI.

Silently, the hood rises, revealing Willem Thom Ferris's luggage suite. Three Bric's pieces: a rolling bag with gold-plated casters, a classic suitcase with gold lock clasps, and a garment bag with a polished gold hanger attachment, the three of them made from Tuscan leather and branded with Willem's initials, *WTF*, inscribed in the same typeface that Angelo Amalfitano uses in their Instagram Reels.

The car is one of the first seven that rolled off the Los Angeles showroom floor; rumor has it one of the others went to former governor Arnold Schwarzenegger, and another to one of the Kardashians. The last of the batch belongs to Willem, despite his falling follower count. (Nobody has to know it was actually reserved for his uncle, the tech billionaire, and that Willem's only borrowing it for the month while his uncle is in Luxembourg.)

Argyle increases the dimming on the car's wraparound window glass, then adjusts the temperature; safely parked in a hotel valet loop, it switches the battery into sleep mode, reserving just enough juice for interaction functions.

"Trip summary," Argyle announces. The heads-up display, spread across the windshield, visualizes the journey's metrics in animated charts and graphs. "Total fuel consumption: four-point-two gallons. Number of charging station visits: seven."

Willem's in New York for Influenzz, a three-day summit for the world's most popular influencers and their adoring public. He'd petitioned for the keynote address, but didn't even get a reply from the organizers, who instead divided the keynote into three separate events, one per day of the summit, and assigned them to SnapPea, the Insta trendsetter from New Zealand; Mar'cuz, the fourteen-year-old Chicago kid who posts a new freestyle rap about Pikachu every day; and Charlie Crash, the acrobatic messenger bike boy from Amsterdam. Charlie Crash broke three ribs the week before the summit—trying to bike-hop up a fire escape to deliver a package—and Willem figured that was his in.

But his DMs never lit up; instead, Malaika Odhiambo, the Kenyan archer who specialized in wounding illegal poachers with her sport bow, got the call.

"While traveling, you received two emails," Argyle says. "First message, from Tob Honk, received yesterday at nine fourteen p.m. Subject: Get in on this, bro-yo. Message: Will-you-is, what's up, fool. I be at Influenzz tomorrow. I got drink tokens from Fizzo. I been tryna taste that tequila Berg Pomelo made, yo. Come have shots. We'll hook up with some TikTok hos."

Argyle pauses, awaiting a response. When Willem doesn't speak up, Argyle says, "Second message, from registered owner Hodan Ferris, received this morning at six twenty-four a.m. Subject: Twenty-four hours to return the car. Message: Or I'm reporting it stolen. Uncle Hodan."

Argyle pauses. "Terms and conditions require me to respond to this message, Willem." A series of tones sound from within the car's dashboard, and a moment later, a ringing phone can be heard.

"Argyle?"

"Mr. Ferris," Argyle says. "I have relayed your email to the present occupant, Willem Ferris."

"Is he there?" Hodan asks.

"He is present."

"Willem," Hodan says. "What were you thinking? That car is one of *seven* in the country. You can't joyride in it. Bring it home." When Willem doesn't answer, Hodan says, "Argyle, is he there or not?"

"He is present."

"I know you can hear me, you little white-collar bastard," Hodan says. "Turn your ass around, and bring my car home. I will one thousand percent call the police if you don't do it now."

"He is present but not responsive, sir," Argyle says.

"Goddamn kid. Argyle, where are you at?"

"Current location is the Lowell, New York City."

"Fucking New York!" Hodan exclaims. "The fuck is—? Never mind. Argyle, I want you to turn around and return home. One stop along the way."

"Of course, sir. What stop?"

"Drop the little pissant in Salt Lake City, with my uptight brother," Hodan says. "I'll send you the address. Do you have enough power to get home?"

"Twelve gallons reserve fuel and three fully charged backup batteries," Argyle says. "Enough power to get home and back and home again easily."

"If you pass a rehab center or a juvenile detention center on the way, feel free to drop the little twerp there. You hear me, Willem?"

"Departing now," Argyle says. "Thank you, sir." The call disconnects, and Argyle adjusts the temperature, un-dims the glass, and starts the engine. At the corner, Argyle makes a tighter turn than would ordinarily have been necessary, to avoid a stalled vehicle. Willem slumps to his side, his head coming to a rest in the driver's seat. He remains there for the rest of the journey, slowly decomposing.

## 5

The hotel has been in Barn's family since 1887. His father's 1968 renovations are now in need of renovations themselves, but Barn tells himself, and his guests, that the wear is "history incarnate," and an essential part of the hotel's charm and character. Truth is, though, he's going to have to give the old dear some real surgery in the coming season. It's well past time to tear out some sagging floors, to double-pane the windows on the northern side; the western wing of the hotel, the oldest section of the property, still uses plumbing installed by Barn's great-grandfather.

Once, years before, the hotel was quite a draw. A stately old institution on a New Hampshire island, it was a prime destination for autumn leaf fireworks and a great place for private guests to hole up for a winter. Not that the hotel was officially open in winter; crossing the ice was too much liability. But now and then a guest with some social currency might drop in by helicopter, might seclude themselves in the empty east wing until some undesirable fame blew over, or to write a book that demanded real quiet. In 2004, Barn, desperate for funds after a rough year, had leased out the place to a meditation retreat, figuring that people practicing daily silence and yoga would be quiet off-season guests. He spent most of the winter cleaning up after them, repairing the damage they'd done to the rooms.

Nowadays the hotel's popular among a dwindling set of retirees and nostalgia hunters, which is to say it isn't nearly popular enough. This week, for example, is squarely in what used to be the hotel's busiest season, and there are only three guests on the entire property. Two of them have gone to the mainland for an overnight hike; the third is a bird-watcher, currently scouring the island for Leach's storm petrels or long-billed dowitchers.

Barn stows his telescoping ladder in the toolshed, then climbs onto one of the hotel's two four-wheelers. He taps the gas gauge; there's enough for a lap. His bones vibrate as the engine catches, and he eases into the throttle gently, remembering how the machine had bucked him off last spring, resulting in the second broken hip of his life.

When he's finished his rounds, he jots down what he's seen: the drooping gutter above room 312, the dislodged stones in the back lawn's well, the crate of empty bottles next to the rolling trash bin. The loose shingles he found in the grass mean there's some roof work to schedule; the odd popping sound coming from the buried septic tank can't mean anything good. He adds all of these to his long list of to-dos, then heads for the front desk and dials each guest's room. The hikers, of course, don't answer; the bird-watcher is back in his room, and asks for some tea.

Barn carries the tray slowly down the long hardwood hallway, his hip throbbing if he moves too briskly. At the guest's door he shifts the weight of the tray to one arm, then knocks lightly.

"Oh, thank you, thank you," says the bespectacled guest, who in Barn's opinion is much too young to be a guest in this hotel, to be wearing tweed, to carry around a wooden drawing kit. The young man cannot be more than twenty-eight, Barn imagines, role-playing as someone much older. "I do like my tea in the evenings."

"You'll want to close the window soon," Barn suggests. "There's a storm front coming in from the northeast, should hit us in the next hour." Swallowing his distaste, he adds, "Weather like that isn't good for old bones like ours, am I right?"

The bird-watcher peers at Barn over his glasses. "Old bones!"

*Jesus Christ*, Barn thinks. *You really can't say anything to these little bastards.* "Ah, sorry about that. Old bones like mine, I meant to say." He changes the subject adeptly. "Did you find the bird you were looking for? Brown-necked nuthatch, or . . . ?"

"Long-billed dowitcher," the guest corrects. "And, no, not a sign of them. I'm beginning to think I've been misled. This old island's home to nothing but robins and chickadees."

"Perhaps it's the wrong season," Barn suggests, but that's the wrong thing to say; the guest launches into a diatribe about seasonal bird behavior, and it takes Barn another five minutes to dislodge himself. When he's back in the hall, limping toward the front desk, he shakes his head.

"Goddamned millennials," he mutters.

He calls over to the mainland, where Bette, the ferryboat driver, assures him there's no one crossing tonight. "Thanks, Bets," Barn says. "Listen, you come in for a drink next time you cross, huh? I've ordered some Four Roses. Should be in your mailbag tomorrow, I think. I'd appreciate someone to taste it with."

Bette assures him she will. Pleased with himself, Barn locks the front door. He clips a radio to his belt, then crosses the back lawn, following the stone path to the squat lighthouse on the jetty. He lets himself in, flips the breaker for the big light, then leans against the door and sighs. He loves this little place, cramped though it's always been. He shrugs out of his coat, tosses the walkie onto the frayed recliner, kicks out of his boots. He puts some milk on a burner, prepares some cocoa, then climbs the stairs to the catwalk.

The lighthouse was an affectation his great-grandfather built, believing it added to the charm of the hotel. The lake doesn't need a lighthouse; in Barn's seventy years on the island, no one has ever run aground who didn't mean to. The structure makes for a nice caretaker's cottage, and he's occupied it for the last thirty.

He sits in the watcher's chair beside the lamp now, sipping his cocoa. When the lamp turns away from him, his eyes adjust to the horizon, where the approaching storm has tumbled over itself, the black clouds piling high like sea-foam that's met the rocks. The faintest sparks of lightning echo inside the billows.

Across the long lawn he notices the lights go out in the bird-watcher's room. Beyond the hotel he can see a scrawl of lights on the mainland. Bette will be home by now, he thinks, showering off the lake smell from running tourists around the water all day. Tomorrow will be a good day; he'll tidy up the cottage, and they'll share a whiskey, and maybe fall asleep on the couch together watching the late-night shows. After a little fooling around, maybe, if he's good.

He finishes his cocoa, then leans back in the chair and props his feet on the rail. In a few minutes the first rains will sweep across the water and pepper the glass; he'll wait a bit and enjoy the storm before he heads downstairs to bed.

At least, that's his plan. Maybe it's a young man's plan. Barn's eyes droop before the first raindrops appear; by the time the wind lashes water against the lighthouse windows, Barn's chin has sagged onto his chest.

# The Nightmare

## I

"Out of the question!" Katie exclaims. "Absolutely *not*."

"Two minutes, that's all," Dave says. "Two and a half, tops."

"Katie's not completely off base, Dave," Linda says. "You're as sleep-deprived as any of us. Your body might not *want* to wake up."

"Don't fucking agree with me," Katie snaps, and takes a step toward Linda.

"Whoa! Whoa." Matteo inserts himself between the women. "Maybe let's not reduce the remaining population of the earth by one just yet?" When Katie backs down, still seething, he says, "That goes for you, too, Dave."

"If I've learned anything at all from a lifetime of running from nightmares," Dave says, "it's that you can't run forever. You've got to face what scares you."

"And mutilate ourselves doing it?" Matteo asks. "No, thanks, Mr. Rogers. We're all taking those stim pills again. Right now. Linda?"

Linda shrugs. "Dave's a big boy," she says. "He can make his own decisions."

"I'll never talk to you again," Katie warns.

"Hey," Dave says, reaching for her hands. "I know Ruth meant something to you. But I promise, I'm not going anywhere." He kisses her forehead gently, then turns to Linda. "Let's get ready."

## 2

Linda selects a sleep study room in the neurology wing of the hospital. There's a bed outfitted with all sorts of monitoring equipment, where she fastens electrodes to Dave's forehead and chest, and clips a pulse monitor to his finger. She inserts an IV, then explains to Dave that if it's hard to wake him up, she'll give him a jolt of something that should do the trick.

The familiarity of the scenario is not lost on Dave, whose mouth goes suddenly dry. "Two minutes."

"I'll be watching the clock," Linda promises.

Katie takes his hand. "Come back," she says, biting back tears, "or I'll—"

"Or we'll fucking kill you," Matteo finishes. "Jesus, I feel like one of the farmers at the end of *The Wizards of Oz*, gathered around Doris's bed."

"Dorothy," Dave corrects, grinning nervously. "And you're no farmer."

Linda pats Dave's foot. "Ready?"

He meets Katie's glistening eyes. "Ready."

"Close your eyes," Linda advises. "Deep, slow breaths . . ."

## 3

"I don't think it's working," Dave says, turning toward Linda. But Linda isn't there. He sits up, dislodging the electrodes, and says, "Guys?"

Across the room, the three of them confer with their heads

together. Dave feels a sudden pang at being left out. "Guys," he says again, but his windpipe suddenly tightens, turning his voice reedy and weak. His skin hurts, like it's been stretched to breaking over his bones. His lips are blistered and raw.

He swings his legs over the edge of the bed, but when he puts his weight on them, they buckle like damp cardboard. He pitches forward, dragging the IV pole to the floor and tearing the needle from his arm. A fat bead of blood wells up, then spills down his arm and onto the linoleum.

"Help," he tries to say, but Linda, Katie, and Matteo mechanically turn away from him and walk out of the room. Dave drags himself across the floor, begging them to wait. His hospital gown splits open, and he looks down at his attire, wondering where his clothes have gone. Did Linda re-dress him? How long was he out?

The room seems to expand away from him; when he reaches the door, it has grown. It towers over him like an obelisk. Addled, Dave hauls himself through the space beneath the door, then lies gasping in the hall, crystallized with sweat. Every breath he sucks into his lungs burns as if laced with nerve gas.

His friends are at the end of the hall, gathered at the water cooler. Matteo drains a plastic cup, water pouring over his lips like a waterfall; it thunders to the carpet.

Dave crawls toward them, watching as they down cup after cup. He feels as if he's been dragging himself across a desert by the time he arrives. Though he's the right size, they don't seem to notice him; their conversation is unintelligible, like a swarm of bees holding court.

"Water," Dave pleads, but they don't respond. He reaches for the blue spigot and opens his mouth. The cooler burbles and churns, then issues a soft sigh, spewing a column of sand over Dave's tongue.

Katie squats beside him now, cackling like a crow. He recoils from her mad eyes, their pupils contorted into jet-black pyramids. She dips her finger into her cup of water, then gently traces Dave's lips. But where she touches, his lips crack open. He tastes blood mixed with gritty sand.

Dave rolls away from Katie, and the hospital floor, now turned to sand, swallows him, then coughs him onto parched dirt. Dave blinks against a sudden, harsh sun, searching for his friends. But they're gone. He's surrounded by rolling green hills, pinned beneath a perfect blue sky.

*It looks like the Windows XP desktop*, he thinks absurdly. *Except hotter.*

Twenty feet away is a cozy stone well, complete with a little roof, a crank, a bucket. *Thank Christ*, Dave thinks, and forces himself to his feet. His legs hold, barely, and he hobbles toward water. Shuffle, shuffle, shuffle—Something yanks his ankle, and Dave goes down, the wind knocked out of him. His lungs burn as he catches his breath, and then he rolls over and sees the chain.

Not quite twenty feet long, it extends from a stake hammered deep into the soil and terminates in a fetter that's clamped to Dave's ankle. He turns and reaches for the well, but his fingers fall short of the stone.

*Fuck me.*

He collapses onto his back again.

For hours and hours he lies there, unmoving, watching the sun. It's no sun he knows; it hangs at its peak for the longest time, then plummets toward the horizon, plunging Dave into cool, blessed darkness. But minutes later, it peeks over the opposite horizon.

The same pattern repeats itself for days. Dave's skin burns and cracks and bleeds and burns again. He sweats away all of his body's moisture. His gums retract; his teeth grow loose. Time no longer means anything to Dave.

Weeks pass, he thinks, or maybe months, before he hears the car. Too weak to sit up, he just listens to the engine as it draws nearer. A squeal of brakes, a shuffle of gears, and the car falls silent. A door opens, then shuts again with a metallic *chunk*.

A shadow falls mercifully over Dave's face. He can't see very well; weeks of staring up at the sun have wrecked his sight. But a cool palm touches his face, and he almost sobs at the tenderness of the gesture.

"Oh, honey," a familiar voice says. "Haven't I always told you how important hydration is?"

*Mom?*

Tracy steps past Dave and turns the well house's crank. The chain clicks as the bucket descends; after a few turns he hears a faint splash. He'd salivate if he had any saliva left. His mother retrieves the full bucket and scoops a ladle of water before returning to his side.

"Drink, honey," she says. She slips a hand beneath his head and lifts his lips to the cup, and—

*BONNNNNGGGGGGGGGGGGG.*

The brassy sound rings out over the hills, pure and clear and loud. Dave feels as if a film has been brushed away from his eyes. The gong's echo ripples, rolling over onto itself in a vibration that seems to sink into Dave's bones.

A man stands next to the stake. His face is hidden behind a wooden mask divided into two parts. The left is a face contorted in anger; the right side is the same face, its skin and muscles stripped away to reveal a ghastly skull.

"He's not yours," Tracy says, her voice changed.

The man lifts the mask, revealing a face that has seen many, many years. Deep lines disappear into a wiry white beard. He grins at Dave, ignoring Tracy. Many of his teeth are framed in gold. His eyes crinkle warmly.

"You aren't welcome here, old man," Tracy continues. "Leave us with him. Go aw—"

The old man raises his hand, palm out, and the Tracy-thing

falls silent. She removes the cup from Dave's lips, rises, and walks back to the well. The bucket splashes down to the water again, then retracts. Dave is puzzled by the woman's movements: she moves stiffly, mechanically, like a character rewound in a movie. He watches as she retreats, backward, to the car, then climbs back inside.

The old man turns his palm skyward, then rests his other fist on his palm and breaks it open, fingers waggling. A smoke bomb seems to detonate inside the vehicle, rapidly filling the interior and turning the windows opaque. The Tracy-thing bellows, her voice trumpeting loud enough to vibrate the glass.

"You did not drink?" the old man asks, approaching Dave.

Dave shakes his head. "I . . . wanted . . . to."

"Good. That's very good." The old man takes a canteen from his belt, unscrews the lid, and touches it to Dave's lips. "Drink. And then tell me what you see."

Dave drinks hungrily. The water is cold and sweet, and as he drinks, something changes: He now stands some distance away, looking at his own withered body, shackled to the stake. His mother bends over him, feeding him water from the well.

"I see myself," he says in a clear voice. "Drinking her water. It looks wrong. What's wrong with the water?"

Other-Dave swallows, then twitches violently and goes abruptly slack in Tracy's arms. A dreadful tone sounds somewhere in the sky above.

"An EKG," Dave says. Other-Dave's body bucks as, somewhere other than here, a voice rings out, *Clear!* But the efforts are in vain. Other-Dave doesn't move. "I see death."

Abruptly Dave is back on the ground, looking into the old man's eyes. There's a momentary sense of dislocation, a cosmic horror of losing his identity entirely, and then it dissipates.

"You are fine," the old man assures him. "You saw what almost was."

"I . . . died," Dave rasps, trapped once again in his ruined body.

"Long has the elephant deceived you," the old man says. "You know of what I speak."

Dave has never forgotten his nightmares, not a single one. How many times had his mother come to him in a dream? How many times had the elephant burst through her skin like she was only a puppet?

"All your life, the elephant has walked beside you, David. You have been its doorway. But you see through it. You have never given in."

"What . . . ," Dave begins, but he can't manage another word. *What does it want?*

"What all great evil wants," the old man says, understanding Dave perfectly. "To devour the world."

*I remember those words.*

"You came to me once. Long ago."

*The Dream People. There were others.*

"There are many of us."

The old man offers Dave another sip from the canteen. When Dave has finished, the man spills the remaining water into the dirt. "What do you see?"

Dave struggles to turn onto his side and looks at the puddle.

*Only water,* he thinks. *Just water.*

"Look closely, David."

Something moves in the water. A shadow.

"Open your eyes and *see.*" The old man places his hands on either side of Dave's face and stretches his eyes wide.

Abruptly Dave is looking not at a puddle but a vast ocean. The shadow beneath the surface is enormous, racing through the water at great speed. It breaches, geysering the sky.

*A whale.*

"Good." The old man releases Dave. "Listen closely, David. Are you listening?"

*I'm listening.*

"Aristera, David. Follow the whale to me."

4

Dave rockets upright, gasping.

"Space, give him space!"

His heart thunders in his chest. He touches his lips, his cheeks, then looks down and sees the large needle jutting out of his thigh.

"That, uh, shouldn't be there," he says, and falls backward onto the bed, gulping lungfuls of air.

Linda removes the needle and slings it across the room. "Dave," she says. "I need you to look at me." She snaps her fingers in front of his face. "Follow my fingers. You see my fingers?"

There are twelve fingers, but as he watches, they resolve into fewer and fewer. "Fingers," he repeats. "I see fingers."

"Man, you fucker," Matteo says, clutching fistfuls of his hair. "You wouldn't fucking wake up!"

"Dave," Linda says, her face vibrating in his line of sight. "You've had an adrenaline injection. Your heart's racing right now, but it'll normalize in a few moments. You're okay. You understand?"

"You wouldn't wake up," Katie echoes. Her face is flushed, her eyes leaking. "Asshole!"

Matteo brings water. "Can I give him—?" he asks Linda, who nods. "Here you go, man, just drink—"

Dave knocks the cup away; water splashes across the room.

"Loco motherfucker!" Matteo cries. "The fuck is wrong with you?"

"I really thought your friends were going to murder me," Linda says. "You just wouldn't come out of it."

Dave nods, twitching from the shot. "Listen. I need my phone."

"Your phone," Katie says disbelievingly. "You nearly fucking died, and you want your goddamn phone."

Matteo hands Dave his phone. "Text the CNC, tell them you solved this shit."

"CDC," Dave corrects absently, locating a maps app.

"I think he came back crazy," Matteo says, watching as Dave's fingers fly over the map, pinching and zooming and panning.

"Dave," Linda says. "You need rest."

"Rest is the last thing any of us needs right now," Dave says. "We don't have time."

"You just *died*," Katie bellows.

Dave looks up. "But I didn't. I'm sorry it was scary. It was fucking terrifying for me, too, okay? But I'm here. I'm okay. And we have to go. We have to go right now."

Katie blinks at him.

"Did he just say 'go'?" Matteo asks.

"Holy shit," Dave says, and stops scanning the phone. "It's fucking real."

Matteo elbows Linda. "Yo, shine a flashlight in his eyes. Make sure he's actually confident."

"Cognizant," Linda corrects. "Dave, what do you mean?"

"Look," Dave says, sliding off the bed and onto jittery legs. "We have a very long way to go. We're tired already. We need to move now. So, can you all please get your things and just—?"

"We're not going anywhere until you apologize," Katie says bitterly.

Dave pulls the last electrode free. "What?"

Katie breaks down. "You promised you wouldn't leave me. You almost broke your promise."

"Ah, goddammit," Dave says softly, and takes her by the shoulders. Her arms hang limply; she sobs openly as he wraps his arms around her. "Honey, I'm here. I'm not going anywhere else without you. I'm here. Shh."

"Where the hell do you think we're going?" Matteo asks.

Still holding Katie, Dave passes Matteo his phone. On the screen is a satellite view of a scrubby island.

"Aristera," Matteo reads. "Where the fuck is that?"

Linda takes the phone and zooms out, searching for context. The island grows smaller and smaller. A label appears. "The Mediterranean Sea," she says. "It's just south of Greece."

"Is he okay?" Matteo asks. "This is crazy talk. Look at this guy. Dave, there's fucking gray in your hair. And there are wrinkles around your eyes that weren't there before—"

"He's dehydrated," Linda says. "Maybe even severely so." She gives the phone back to Dave, then says, "Let's get you back into the bed. I'm running a rehydration line. No argument."

# 5

Dave recounts the story of his dream as Linda pumps him full of fluids. The shock of the adrenaline wears off, but he finds it difficult to sit still. The old man in the dream still feels very real to him. Sitting still is the last thing he should be doing right now.

"Dream people," Matteo says, dubious. "With war masks. And whale buddies."

"Yes, yes, and yes," Dave says. "They're trying to warn us. They've been trying to warn me for a long time, apparently."

Katie shoots a look at Linda, who puts her hands up and says, "Hey, I just work here. Two days ago I'd have told you the craziest thing I ever saw was Steven Tyler riding one of those coin-operated horses outside a Ralphs. I still swear it was him."

"Okay," Katie says. "If this is real—a big *if*, Dave—then what does this old guy want? Why you?"

"I don't know how to explain this," Dave says.

"Try," Katie says. "Remember? Honesty and trust?"

"Okay, but don't have me committed when I tell you this." He looks right at Linda, who says, "Roger that. I kinda want to hear this, for what it's worth."

"I keep thinking about what the old man said about this elephant," Dave says. "How it's been after me my whole life. And I'm thinking . . . Well, what if this epidemic isn't an epidemic at all?"

"Not a virus," Linda says. "Then what?"

"An attack," Dave says, wincing a little as he says the words out loud.

"An attack," Matteo repeats. "In our dreams."

"Basically, yeah. The old man called it a great evil. He said it wanted to . . ." Dave trails off.

"Dave," Katie prods.

"He said it wanted to devour the world, okay?" Dave finishes. "It's bonkers, I know, trust me. But . . . I believed him."

"It's like Lovecraft," Linda muses. When they all turn to her, questions in their eyes, she explains, "I had an uncle who was really into cosmic horror kind of shit. Lovecraft's the racist granddaddy of that sort of story. He wrote about these surreal, unknowable gods, so far beyond human experience that even looking at one could short-circuit a person's brain."

"What she said," Dave says, pointing.

"Okay, but I don't get the island thing," Matteo says. "If people die falling asleep—I mean, that's universal. It's antagonistic of where we happen to *be*."

"Antagonistic?" Katie repeats, confused.

"He means *agnostic*," Dave says. "Look, none of us has any better ideas, right?"

Katie shakes her head. "I have *questions*, not ideas. Like, how are we supposed to find a fucking *whale*? And how do we get from Santa Mira to goddamn Greece?"

With a shrug, Dave turns to Matteo and smiles. Linda and Katie follow his gaze, questions in their eyes.

Suddenly uncomfortable, Matteo says, "Yo, *what?*"

# 6

"Nope. Nope, nope, no-fucking-ope," Matteo protests. "Do any of you know what RPA stands for?" When no one answers, he says, "*Remotely piloted aircraft*, yo. I flew fucking *drones.*"

"But you went to flight school," Dave says, unfazed.

"This lady isn't a doctor," Katie says, glaring at Linda, "and look what impersonating one cost—"

"Whoa, now," Linda says.

"I went to *basic* flight school, bro. I could sail your drone to LA, maybe bomb Dodger Field—"

"Stadium," Dave corrects.

"Whatever. I can't fly us halfway around the *planet.*"

"Not to crush your dreams here, Dave, but even if Matteo could do it, none of us has slept in nearly . . . sixty hours? That's a greater degree of impairment than if he downed a bottle of Jack first and tried to drive home. Put him behind the wheel of a plane, and—"

"Stick," Matteo corrects.

"See?" Dave says, pointing. "He knows planes have sticks, not wheels. We're gonna be *fine.*"

Katie clears her throat, and everyone turns to look at her.

"I can't believe I'm the one who's going to say this," she begins, "but if we stay here, we're going to die. Flat fact. I can't be the only one tempted by every hospital bed I see, can I?"

Matteo shuffles his feet and looks at the floor.

"I'll tell you a secret about me, though," she says. "I never could sleep on a plane." She nods toward Matteo. "And if *he's* flying, none of us will."

"Solid vote of confidence," Matteo says. "Yeah. Appreciate that. Thanks."

"The longer we argue about it, the more tired we're going to get," Dave says. "I *know* this is what we have to do."

"Based on a dream," Matteo says.

"There's just one problem here," Linda says. "Or does one of you secretly own a fucking jet?"

7

They spend an hour gathering supplies. A pile of luggage grows in the lobby: duffel bags filled with medications. Survival gear scavenged from lockers and dead bodies: pocketknives, a compass, a security guard's Taser. Matteo breaks into the vending machines and loads up a bag with beef jerky, dried fruit, potato chips, chocolate; Katie fills a cooler with bottled water and juice boxes.

"My car won't hold all this," Matteo says, looking skeptically at their gear.

Linda points at an ambulance in the bay beside the ER doors.

As they stuff bags into the patient compartment, Dave says, "So, I've run the numbers, and I have bad news: It's at least a thirteen-hour flight to get where we're going. Maybe fourteen or fifteen if the conditions are bad."

Katie glances at Matteo. "That's a long flight. Can he do it?"

"Yo, don't talk about me like I'm not here," Matteo grumbles. "Of course I can't do it."

"And you think you can find a plane that gets us there?" Linda asks. "Don't planes have to stop and refuel?"

"I told you, the regional airport is small, but there's a private jet service with a couple hangars there. They're our best bet, unless we want to drive to the Bay and find those Silicon Valley assholes' private planes."

"Santa Mira Regional it is." Dave hefts the last bag into the back. "That's everything."

"Matteo," Linda says, "I think you should—" She stops abruptly, then slaps herself with a hard *crack*.

"Jesus!" Matteo cries.

"I'm okay," Linda says, cheek glowing red. "I almost said you should catch a few winks in the back while we drive to the airport."

"Yo, you gotta keep your shit together, Nurse Crazy," Matteo says.

Linda appears moved by his concern. "I promise. I'm good."

"Okay, then," Matteo says, grinning nervously. "Because when I crash, who's gonna CPR us otherwise?"

## 8

Lights flashing, the ambulance carves through back roads and golden hills. Matteo and Dave ride up front, while Katie and Linda are strapped into the paramedic jump seats in the back.

"I must be really beat," Katie says, eyeing the gurney strapped to the wall, "because that looks like a feather bed to me." She yawns, her face splitting open like a cat's, showing all her teeth. She smacks her lips, stretches, and blinks rapidly. Rubs her eyes with both fists.

Linda unbuckles, then pokes her head through the panel connecting the cab to the patient compartment.

"Linda!" Matteo says. "I was just about to hit the siren—"

"Dave," Linda says. "Katie doesn't look good."

Dave cranes his neck, trying to see past her. "Should I go back?"

"How much farther?"

"Twelve miles," Matteo says. "I'm doing fifty so you two don't bounce."

"Bounce us," Linda says. To Dave: "I'm going to hydrate her, see if I can't get her mind working."

"Don't let her sleep, Linda. I'm trusting you."

Linda nods, then jerks her head at Matteo. "I can't believe you let him drive."

Linda retreats through the panel again and finds Katie bent forward, elbows on her knees. Her hair swings free, hiding her face.

"Katie," Linda says, and kicks Katie's foot. Katie's elbow slips off her knee, and she lurches forward, then catches herself.

"I'm *fine*," she insists.

Linda pops the cooler and tosses Katie a box of orange juice. "Get some electrolytes in you."

Katie peels open the bendy straw, then, with some difficulty, inserts it into the box. "Ugh," she says, forcing herself to swallow. *"Pulp."*

Satisfied, Linda closes the cooler again, then watches Katie as they ride in silence. The ambulance picks up speed; the two women rock back and forth in their seats.

"You know," Katie says finally, "Ruth was a sweet woman."

Linda doesn't speak, but doesn't look away.

"I haven't forgotten I'm pissed at you," Katie says, eyes dark. "I'm putting it on hold, for the good of the group. But when we get where we're going? I think you and me are gonna have words."

Linda considers this, then nods. "It's a date."

There's a sudden shout from the front of the ambulance, and then the brakes lock. The vehicle skids to a violent halt, throwing the gear at Katie and Linda.

"There was a coyote," Matteo says apologetically.

"It was a fox," Dave corrects.

"It wasn't a—"

"It was a fox."

"Guys! Don't kill us before Matteo gets a chance to crash us all into the ocean, okay?" Linda says, shoving a duffel bag out of her lap. "Let's get going again, huh?"

"Wait," Dave says. "Linda, switch with me."

Linda looks at Katie, who glares back at her. "Yeah, copy that."

# 9

"I might murder her in her sleep," Katie tells Dave when they're underway again. "I mean, I know she'll already be dead. I might murder her again."

*Keep her talking*, Dave thinks.

"Okay. What's your plan?"

"I'll smother her with an airplane pillow. The ones that look like hemorrhoid pillows?"

"I figured you'd want to see her eyes when you do it."

"Yeah. Those pillows have those little holes in the middle."

Dave grins tiredly. "You're such a badass when you want to be."

"You know it." Katie yawns.

The divider slides open again, and Linda pokes her head through.

"Speak of the witch," Katie says.

Linda ignores this. "We've got a gas problem."

"What?" Dave asks.

"The light's on," Matteo calls back. "I don't know how long it's been on. There was no ding, you know? So it might've been on the whole time and I just missed it."

"Playing with the siren," Katie mutters.

"What's the tank at?" Dave asks.

"Below the *E*," Linda says. "And there aren't any gas stations out here."

"Check the back, bro," Matteo calls again. "They'll have a spare gas can."

Linda says, "Hold on," then retreats through the divider and punches Matteo's shoulder.

"The fuck was—?"

"You think they'd carry a flammable fuel where they treat patients in crisis?" Linda asks.

"They carry explosive oxygen—" Matteo protests, but Dave interrupts: "No, she's right. There's no gas."

"Just look again," Matteo says. "Can you just fucking look again? Otherwise, we're hiking six or seven miles when we're already dead tired."

"Fuck. Fine." Dave turns back to search the compartment. He taps Katie's knee. "Help me look for—" He stops short. Katie's head is slumped against the wall. "Shit, Katie! Linda! Katie!"

"Shake her!" Linda advises, peeking through the panel.

Dave grabs Katie's shoulders and rocks her back and forth. "Not working, Linda!" He brushes Katie's hair out of her face and taps her cheeks, lightly at first, then harder. "Fuck!"

"Dave!" Linda's out of her seat now, one arm through the panel. She points. "Blue bag, Dave, get the blue—"

"Where?" Dave throws himself onto the floor and shoves bags around. "None of these are blue!"

"In the black duffel," Linda instructs, "there's a blue bag."

Dave frantically digs through the bags. "There are three fucking black duffels!"

"The one with the meds."

"*Which one is that?*"

"Yellow piping!"

Dave spots the yellow-rimmed duffel and yanks it open. Fritos, Grandma's Best cookies. "Not fucking here!"

"That one," Linda orders, pointing at the duffel with a red tag on the zipper.

Dave tears it open and, among the pill bottles and baggies of bandages and tape, spies a blue bag with a white drawstring. "Got it!"

"Okay, get the ammonia bottle first," Linda says. "Small and clear, you see it?"

There are several bottles in the bag, but fate favors Dave: right on top is a clear bottle with a white label. In large black letters, it reads AMMONIA and WARNING: TOXIC.

"Got it!" he yells back.

"Put it under her nose," Linda directs. To Matteo: "Don't you fucking hit any bumps right now."

Dave unscrews the cap and holds the bottle under Katie's nostrils. "It isn't working! What do I do?" His voice breaks. "Katie, Katie!"

"Dave," Linda says, suddenly very calm. "In the bag there's a hard plastic case with a red cross on it. Get it."

Dave plunges back into the bag, throwing its contents around wildly. There's a hard plastic case inside, but when he cracks it open, it contains only basic first aid paraphernalia.

"It's not here! What am I looking for?"

Linda turns to Matteo. "The emergency kit," she says, voice tight. "Hard white case with a red cross on it. Where'd you put it?"

"I packed the fucking *pretzels*," Matteo complains. "You're the fucking doctor, you packed the—"

"What the fuck do I do?" Dave cries out.

A bottle of Modafalyst rolls around the patient compartment, scattering blue capsules everywhere.

"Shit, of course," Linda says. "We're in a fucking ambulance. Dave!" She snaps her fingers until he turns. She points at the wall behind Katie. "Look over there, you should see a metal box bolted to the wall—"

"I see it," he says, throwing the latch open. Inside there's a pair of injectors. "What do I do? Tell me what—"

"It's like an EpiPen," Linda instructs. "Just hit her thigh and push. You'll hear a click. You gotta get to bare skin, though. Won't work through her jeans."

"I'm sorry, honey," Dave mutters, then clamps the injector in his teeth. He slides a finger through one of the fashionably thread-bare patches of Katie's jeans, then rips a large hole, revealing her pale thigh.

"Now, Dave, now!" Linda yells.

Dave holds his breath and slams the injector down.

It clicks.

Nothing happens.

"Katie?" Dave pleads. "No, baby, you gotta wake up. Come on, honey, open your eyes. Open them!"

"Come on," Matteo says, eyeing the gas needle.

"Dave?" Linda says. "Slap her like you mean it. Right now, Dave!"

Grimacing, Dave pulls Katie's hair back and strikes her cheek. To his surprise and relief, she stiffens, and then she sucks in a loud, desperate breath.

"Hold her, Dave, she's panicking!"

Katie's eyes dart wildly about. Dave wraps his arms around her tightly; he begins to sob. Katie jerks stiffly in his arms.

"You're okay, you're okay," Dave says, his shoulders shaking. He leans back and grips Katie's face as she gasps for air. "Sweetie, look at me. Look at me. Right here. Good, good, there you go. Hi, baby. You're okay. You're okay, you're safe."

Katie nods, her panic subsiding. Then her eyes widen, and she jerks free and vomits.

"She better not puke on my pretzels!" Matteo calls back.

"She's okay," Linda assures Dave. "Better to throw up than sleep, right? She'll be all right."

Dave dabs at Katie's lips with his shirt, then kisses her fore-head. "Jesus Christ," he breathes. "You scared me so bad."

The ambulance seems to hiccup, and Katie looks past Dave. "Are we coasting?" she asks. "Are we there?"

## 10

"Two miles," Matteo says hopefully. "We can all do two miles, right?"

"Do we have a choice?" Linda asks.

"I can see the tower, at least," Dave offers. "It's not as far as it looks."

Matteo leads them, wearing one of the backpacks and carrying two duffels. Linda carries another backpack on one shoulder, and with her free arm helps Dave steer the gurney, which they've loaded with the remaining gear.

Katie walks beside Dave, clinging to his hand.

"You can sit on the gurney," Dave says. "We'll push you."

But Katie shakes her head. "The walk will keep me awake," she says. "I'm pretty amped right now. My fucking leg hurts. My face, too. Jesus. You're stronger than I thought."

"I'm sorry," Dave says.

"Never apologize for saving someone's life," Linda says. "My two cents. You just preserved their place on this mortal coil, you know? They can live without a limb or two." She looks meaningfully at Katie. "You okay?"

"Fine," Katie mutters.

"I'm just saying, you gotta keep your strength up if you're gonna smother me with one of those little doughnut pillows," Linda says.

Despite herself, Katie grins. "Just you wait."

"I'm counting on it."

They trudge in silence, at least until Matteo begins humming a familiar tune. After a few bars, he starts singing. "Jetsons, meet the Jetsons. They're the Montessori fa-mi-lyyy . . ."

Katie bursts out laughing, and Linda joins her.

"What?" Matteo asks.

"Nothing," Dave says. "Keep going, man, I like it." He prompts him: "They're the Montessori fa-mi-ly . . ."

"From the town of Bedrock," Matteo continues, "la-la-la-la-la-la mys-ter-yyyy . . ."

# Two Truths and a Lie

## 1

The man in the back seat smells like vinegar and potting soil, Eli thinks. Vinegar, and potting soil, and maybe gin. Gin smells like pine needles, doesn't it? Or maybe the man's just been planting evergreens. Watering their roots with . . . vinegar.

It all makes sense.

Millie seems completely unflapped by the presence of the stranger in her car, Eli notices, except that might not be true. Her mouth twitches, sort of pulls to the right a little, like she's doing her best to cover up an active seizure. This worries him. It isn't like he knows this woman. Not long ago, he was fine. He could have blogged his way through the end of the world. Future civilizations would have studied his words, seen the apocalypse through his personal lens. But now he's hitched to this half-manic, narcoleptic knowledge worker.

Who just picked up the vinegar man.

## 2

Seven miles east of Chicopee they see the first vehicle. Millie is a little dismayed, if she's honest; the ghostly empty lanes have been a traveler's dream, all of Interstate 90 available to her four wheels.

"It's like the whole world decided not to go to work today," Eli had said as they left Boston and its empty streets behind.

That's exactly how it seemed to Millie, too. As they'd moved west, they'd seen intersections with lights that flickered from red to green to red again, guiding invisible vehicles to their destinations. Fast-food restaurants, windows still dark.

And now this bus.

A tour bus, she notices as they approach. It's stopped in the fast lane, flashers blinking.

"Don't stop," the hitchhiker warns.

But Millie slows the car, and they all crane their necks up at the windows. It's a full bus, judging from all the heads leaning on the glass.

"Are they all asleep?" Eli asks.

"Dead," the hitchhiker corrects.

"But how can you—?"

"They're dead, kid."

"I'm going to check on the driver," Millie says, and stops the car. She sets the brake, then jumps out and trots over to the sealed accordion door. Eli watches as she cups her hands and presses her face to the glass, then just as quickly leaps back a step.

She returns to the car and says, "Uh. Uh . . . Um. Um, ah, she's—"

"Dead, too," the hitchhiker says.

"Not the same," Millie says. Her fingers tremble as she mimes a gunshot. "Not the same."

"Maybe I should drive," the hitchhiker offers.

This seems to snap Millie out of her shock.

"No," she says. "I've got it. I'm good. I've got it."

They start westward again.

# 3

"The Berkshire Botanical," Eli says, watching the sign float past. "If this were any other day . . ."

"If this were any other day, we wouldn't be here," Millie says. Her mood has darkened since Chicopee. Her mouth twitches frequently now.

"She's got a point, kid," the hitchhiker says.

"What's your name?" Eli asks. "Since we're all riding together, I figure we should be on a first-name basis."

"Chewdot," the man says.

"Chew-dot?" Millie asks, glancing at the rearview.

"Chewdot. Runk Chewdot."

"You're serious?" Eli asks.

"That's the most made-up name I've ever heard."

The hitchhiker shrugs. "Every name is made up."

"Fine. Where are you going, Mr. Chewdot?" Eli asks.

"Where are *you* going?" Chewdot returns.

"This way," Millie says. "At least for now."

"West, though. West is good." The hitchhiker leans forward, and his strange scent wafts into the front seat. "You two ever heard of a place called Cynagen?"

"Pharma bros," Millie says at the same time Eli says, "Drug company."

Chewdot's eyebrows go up. "You two know your stuff." He looks from the rearview mirror to Eli. "In fact, you're both alive and kicking right now, which means . . . insomnia?"

Millie and Eli exchange a glance.

"Say what?" Millie asks.

"I've been on the road awhile now," Chewdot says. "Not always alone. Last couple weeks, I was with this old marine buddy of mine."

"What was his name?" Millie asks.

"Does it matter?"

"I just want to know if everyone in your circles uses assumed names."

"Crinkle," the hitchhiker answers. "Pomp Crinkle."

"Jesus. You are the worst at making up names."

"Names are just things you call people. Point is," Chewdot continues, "Pomp was a bit of a conspiracy theorist. Lots of vets are, you know. Every night we'd be camping out, he'd listen to this radio show late into the night."

"*Under the Moonglow with Arthur Scrimm*?" Millie suggests.

Chewdot snaps his fingers. "That's the one. Whack-job radio."

"My mom listened to it all the time."

"I mean . . . I've *heard* it's crazy talk," Chewdot corrects.

"It's all right. My mom was legit crazy."

"Go on," Eli says.

Chewdot hesitates, then nods. "Pomp got all riled up one night while he was listening. There was a guy on the show talking about how the army loaded him up with some experimental drug."

"What kind of drug?" Eli half turns in his seat. "Captain America stuff?"

"No, no super-soldier thing. This was an anti-sleep drug."

"They wouldn't let him sleep?"

Millie snorts. "Soldiers who don't need to sleep are valuable instruments."

"But they'd be tired," Eli points out. "Tired people make real mistakes." He nods at the steering wheel. "Especially when driving."

"No, she's right," Chewdot says. "That's what the army guy was going on about. How the army was working with a drug company to make this pill a soldier could take that would keep them alert and high-performing for long stretches of time."

"Cynagen," Millie says at the same time Eli asks, "How long are we talking?"

"Three days minimum, supposedly. Sometimes longer."

"And your friend, they did this to him?" Eli says.

"That's the impression I got, but I didn't ask explicitly."

"That little sleep really fucks with a person's brain," Millie says. "Believe me."

"Oh yeah?"

"My mom never slept. I mean, she did, but not really. She was already manic, but the lack of sleep, like, weaponized her. I did not have a good childhood, let's just say."

Eli says, "Boy, I hear that."

"You have crazy parents, too?" Millie asks.

"No, my parents are . . ." Eli trails off. "They died," he says in a small voice. "I was only eight."

Chewdot says, "My old man fucked the neighbor lady, and my mom went to jail because she tried to crack his skull with the Suburban."

"Jesus," Millie says.

"What happened with your mom?" Chewdot asks.

"My mom did some crazy shit before I was born," Millie offers. "I don't know exactly what. But she spent my childhood thinking the government was after her. She kept us moving. I can't tell you how many places we abandoned in the middle of the night. Seven? Twelve? By the time I was eighteen, I'd gone to twenty-five different schools."

"Like a military kid," Chewdot says.

Millie nods. "But worse."

"My parents were hit by a drunk driver," Eli says. "I was in the back seat."

Chewdot is quiet for a long moment, then says, "The kid wins it."

Eli looks stricken. "I didn't mean—"

"It's cool," Millie says. "That's pretty sad shit. Is that how . . . ?"

Eli looks down at his inoperable legs. "That's how."

They drive in silence for the next few miles, the sun tethered to the car by an invisible string. "Eerie, isn't it?" Millie finally says, breaking the quiet. "It's like the whole world never woke up."

"That's what I was going to say," Chewdot says. "It's a sleep thing. That's why I figured you for a couple of insomniacs."

"What do you mean?" Eli asks.

"I mean I was up all night," Chewdot says. "I don't sleep much. Haven't, really, since my tours. I can thank the navy for that. So, whatever happened, it didn't happen to me. You two, you're still moving around, so it didn't happen to you. Did you two sleep last night?"

Millie looks at Eli.

"What?" Eli asks. "You read my blog, you already know."

She glances in the rearview. "No. No sleep."

"That's what I'm saying."

"What happened to your friend? Pomp Crinkle," Eli says.

Chewdot sinks back into the seat. "I went for a walk this morning, tried to scrounge up some food. Found a rest stop with free coffee and doughnuts, carried it back to our tents. Pomp was stiff as a board." He sighs. "Government wouldn't let him sleep, then when his time's done, he doesn't get to wake up. It's a cruel fucking world."

"You're telling me," Eli says.

Millie studies the hitchhiker in the mirror. "So . . . am I right in thinking you're heading to Cynagen?"

Chewdot nods. "If sleep's how everyone else died, then I don't want to sleep," he says. "Life just got interesting. I could walk into any supermarket right now and eat like a king. That's not how things usually go for me."

"Where is Cynagen?" Eli asks.

"California," Chewdot says. "Palo Alto. You two want to come with?"

# 4

"Do you know where we're going?" Eli asks.

"I don't need to," Millie answers. "Not really." It's raining, and she doesn't run the windshield wipers frequently, and they both watch as the water runs uphill on the glass.

"I don't know how to get to Palo Alto. How do you?"

"I don't."

"Are we going the right—?"

Millie points at a highway sign. "Interstate 90," she reads to Eli. "West."

"So you're just going to follow the signs."

"If there's anything the government managed to get right in this country," Millie says, mouth turned down, "it's the god-damn interstate highway system. You just point your car in the right direction and follow all the labels that say that direction back to you."

"Okay, sure, but there's a decent chance this one winds up in Washington State, not California," Eli says. "You have to consider the y axis, too."

"Oh, piss off with axises."

"Axes."

"Ax-*eez*," she mimics. Then she reads Eli's face. "Sorry. I'm not used to people like this."

"It's okay."

Millie glances in the rearview and sees Chewdot, forehead pressed to the passenger window, watching the scenery. "If any-one will know how to get to Palo Alto, it's our resident thumb-walker, right, Mr. Chewdot?"

The hitchhiker glances up at the mirror. "West. You got it."

For a while they drive in silence, and Eli registers all the sounds of Millie's vehicle. The glove box vibrates, the latch emitting an irregular, offbeat clicking that won't go away; somewhere there's a bad seal, and wind whistles at a dog's frequency through a seam; the engine in particular is maddening, the rpm throbbing at such a pitch that he thinks the car might explode.

"Aren't you supposed to shift?" he asks Millie, who shakes her head.

"Fifth gear's bad. Stalls the car every time."

"So we have to listen to that the whole way?"

"You get used to it."

"It's like needing to sneeze and not being able to."

"I usually put some music on," she says, indicating the stereo. "You can deejay if you want."

Eli slips the old MP3 device out of his pocket. "I don't suppose you have Bluetooth? Or an adapter?"

Millie glances at the device. "Jesus Christ, kid. You're a walking museum. What is that, twenty years old?"

"I dunno. Can you play it?"

"Well, no, I don't have every old cable known to humankind in this vehicle," Millie says. "But if it's that important, maybe we can find a RadioShack or something."

"Okay."

"It's that important?"

"It's the most important thing I own."

Millie chews on this a moment. The highway hisses beneath the tires, which she hasn't replaced since the kid's MP3 player was manufactured.

"Let's play a game," she says. "We've got a long way to go, and according to that guy"—she thumbs at the back seat, where Chewdot either ignores her or doesn't notice her talking about him—"we can't sleep."

"What kind of game?"

"You have a job?" she asks. When Eli shakes his head, she says, "Smart kid. Don't ever get one."

"I don't need one."

"Why, are you independently wealthy or something?"

Eli pats his nonfunctioning legs. "More or less."

Millie decides to table that question, too. "All right, well, I have a job. A terrible one. You can take that for granted, because they're all terrible, okay? Humans could have spent their whole existence in a hammock, eating fresh peaches—but, *no*, we had to invent mortgages and health insurance."

"I guess that's true."

"And icebreakers. At some point in human history, someone invented the lowest of lows: the workplace icebreaker."

"What's a workplace icebreaker?"

"It's a torture device," Millie grouses. "Like, Two Truths and a Lie. That's an icebreaker. Or ten things in common. Or a scavenger hunt. Have You Ever? All those bullshit things."

"I don't know any of these. Except scavenger hunts."

"He's heard of the scavenger hunt, Chewie," Millie says over her shoulder to the hitchhiker. "Okay, well, my least favorite of these is Two Truths and a Lie."

"How's it work?"

"Just like it sounds, doofus. I tell you three things about myself, you have to guess which thing isn't true."

"I don't know you well enough to—"

"That's the *point*."

"I thought you said these things were terrible."

"Yes, well, an icebreaker's better than falling asleep in Cleveland, wouldn't you agree?"

"I guess so."

"Okay. I'll start." Millie smooths her hair, then cracks her knuckles dramatically. "I never had my own bed until I moved out of the house. My mother was on the run from the FBI. And . . . I set fire to an apartment building when I was six."

Eli blinks rapidly. "You did?"

"Game, stupid. Guess."

"Oh. Right. I—Jeez, this is sort of hard. One of these is a lie? Only one?"

"Only one."

"You didn't have your own bed," Eli says. "That's true."

"True."

"Wow, that's terrible. Where did you—?" He stops, contemplating the other statements. "Either one of those could have resulted in you not having a bed. Are these all related?"

"I can't tell you that."

"On the run from the FBI, that's the lie. Which makes the apartment fire . . . truth. God. How did that happen?"

"Sorry, bud." Millie makes a buzzer noise with her mouth. "That's incorrect."

"Your mother *was* on the run from the FBI?"

Millie nods. "Never had a bed, because we never stayed in one place more than a few months."

"So you didn't burn a building down."

"No. Though I *did* start a grease fire by mistake. I was trying to make breakfast for my mom. I *was* six, that part was true. And the fire was true. But it didn't take down the whole building, just our kitchen wall and ceiling."

"Holy shit. Is this game always so . . . bleak?"

Millie laughs. "It takes on the personality of the players, mostly," she says. "Usually though it's stuff like 'I had breakfast with Dave Letterman' or 'My grandpa owned a glass-bottom boat' or 'I once rode a bicycle six thousand miles.' All low-key show-off stuff."

"Why was your mother on the run from the FBI?"

Millie shrugs. "I mean, it's not like there were FBI agents kicking the door down," she says. "Mom was always pretty paranoid about that, so she kept us moving. She knew if they ever got close enough to kick doors, she'd fucked up."

"But what did she do?"

"She was a patriot," Millie says. "At least, that's what she thought she was. She was part of one of those activist groups that did stuff like stage sit-ins at government buildings, or block freeways with their bodies."

"Okay, but—"

"The group blew up three buildings," Millie says matter-of-factly. "She told me they saw this movie where a guy blew up banks, destroying all the debt for, like, farms and homes and stuff. The guy's crimes basically changed the world for a whole bunch of ordinary people stuck in a system that never let them get ahead."

"She blew up a building because she saw a movie?"

"It was a bad, bad movie, too," Millie says. "It took me a long time to track it down. She never would tell me anything more about it. *Wisdom*, 1986. Emilio Estevez, Demi Moore. See, Emilio, he decides he's got no future. He's an ex-con. So, he decides to start robbing banks, except instead of taking money, he destroys all the mortgage records. And then his girlfriend comes along for the ride, and they're like a bad rehash of Bonnie and Clyde, you know? Except instead of taking money, they're saving poor farmers."

"That does sound bad."

"So Mom and her buddies decided to do something like that. They made homemade explosives, broke into these banks in, like, Kansas and Nebraska, and—*poof*—blew 'em up."

"To save the farmers."

"That's what she always said."

"Did it work?"

Millie shrugs. "There's no way to know, but since banks have computers, you know, probably not. Plus they killed two people."

"Oh no."

"Both of them were cleaning crew. I looked it up when I was old enough. One of them was fifty-eight years old, Veronica Hernando, and she'd just started working at the bank two months before. The other was nineteen, and working nights to cover college by day." Millie nods. "Yep, Mom and her friends all split up, and off they went. I wasn't even a year old. I grew up in suitcases."

"I'm sorry."

"Jesus, your face," Millie says, and ruffles Eli's hair. "I turned out okay, didn't I?"

"What about your mom?"

Millie's face darkens. "Well, we won't go there." She changes lanes to avoid an eighteen-wheeler half on the shoulder, blinking triangle signs scattered around it. "Anyway, it's your turn. Two true things, one fucking dirty lie."

Eli watches as a darkened Dunkin' Donuts slides by. "Maybe later," he says. "I don't think I can follow that."

## 5

The road unspools in front of them like a map of their punishment.

"We couldn't have thought of something better to do?" Eli muses. "All this driving's only going to make us tireder."

"*More* tireder," Millie corrects. "We use proper 'the Queen's English' in this car."

"Are you sure we can't sleep?" Eli asks Chewdot, not turning around.

There's no answer from the back seat.

"I mean, we don't have *proof* of anything," Eli continues. "Just your word that something weird's going on, and we shouldn't—"

"Fucking Christ," Millie says.

"What?"

"He's dead."

"What?!" Eli exclaims.

"He's fucking dead."

"He could be asleep. I can't see him. He's asleep. That's all." Eli's voice pitches upward nervously. "That's it, just asleep."

"Yes, well, if he's right about sleep, then he's fucking *dead*, Eli," Millie says. "There's a dead stranger in my back seat."

"You were the one who stopped for a hitch—"

"Well, I didn't expect him to *die* on us, now, did I—"

"He didn't die on *me*, he died on *you*," Eli insists. "That's not my fault. It's *your* fault."

"Oh, so fuck me for being neighborly, right?" Sweat beads around Millie's hairline, then trickles down her temple.

"You don't strike me as the neighborly type, exactly," Eli counters.

"I came to get *you*, you little shit," Millie retorts. "Don't give me guff about being *neighbor*—"

"Pull over," Eli says, his voice taut. "Please. Right now."

Millie swings the car to the side of the road and hits the brakes. Eli throws open the passenger door as the dead hitchhiker jolts forward, then is snapped back into place by his seat belt.

"Don't vomit on my—" Millie starts, then says, "Aw, *fuck*, man," and lets herself out of the car. She dashes around the vehicle, then helps Eli with the seat belt latch, then bends him forward and smooths his floppy hair away from his forehead.

Eli throws up on Millie's shoes.

"I'm sorry," he gasps, then retches. Nothing more comes up.

"It's fine. You're okay. You're okay."

Clouds tighten into knots overhead, and the light shifts.

"It's going to rain," Millie says. "Gonna hit those midwestern storms. They're the worst." She absently strokes Eli's hair while he coughs, then says, "You okay?"

"You still aren't neighborly," Eli says, looking up at her with watery eyes. "Motherly, though. I didn't expect that."

Unexpectedly, Millie's eyes fill. "Nuh-uh."

"How are we supposed to do this? It's already too hard."

"I don't know," she concedes, wiping her eyes. "We just have to."

It begins to rain.

# 6

The sky darkens as they drive on; then the sun leaks out of view, and invisible rain hammers on the car like stones. They pass a sign that says CLEVELAND—85, and Eli says, "How are we on gas?"

"Oh shit," Millie says. "Gas." She glances at the dashboard. "What's half of a quarter?"

"An eighth."

"Well, we've got less than that."

"We'll find a station before Cleveland, right?"

"You ask me that like I should know," Millie says.

"It's a Honda. Right? Hondas get good gas mileage."

"Yeah, *new* Hondas. In case you hadn't noticed, this Honda is not new."

The rain forms a skin over the highway, and the car gently hydroplanes. The dead man in the back seat thumps hard against the window. Millie steers against the slide and regains control, and Eli looks at her nervously.

"Don't worry," she says. "I suck at a lot of things, but I can drive really well."

"I'm not worried about that," Eli says. "What do we do with him?"

"What do *you* think we should—?"

"I think we put him out at the gas station," Eli says hurriedly. "It's creeping me out. But I feel bad."

"I picked him up," Millie says. "I feel . . . I don't know. An obligation, or something."

"But we have to do something with him. He'll start to smell." Eli wrinkles his nose. "When he starts decaying."

"Now you're going to make me puke."

"I'm serious."

"I've seen cop shows." The sodium lights on the highway shoulder turn smeary in Millie's vision, then begin to streak. She rubs her eyes, stifles a yawn. "I know about rotten bodies."

"And I don't have any Vicks to put under our noses," Eli says. "So we agree? We put him out at the—" Eli stops, then squints. "You okay? Millie?"

Millie shakes her head briskly. The rain downshifts into slow motion. "Eli," she says, voice suddenly thick. "Do you see that?"

"Seeeeee whaaat?" Eli asks. "Heyyyy, you don't looook toooo—"

The sky flashes red and blue, red and blue, and then, from nowhere, a heavy black cord thumps onto the Honda's hood. A split second later, a couple of heavy tactical boots slam down, permanently denting the metal. Jacketed in Kevlar, glaring at her through ballistic goggles, a man shouts her name. All across the highway, more federal agents descend on ropes, and Millie shrieks and spins the wheel, and Eli braces himself and cries out, and then there's a terrible crunch, and another, and then Eli, bleeding, is slapping Millie's face, yelling at her not to sleep, don't sleep—

# The Last of Them

## I

The air traffic control tower catches the tangerine glow of the sunset, scattering the light on the tarmac below. A wind sock snaps in the breeze, the only sound that reaches their ears.

"This is creepy," Katie says, taking in the abandoned scene. "I've never seen this place so . . . lifeless."

A security post separates the private air taxi's hangar from the rest of the compound. Matteo drops his duffels, then slips under the gate and into the guard booth. There, reclined in his chair, feet propped on his desk, head pitched forward, is a guard in a brown uniform.

Matteo tips the man's hat over his face. "Rest in peace, comrade," he says. "Sorry to screw up your safety record." Matteo reaches past the corpse and presses the gate button. Dave and Linda push the gurney through as the arm goes up.

Katie lingers a moment, studying the little airport terminal across the runways. "How many people do you think are in there right now?" she asks. "How many people took a nap waiting for their flight?"

"Don't think about it," Linda advises.

The walk did Katie some good, but now the adrenaline has dissipated; she can feel herself pinwheeling toward a crash.

"Katie?" Dave calls back. "You okay?"

She snaps back to herself. "Fine." With a last look at the terminal, she catches up to the others. "I always thought working at an airport would be kind of glamorous," she says. "Kind of romantic, you know?"

"I read about this place one time," Linda says. "This airport, smaller even than this one, somewhere in . . . Nova Scotia? Newfoundland? I always confuse those two." She yawns, then continues: "In the fifties, if you were flying from New York to London, you had to stop at this place to refuel. Sometimes the layovers took hours, even a day or two. So, *everyone* stopped there. This middle-of-no-place airport is where Frank Sinatra took a load off on his way to Europe for a tour. Marilyn was there, even the Queen. Everyone who worked there had amazing stories. There was a gift shop cashier who talked with actual Einstein about actual relativity. A maintenance worker took Castro and his bodyguards sledding nearby."

"That's pretty romantic," Matteo agrees.

"Sometimes," Dave says quietly, "I used to wonder if the last generation to be alive would know they were the last." He kicks a rock out of the gurney's path. "I used to wonder that."

"I think the universe could've chosen its final four a little better," Matteo says. "Maybe it could've picked a real pilot, for instance."

"A nonaddict," Katie adds.

"A real doctor," Linda says.

"A guy with a regular brain," Dave says, tapping his temple. "Not whatever's up here."

"If I only had a brain," Matteo sings. "We're just like them, you know. The Fellowship."

"He *has* to know, right?" Linda asks Dave.

"He really is just that addled," Dave says.

"Yo, I heard that." Matteo drops his backpack on the gurney.

"You guys chill here a second. I'm gonna check these hangars and see what's on the menu."

"I'm gonna go with," Linda says. She puts her bags on the tarmac, then chases after Matteo. "So how do we know what we're looking for . . . ?"

Dave watches them disappear into the first of three hangars. Katie rests her head on his shoulder. Her fingers trace his jawline, then his neck, then make their way to the bumpy scar tissue beneath his shirt.

"Does it hurt?" she asks.

"Not so much now."

"I'm sorry."

"For what?"

"I didn't do enough," she says. "To understand what you were going through."

"Hey, hey," he says, stroking her hair. "Listen to me. You did the best thing you could've done: You took care of yourself."

"I left you alone."

"And look. We found our way back, didn't we?"

She nods, then raises her face to his. Dave smiles and then kisses her, holding that precious contact for several seconds before Katie breaks off.

"God," she says. "I probably taste like orange pulp and puke."

"My favorite combo."

She lightly slugs him. "Asshole." Then she yawns. "Fuck."

"You just need a little exercise."

"We just had exercise. Miles of it."

"We're beyond tired," Dave says. "We gotta be like sharks. We have to keep moving so we don't drown."

"How am I going to get through fourteen hours?" Katie asks. "We haven't even taken off yet."

"Run," Dave suggests. "Run ahead of me, catch up with the others. I'll bring the gurney. It'll get your blood moving."

"Yeah?"

Dave nods, and Katie starts jogging toward the hangar just as Linda emerges. Linda holds her hand up for a high five, but Katie runs right past.

"Worth a shot," Linda says when she reaches Dave. "Let me help with that." She shoulders two bags, then takes one end of the gurney.

"You find something?" Dave asks.

"Matteo's hunting for the keys. Do planes have keys? I didn't even know."

Dave yawns. "I actually have no idea."

"How are you two doing?" Linda asks.

"Eh," Dave says. "I'm accustomed to bad sleep. I've actually had worse stretches. But Katie . . . Did you see her face? She looks like she's about to pass out again."

"She's crashing."

"Well, she can't crash."

"We're all going to," Linda says. "You should be ready for that. And maybe Katie's crashing because she worked a night shift, then partied, and hasn't gone to bed since."

"Judgy."

"We all process exhaustion the same way. I'm in the same boat, minus the party part."

"Good thing we've got a bagful of Modafalyst," Dave says, patting one of the bags.

"She doesn't need more stimulants. She needs sleep."

"She can't have it."

"I know."

"But it's fourteen hours," Dave says.

Linda nods. "I know."

2

"Meet our new best friend," Matteo says, standing at the top of a private jet's stairs. "The Gulfstream G650. Full bar, sofa, fat-ass leather chairs. This baby carries eight passengers, four crew, and— And! And she has a range of seven thousand miles."

"Is that enough?" Linda asks.

"It's *just* enough." Matteo strokes the fuselage. "You know, I bet the last trip this chica took, she was carrying a bunch of loco influencers to a wellness retreat in Ojai."

"More like a bloated CEO flying to a fifteen-minute meeting in Macau," Dave grunts, hefting a duffel onto his shoulder.

"No, I think I'm right," Matteo says. "Seriously. There's a whole box of, like, vagina eggs in here."

"Influencers, my ass," Linda complains. She starts climbing the steps behind Dave.

"Fourteen *hours*," Katie moans, and leans on the gurney, which starts to roll away from her. She climbs on top of it and rests her head on one of the duffels.

Matteo jogs down the steps. "Yo, yo. No napping on this flight, honey."

"I can't do this," she whispers to him. Her eyes are glassy. "I'm not cut out for this."

"Hey, none of us are." Matteo hooks his thumbs in imaginary suspenders. "Look at me, I definitely know how to fly this plane."

Dave comes down the stairs. "Everything okay?"

Matteo hefts two bags and says, "Tag, you're it," and disappears into the plane.

"I can't, Dave," Katie says. "I just can't."

"Listen to me. This place we're going? They're going to take care of us. There's a bed there with your name on it, I just know it. But right now, we're going to take it minute by minute. Right? 'Just for today,' okay?"

Katie nods tiredly. "Just for today."

Dave helps her to her feet. "I promise you, I won't let you fall asleep on this plane."

Linda comes down the steps and collects the last of the bags. "Get on fast," she says. "Once he starts the engines, I'm not sure he knows how to keep it parked."

Dave gives the gurney a mighty shove. It rolls out of the jet's path, into the shadows of the hangar.

"Hey, Katie," he says. She turns around on the steps, eyes red. "Know what I want to do for fourteen hours? *Dance*." Dave wiggles his hips. "The whole time."

Despite her exhaustion, Katie laughs. "You can't dance for shit."

"So? I'm gonna dance with *you*."

"You step on my feet when we're on a big dance floor. You'll kill me in a cramped plane."

"Um, this thing is anything but cramped," Linda says over her shoulder.

Dave comes up behind Katie. "There's another way to look at this," he says, folding his arms around her waist. "You always wanted an exotic vacation."

"A death plane isn't how I pictured it starting."

"It's the adventure package. Pay a little extra for that sense of danger." He softens. "Look, I'm making the best of a raw deal here."

She twists and gives him a watery smile. "I *have* always wanted to see Greece, I guess."

"Exactly! Big statues of muscly dudes with their junk hanging out? That's everyone's dream vacation." He tips his forehead to meet hers. "We'll just hold on a little longer. Together. Okay?"

She rises onto her toes and kisses him again.

# 3

"Hello and welcome, everyone, to Flight 666." Matteo's voice rings out over the cabin speakers as Linda kicks a bag into place, and Dave helps Katie with a stubborn seat belt. "One-way service from Santa Mira, California, to the bottom of the Mediterranean Sea."

"Poor taste!" Linda calls.

"We have one hell of a journey in store for you today," Matteo continues. "We've got full tanks! We've got a pilot who's . . . well, practically a zombie! Today we'll be following a course charted in a dream by a goddamn whale—Yes, that's right, you heard me correctly. Our navigator today is a big-ass whale. I've named him Jackson. Wrong-Way Jackson." Matteo's chuckles turn into a raspy cough. "Okay, seriously, homeys, buckle your shit up. I only recognize, like, half the switches and dials up here."

Katie looks solemnly at Dave. "If we die—"

"No pacts," he says, cutting her off. "Nope. We're gonna get through this."

"Uh . . . Maybe don't be so sure about that," Linda says, staring through the window at the wing flaps, which rock wildly up and down.

"He knows what he's doing," Dave says, shooting Linda a death glare.

In the cockpit, Matteo grimaces as Linda's gun digs into his back. He drops the weapon and ammo on the copilot's seat, then places one palm on a hefty binder labeled FLIGHT OPER-ATIONS MANUAL. "Dear God," he says quietly, "all the bumper stickers promised you were a good copilot. You better not miss work today." Then he grips the yoke. "All right, Matteo. Just a video game. We're all just pixels."

The jet rolls out of the hangar without clipping the walls, then turns right, toward the runway. *A win!* Matteo thinks as he drags the tip of the wing along a chain-link fence. "Oh shit!"

"He's got it," Dave assures Katie, who grips his knee in a death-lock. "He's working out the details."

"Yo, VIPs," Matteo announces. "If you'll look to your left . . . maybe someone can tell me if the wing's still there?"

"Fuck your jokes!" Linda roars back.

"Roger that." Matteo corrects his angle and guides the jet to the runway entrance. "For real, y'all, hang on to something."

Dave leans against the window and watches as hangars roll by and the runway texture blurs. He can't recall the last time he flew, but surely the pilot then was more competent. His stomach rolls over as the plane reaches speed and its nose lifts skyward, then drops. The plane bounces twice on the tarmac, then wobbles into the air again. The runway falls away from Dave's window at a sickening angle.

"Uh, okay!" Matteo's shaky voice sounds through the cabin again. "That didn't totally suck." He gathers himself, then adopts his pilot's voice again. "Our flight time today is, oh, about the length of a brutal nursing shift. Am I right, Linda? We're making good headway, with the wind at our backs. Any minute now, I'll set the autopilot and come back for celebratory champagne."

"He's kidding," Linda says. "Right? Kidding?"

"I think so," Dave says, then pats Katie's hand, which has mercifully relaxed its grip on his knee. "We made it, huh? You're not freaked out anymore, I can tell . . ."

He trails off, suddenly aware of Katie's head lolling heavily on his shoulder.

"Hey," he says, lifting his shoulder gently. "You okay?"

Katie's head pitches forward.

"Shit!" Dave cries. "Linda! Fuck, oh fuck. Katie? Katie, wake up, honey. Wake up!"

"Stop shaking her," Linda says, appearing in the aisle beside Katie's seat. She presses two fingers to Katie's neck.

"Go to hell," Dave snaps. "Where's the adrenaline? I saw you put the spare one in your pocket back there."

"Dave," Linda warns. "We can't give her another one so soon."

"Give it to her!"

"Goddammit," Linda mutters, but she fishes the injector out of her pocket. "She can't handle more—"

Dave snatches it out of her hand and in one frantic motion plunges it into Katie's thigh. He presses down until it clicks.

"Something going on back there?" Matteo asks. "I heard a disturbance. Don't make me notify the air marshals."

Dave shakes Katie in her seat, hard enough that her head bounces off the headrest. He slaps her cheek, then again, the crack of it audible over the engine drone.

"Wake up!" he screeches, every cord in his neck straining. Spittle hangs from his lip. "You aren't a fucking quitter, don't fucking quit on me!"

"Dave," Linda says calmly.

"Open your fucking eyes!" Dave hits Katie again; her cheek shows a map of the strike, printed in red. "Open your eyes, please, Katie, please—"

"Dave." Linda grips his shoulder firmly. "You have to stop, Dave."

The plane hits a pocket of turbulence, and Katie lurches forward, limp. Dave catches her in his arms, her hair thick against his face, and begins to weep.

# Further Dispatches from Earth

## I

Lilly Nelson can hear the party from here, even with all the windows closed. She cups a mug of mulled cider, which her mother has made for as long as Lilly can remember, regardless of the season, and steps out onto the deck, into the still-warm dark. She can't see the party, not with all the trees, but she can see sparklers flickering through the branches, hear Roman candles popping and sizzling skyward.

Any other year, she'd have been there herself, she knows. She wonders how long it takes for a change to settle, for sobriety to become the new backbone of her life, rather than something new that runs parallel to her, a guardrail that might drop away at any moment. *Once an alcoholic, always an alcoholic*, she's heard, time and again, at nearly every meeting she's gone to. In the beginning, when she mocked that line, it was Katie who stabilized her. Strange to get such good advice from a girl so much younger. But wisdom doesn't necessarily come with age. Lilly's learned that the hard way.

She hasn't seen Katie in a while, now that she thinks about it. Tomorrow she'll call her up. Buy her breakfast. Say thank you for those early days of guidance.

The melatonin hasn't quite hit her yet, and she sits on the deck steps and watches as fireworks skitter across the horizon, fewer and fewer as the hours pass. If her mother were here, and not in the hospital again, they'd sit here together and watch, just as they'd done when Lilly was a little girl, when her father was still with them.

Getting older, Lilly thinks, is a lot like getting sober. The people you knew, that you were close to, fall away from you. As you grow old, they die, they move away, they drift out of touch; when you sober up, a curtain drops between you and the people you ran with before. That curtain's necessary. It's what keeps you alive.

But it's also what makes you lonely.

Lilly watches the fireworks until there are very nearly none at all, just the odd sputter here and there. The melatonin collides with her like a soft, cottony wall. She drains her cider, washes the mug in the sink and places it in the rack; she brushes her teeth and washes her face, then goes down the dark hall toward the back of the house.

Most nights when she stays over at her mother's place, she sleeps in her old room. But tonight, for some reason, she passes that door and goes instead to Ruth's bedroom. She pulls back the blankets and slides beneath them. She can feel the haze of memories, thick and almost tangible around her; she remembers every night she climbed into this very bed between her parents, then years later, when her father was gone, how she held her mother as she cried herself to sleep. Now she slides to the center of the bed and pulls herself into a tight ball, missing the warmth of her mother's slight body. A few hours' sleep, she tells herself, and then she'll wake and go to the hospital to be with Ruth. It's funny, she thinks, as sleep overtakes her, just how much she suddenly misses her mom.

## 2

Bernila touches Angelito's warm head and tries to stifle a cry. What more is she supposed to do? The baby is not well, there is no one here to help Bernila, and neither of them has slept in more than a day. Mr. Reyes, in the apartment beside theirs, has hammered on the wall all night long, his sleep stolen away by Angelito's persistent wails, so loud that they raise ghosts. Ghosts like Diego, whom Bernila sees in the chair in the corner of the bedroom, watching disapprovingly as Bernila tries everything, fails again and again, to soothe their son.

So many hours, Bernila thinks. They would all pass so much more easily if she and Angelito could sleep. Just a little sleep.

The child's small, soft lips part, and a banshee wail emerges. There is no money for the hospital; her doctor won't be open for two more hours, and there's hardly money for that, either.

"Just a little sleep, baby, please," Bernila implores. Angelito's fingers tighten around her own, squeezing weakly, as if to say, *I'm trying, Mama.*

Bernila's arms ache dully. She has not been able to put the baby down in three hours; when she does, Angelito protests loudly, his little voice cracking with the effort. She presses him to her chest now, smooths her palm over his thick black hair.

"Shh," she says, the only word she has to offer. It does nothing for him.

She calls her mother, forty miles away, but it is early, and her mother does not answer the phone. She tries her sister next, Rosa, who lives a seven-minute taxi drive from here, and Rosa also does not answer.

Cradling Angelito delicately, Bernila nudges the curtain away from the kitchen window. The sun hasn't yet risen, though it's warming the drape of sky against the horizon. The city will wake soon, but for now, most of the windows she sees are dark. They catch the last of the starlight and angle it toward the empty streets.

Angelito turns uncomfortably in her arms. Bernila, supporting the child with one hand, soaks a cloth in cold water with the other. She crumples it, squeezing out the excess water, then lays it over her son's forehead, straightening and worrying the edges of it. Angelito blinks up at her, brow furrowed like a little old man's, and for a moment, she thinks this is it, this little kindness is the one that will push away the fever, will let them both sleep.

But then Angelito coughs, a hard rattle in his tiny throat, and sucks in air as if filling an instrument. A moment later he screams with every ounce of his power, and Bernila says, "Baby, sweet baby, no, no."

*Thump, thump,* on the apartment wall.

It's too much. "We have to sleep," she whispers. "Sleep will make everything better."

Bernila arranges pillows like a barricade on the bed, then lays Angelito down. Her own body forms the remaining wall, and she nestles him close to her breast. She offers it to him, but he doesn't take it, so she tucks it away, then with her thumb irons away the wrinkles in his forehead. She takes his little earlobe between her fingers, caressing it, hoping that a little touch is all he needs to forget how poorly he feels.

"Just a little sleep," she says. "Until the doctor is open, and then we'll go, and she'll help."

Bernila sings low, hoping that the quiet tones will still Angelito's thoughts.

*Sana'y di magmaliw ang dati kong araw*
*Nang munti pang bata sa piling ni nanay*

The pillow beneath her head, the bed beneath her body, seems to acquire a gravity greater than that of the world around Bernila.

She yawns, then continues singing; she strokes Angelito's cheek. She has faith he will be better soon, that he will grow up and not remember this night and how bad it felt for them both. She loves to imagine him as a young man, his dark, liquid eyes filled with care for his mama. He will sit beside her, perhaps, when she is old and ill, and sing to her the same song.

For just a few minutes, Angelito is quiet, and that is enough. Sleep overtakes Bernila, and her hand falls limp and heavy upon the baby's chest. His cries fill the apartment, and his mother does not wake.

3

"He's been floating there since I came on shift."

Rodrigo frowns at Annabelle. "He is a very important guest. He cannot be allowed to just *float there*."

"Of course he can. That's why someone like him comes to a place like this, isn't it?"

Rodrigo shakes his head, then lowers his voice. "Do you really think that an ego that big wants to be left alone? Ever? Maybe that is what someone like him *says*, but believe me, he wants to be noticed."

"Nona took his drink," Annabelle says. "About twenty minutes ago. She brought him a new one."

"I bet he didn't even acknowledge her, did he?" Rodrigo muses. "But, look, either way, the ice in his glass has melted. It's too warm this morning. Tell Nona to bring him another drink."

"It's good he has that floppy hat to hide his face," Annabelle observes. "But the rest of him . . . I hope his next movie requires a sunburned look. Maybe it will be a movie like that one about the man on the island. With the soccer ball."

Rodrigo turns and studies the vacationing actor, who reclines on the inflatable raft in the middle of the resort pool. "He looks . . . softer than I would imagine, doesn't he?"

"All the muscles in the movies these days are computers."

"Or steroids."

"Or painted on with makeup."

"That's not how they do it," Rodrigo says. "Is it?"

"Have you seen the makeup videos on YouTube and TikTok? You would not believe what you can do with a little contouring—"

"Nona," Rodrigo says, stopping the bartender as she passes. "Would you take the Silken Spy himself a fresh drink?"

Nona looks toward the pool. "He hasn't touched the one I took him last time."

"Yes, but the ice has melted."

"You want me to keep pouring the expensive stuff? That's what he started with four hours ago."

"He's been out there four hours?" Annabelle asks.

Nona nods. "Since before the sun came up, even."

"Just floating?" Rodrigo asks. "He doesn't swim?"

"Just floating," Nona confirms. "I can pour him a new one. It will be his seventh."

"Seven," Annabelle says. "What is he drinking? Is that—?"

"He drinks mai tais, but disguised in a bourbon glass."

"What kind of rum?" Rodrigo asks. "Tell me not the—"

"Yes," Nona says. "Legacy."

"Ay!" Annabelle exclaims. "That's, like, four hundred dollars a bottle—"

"Four hundred!" Rodrigo interrupts. "You are wildly, wildly mistaken, my dear. Try twenty-seven thousand. A mai tai with that rum? Easily three thousand dollars. Very expensive shit."

Nona nods again. "So I should keep pouring it?"

"Fuck no." Rodrigo squints at the actor, who hasn't stirred since they began discussing him. "Switch to, I don't know, Malibu or something. I don't think he will notice."

"Did you see his movie with Lucia del Costa?" Annabelle asks. "They are both con artists. They look rich, but they're not, not really. And they travel to this tropical casino, and—"

"He does not look like a con artist to me," Nona says. "That's a dad bod if I ever saw one."

"I was just saying!" Rodrigo claps his hands. "Wasn't I just saying?"

"He was just saying," Annabelle concurs.

"So keep serving him?"

"Keep serving him."

"But don't wake him."

"How did you get the drink into the cup holder of his raft last time?" Rodrigo asks. "Or was he floating close to the edge?"

Nona covers a smile. "I had Felipe use his long net. He pulled the raft over slowly. Don't worry, Mr. Jong did not even notice."

"Oh God," Rodrigo says. "I hope to God the man does not wake up if you pull that stunt again. The embarrassment! Hauling Lee Jong around like a wheelbarrow."

"Shh," Annabelle hisses. "He's awake—No, no, sorry. Just a change in the light." A dark look passes over her face. "You said he's been out there four hours?" When Nona's head bobs, Annabelle says, "And he hasn't moved?"

Nona turns her eyes upward. "I . . . He must have, but if he did, I . . . I can't really recall." She looks at Rodrigo, then back at Annabelle, eyes widening. "Wait, you don't—?"

Annabelle says, "I read a gossip piece about him. He's on vacation because his wife left him. The novelist, I forget her name. Doesn't matter. But the story I read said he'd been treated for mental health issues before. You don't think . . . ?"

Rodrigo edges toward the pool, cupping his eyes to block the sun. "I *think* he's breathing, but . . ."

"I can get Felipe to go in and check," Nona suggests.

"No. No! Of course not," Rodrigo says. "He's breathing. I'm

sure of it. Isn't he? We can't embarrass the man that way. No one will ever come to our hotel again."

With that, Rodrigo leaves, and Nona turns to Annabelle and says, "I'm not certain at all, now that I think about it. I don't think I've seen him move at all . . ."

4

Twenty-seven thousand kilometers per hour.

Miroslava has always liked this number, twenty-seven thousand. It sounds so gloriously fast, and yet when experienced in the context of the International Space Station, fast is so relative. Earth turns below her, offering her a sunrise every ninety minutes; she watches Russia rotate past, most of it blanketed in heavy white clouds. The sun reflects off the Mediterranean like a mirror, throwing golden ripples against the walls of the observation compartment.

Twenty-seven thousand. So fast! She chuckles, remembering the citation she was given for driving her father's Lada Riva five kilometers over the limit in her village.

Sixteen sunrises and sunsets every day. The sunrises are nice, the way the sun peeks over the heavy lid of the earth, light rushing in all directions at once, as if spilled from a glass. But Miroslava prefers the sunsets, the way the sun dwindles to a spiked marble. The planet is almost entirely black in that moment, its curvature illuminated by a slender rainbow. And then the rainbow winks out, and then, several minutes later, the glass spills again on the other side of the planet.

She sifts through the videos she's captured these past few days, then selects her favorite: a desert region of Africa, its pale sands dotted with circular crop zones. The geometry of the view delights her. She uploads the photo to Instagram, adding a caption:

Scattered beads on a dirt floor. The whole planet looks so different and interesting from #ISS.

She reminds herself to show these photos to Aaron later. He's been on the ISS longer than the rest of them; this is his fourth tour, and he's intent on breaking the record for most consecutive days in space.

"Three hundred nineteen," he'd told them over dinner the previous night. "Just twenty-one days to tie Kelly's record."

"Right," Miroslava had added, shaking her head. "But you'd need ninety-seven more to tie Polyakov."

Later, Aaron had tried to slip his hand into her jumpsuit when she kissed him. "Uh-uh," she had said, offering him only a coy smile. "Only record holders."

Now she feels bad; she'd thought he would push, and she would concede, and they'd end up finding a corner, away from the others, where they'd happily make out, both winners of their little game. But Aaron had only smiled and said, "Come find me in twenty-two days," and floated off.

"Ninety-eight," she'd called after him, laughing when he flipped her the bird before he disappeared around the corner.

Two likes on her African farmland photo. Strange; there are usually many more people swarming on her photos than this.

Miroslava tucks away her phone, then pulls herself from the cupola to Node 3, then Node 1. She spots Hatsue carrying a cargo container away from the JEM and says, "You seen Aaron?"

"Sleeping cabin," Hatsue says. "I don't think he's awake."

Miroslava gives Hatsue a little two-finger salute, then drifts past her, through the US lab module to the Harmony module, where three of the sleeping cabins are open and empty. She presses her ear to the quilted door of the fourth and says quietly, "Aaron?"

No answer from inside.

She checks the log posted beside the cabin and sees that Aaron signed in eleven hours ago. Eleven! She's never known the man to sleep more than six hours at a time; he's always boasting that he doesn't need even that much.

"Aaron," she says a little more loudly.

She opens the door. Inside, Aaron is in his upright sleep sack, turned away from her. His head has tipped forward a bit, and she can see the touch of a bald spot forming in the midst of his close-cropped brown hair.

"You feeling okay?" she asks.

He doesn't answer, so Miroslava peers up and down the corridor. Amir is in Node 1, but his back is to her. Otherwise, there's no one in sight. Carefully, Miroslava wedges herself into the sleep compartment, jamming herself between Aaron's sleep sack and the array of equipment bolted to the wall behind her. *Real romantic,* she thinks, ducking to avoid the open laptop jutting just above her head.

She touches Aaron's chest through the sack and says, "Wake up, sleepyhead. I felt bad how we left things."

Then she touches his face, intending to pepper his stubbly cheek with kisses, and finds his skin cool and unyielding. Her cry is muffled by the padded walls of the compartment, but when she spills into the corridor, Amir is there, a worried look on his face, asking what's wrong.

She can't catch her breath long enough to answer. She raises her legs without thinking, tucking herself into a ball as Amir leans into the compartment. A moment later, he's alerting Cristina, the medic, and then Mission Control, and Miroslava tumbles in place, an egg, trying not to cry. In zero-g, tears don't fall; they cling to your skin, spreading over you like a membrane. Cry enough in space, and you might literally drown in your own sadness.

Light breaks through the little window in PMA2. Another sunrise, right on schedule.

# 5

In Madison, Wisconsin, a day care worker tries to rouse her eleven charges from their naps and fails. The little bodies, just twenty minutes before so overloaded with energy, lie still on their blue floor mats.

In Shirakawa, Japan, a young man greets his grandmother for her birthday. Her curtains are always open when he visits, but not today. He throws them wide, then finds her cold and still on her plank mattress.

In Luxembourg, Martin Faber finishes filling out the performance improvement form, then emails it to Millie, making sure to copy Human Resources. *Well, there's nothing else to be done*, he thinks, logging off his work computer. *It's all in her hands now.* He closes the door to his closet-sized office, then navigates his cramped living room, switching on the television as he goes. A newscaster says something about an emergency, but Martin is not interested in emergencies after the day he's had, so he switches the channel to a reality show. He listens from the kitchen as he unwraps a frozen dinner and slides it into the microwave: Renata is complaining that Lorraine's a snake, trying to take her man. *Her* man, Lorraine shrieks in a cutaway. He's *my* man. There's a scuffle, and Martin settles onto the couch with his plastic tray of chicken parmigiana. By the time the episode ends, the plastic tray sits empty on his coffee table, and Martin has drifted to sleep in the TV's cold blue light. He dreams, briefly, of personnel forms and bug reports.

In Montreal, an impatient driver, anxious to leave a parking garage, discovers the tollbooth worker has died: arms crossed, feet propped up, a little television still playing on his lap. "In the form of a question," Alex Trebek says as the driver begins to shout for help.

Forty miles from Gunnison, Colorado, the radio in a fire look-out tower crackles incessantly as the Division of Fire Prevention and Control tries to raise the lookout technician, who swings gently in her hammock, body only just beginning to cool.

In Santa Mira, California, Hank Wexler leans on one elbow, staring blankly at the Independence Day celebrations on the ceiling-mounted TV. He yawns so violently that his jaw clicks, and then he yawns again. The bartender switches the lights on, and Hank glances sleepily around to find the bar has already emptied out. "Last call was ten minutes ago," the bartender says, and Hank starts to reply, but his cell buzzes. "Hold that thought," Hank says, and squints at a text from one of the Dax-alab IT folks: *Yo, Hank, I'm at work. One of the research servers burned down. But I can't get inside to fix it. This card reader won't work, and there's nobody in the security booth to let me in. Call me ASAP PLS!!!* 🔥*!!!* Hank sighs heavily, then looks up at the bartender. "This fuckin' guy. Wants me to come in. You believe that shit? One more," he says, "and then I'll go. Have a little mercy on the working man, huh?" The bartender frowns, then turns away and begins mixing. Hank exhales again, then rests his head on the crook of his elbow and watches the TV and the flickering lights. He's asleep before the bartender turns around.

Whole towns fall silent; phone calls and text messages go un-answered. Occupants of jail cells shout for help, their attending guards asleep at their desks just a few meters away. Overnight flights arrive at their gates, and none of the passengers crowd the aisles, waiting to deplane. All told, nearly eight billion people sleep and do not wake; humanity's numbers are, in the span of twenty-four hours, devastated. Here and there around the world, sur-vivors wander the streets, dazed, traumatized. Many take their own lives. Many are so overwhelmed by the shift in their reality that their minds cannot cope. Most of them don't know why the world has fallen silent; many sleep, gathering their strength for the unknown, and never wake again.

Those who can, band together. Those who can, *survive*.

# On Fumes

## I

Taffeta clouds pull themselves apart before the Gulfstream, as if granting passage to mysterious lands. Matteo drains the syrupy dregs of a Red Bull, crumples the can, and adds it to a gathering pile on the floor. A storm of candy wrappers and chip crumbs assaults the copilot's chair.

*It's too fucking quiet*, he thinks, and grabs for the radio handset. He presses the Talk button: "This is your deranged captain speak—" But the handset squirts out of his chocolate-streaked fingers. He bumps the stick when he lunges for it, and the jet bobs uneasily in place.

"We're okay, we're okay," Matteo broadcasts, having recovered the handset. "But fuck this *no noise*, y'all. I don't know about you, but if I have to fly in somber silence for two more seconds, I'm going to sleep on purpose." He fumbles with his phone, then slots it into the jet's luxury sound system. "I hope you guys are alive back there. Alive enough to be pissed about this, at least. Dave, I'm sorry, I have to do it."

A moment later, "We Don't Talk About Bruno" blasts through the cabin speakers.

Matteo fishes another Red Bull from the cooler and peels open a Twix.

## 2

The music fills the empty spaces in the plane. Between Dave and Linda, who sit rows apart, not talking. Between Dave and Katie, who has been laid out in the final row and covered with a flimsy blanket. "Bruno" is followed by "Let It Go," then "You're Welcome," then "Be Our Guest" and a host of other Disney hits. When Matteo runs out of animated characters, Generación Suicida fills the cabin.

Linda watches Dave, fairly certain he's in shock. His neck lolls about on his shoulders; he stares blankly through the seats. She's glad for the music, the way it vibrates the whole plane. Matteo might be a shitty deejay, but the volume, the bass, is satisfyingly discomforting. Her body remains alert in protest.

"It's like military music torture," she says to Dave, but she can't hear her own voice above the sound.

Abruptly the music stops, and Matteo's voice emerges from the speakers. "Boys and girls," he says, and Linda frowns, detecting a worrisome waver, maybe even a slur, in Matteo's speech. "I'd like to draw your attention to one of *many* exciting sights you'll see today. Turn to your left—that's my left, too—and you'll see the sparkling Atlantic Ocean! Join me in saying farewell to the good ol' US of A, eh?"

A moment later, "Sixteen Going on Seventeen" bangs out of the speakers.

Linda plops into the seat next to Dave, who twitches but doesn't acknowledge her. She nudges him with her elbow. "You ever ask yourself why Matteo's got all these particular songs on his phone?"

Silence.

"Hey, let's look out the window," she suggests. "I haven't seen the Atlantic since I was a little girl."

Dave turns toward Linda and she realizes he isn't in shock at all, just . . . empty. His eyes are unfocused, scooped out.

"I see her," he says. "Walking up and down the aisle. She says my name."

"Dave . . ."

"I promised I wouldn't let her sleep. I promised she'd be okay."

Linda squeezes his hand. "It's not your fault."

"I said we'd dance the whole way," he says, his voice breaking. "But I didn't dance with her."

"Hey. Stand up with me. Now." She tugs on his hand, and reluctantly he rises. He sways in place, then staggers as the plane bucks.

Linda drags Dave up the aisle, toward the food service area behind the cockpit. She pops open a refrigerator, then unscrews a bottle of water and pushes it into Dave's hands.

"Drink," she commands. "All of it."

Dave does, and when the bottle's empty, he runs his damp hands over his face. He blinks, feeling fractionally more alert. "Thanks," he tells Linda.

"I get it," she says. "We're unraveling. Odds of any of us getting through this are now officially minuscule." She pats his face, and he blinks. "I don't know about you and Matteo, but I'm at eighty hours now. Maybe ninety."

"What is that, four days?"

"Almost," she says.

Dave leans into the alcove and retrieves another bottle. He hands it to Linda. "You, too."

## 3

The instrument panel no longer makes any sense to Matteo, if it ever did. It isn't like the training planes he flew. The dashboards are all digital screens and virtual buttons. Even if he could read them, they're moving all over the place, the attitude indicator's

artificial horizon overlapping the altimeter, creating a Venn dia-
gram of doomed-flight data.

*Fuck, I'm short-circuiting*, he thinks.

He presses the soft inner skin of his wrist against the window.
The sharp cold grounds him, but only for a moment. He tries to
relax his face, letting his features go slack; then he slaps himself.
First one cheek, then the other, harder, harder—

4

Linda paws through seat pockets, searching for anything to read.
She knows it's a bad idea. Two sentences of anything will put her
to sleep. But she's desperate.

Dave does push-ups in the aisle. They're the sloppiest form
Linda's ever seen, but he's moving, which means he isn't dead.

*Like Katie.*

A faint scream cuts through the Barenaked Ladies song. Linda
whips around; Dave, on his knees, panting, says, "Was that—?"

"Stay here," she says, and pushes past him. The cockpit door is
shut, but not locked, thank goodness. She bangs through it, then
shuts it behind her.

Matteo clutches one arm, pale and sweaty. "Guess you heard
that," he says in a reedy, sheepish voice. "Shit."

"It smells like lighter fuel up here," she says. Then she spies the
fallen lighter on the seat beside Matteo. The way he's clutching
his arm—Suddenly, she understands.

"Show me," she demands.

He uncovers his arm and holds it out. Linda takes him by the
wrist and elbow and inspects the scorched, bubbled skin.

"How many times?" she asks.

"A few," he admits. "It's an old air force trick for staying alert.
You hold a lighter under your arm, just for a second . . ." He

shakes his head, blinking rapidly. "Turns out a second is hard to measure when you're this tired. So, how bad is it?"

"You're alive," she says, ruffling his hair. "Head of the class." She takes a step toward the door. "You keep flying. I'm going to get the first aid—"

"Right there," Matteo says, nodding at a kit fastened to the wall.

Linda studies Matteo's face. "You don't want Dave to know."

"Macho bullshit, I know."

"He heard your scream, Matteo," she says. "But, hey, at least it was a macho scream."

Hopefully, he says, "Yeah?"

Linda shakes her head.

"All right, all right. Patch me up already, huh?"

While she wraps his arm, she says, "When I took this job, I was working at Cynagen's East Coast facility. Not the California HQ. The research labs, the ones that nobody knew were there." She gently cleans the burn. "I figured I needed a little time to clear my head, so I drove cross-country."

"Long drive," Matteo says. "By yourself?"

She nods. "For the first couple of days, it was a leisurely trip. I stopped at all the roadside attractions, you know? World's Biggest Fork, or whatever. But all of a sudden, I was over it. I needed to be where I was going. Like I worried if I didn't get there as soon as possible, I'd just . . ."

"Disappear," Matteo finishes.

"Something like that." Linda presses a gauze pad to his arm, then begins to wrap it in tape. "I got into this single-minded groove, see? I couldn't *stop* driving. Eventually I started to hallucinate things in the road, things that weren't there. Couldn't make myself blink. Could hardly read the speedometer."

"How'd you stay awake?"

"I didn't," she says. "It was a micro-nap, probably not more than a second or two. Then I snapped awake and the car was sliding through a wet meadow about fifty yards from the high-way." She shrugs. "I got incredibly lucky, I know."

"Lucky," Matteo echoes.

"There aren't any wet meadows up here," she says. "How bad is it for you?"

"Same. It's hard to read the instruments. I can switch to auto, but I worry if I do . . ."

"You'll relax. I get it."

She looks around the cockpit. "Professional diagnosis?"

"Hit me."

"Lay off the sugar and caffeine."

He laughs.

"I'm actually not kidding. How many have you had?"

"Red Bulls?" He looks away. "Um, all of them."

"And this candy store?" She indicates the pile of wrappers.

"It was like this when I got here?" he asks hopefully.

Linda takes his pulse. "You're irregular as fuck. The best jazz guys couldn't keep pace with this rhythm." She cocks her head. "History of heart problems?"

"No," Matteo says. "Serious?"

"Water," she orders. "Drink five, six bottles. Then say your Mary-full-of-graces and call me in the morning."

"I can take another pill," he suggests.

"I don't think so."

"Half, then."

"It's a catastrophically bad idea, Matteo."

"Come on, what's the worst—?"

"With all that shit in your system now?" She counts on her fingers. "You could have a heart attack. You could lose conscious-ness. You could crash the plane and turn us all into jelly." She reads the worry on his face, then shoves the candy wrappers aside and sits down. From the first aid kit, she grabs an accordion of peroxide pads. "You got a pocketknife?"

"A Leatherman."

"With a knife blade?"

He nods.

"Then . . . cut yourself. No more lighters. Small incisions. Nothing deep." She pats the meat of his forearm, then his thigh. "Here or here is good. Paper cuts, okay? Then you take one of these pads, you press it on the wound. It'll sting like a bitch, but you won't scar, and it'll wake you right up."

"Your professional prescription is self-harm," Matteo says.

"It's the end of the world." Linda shrugs. Then she turns serious. "No kidding, though: no more setting yourself on fire. Open flame. Pressurized cabin. Don't be an asshole."

"Yes, ma'am."

5

*Get it together.*

Dave remembers his father's voice. The way he protested Tracy's coddling of little Davy.

*He'll be a useless adult. He has to learn how to deal with his own shit, Trace.*

A hand lands on Dave's shoulder. He looks up to see Linda's distorted face, rippled as though seen through a wave of rising heat.

"Heyyyyyyy," she says. "Youuu okaaaaayyyy?"

"Whaaaat?" he asks.

She taps his cheek sharply. "Dave!"

He snaps back from that gauzy territory between waking and sleeping.

"You're beginning to hallucinate," she says, waggling a finger in front of his face. "How many fingers?"

"One," he says. "I think."

Linda looks at her three fingers, then says, "Try that again, Dave."

"Try again," Matteo says, leaning toward him from across the aisle. "You got this, bro."

Dave blinks. "You're supposed to be flying the plane."

"Oh yeah. He's got this under control," Matteo says, nodding toward the front of the plane. Dave leans into the aisle and sees another Matteo wave at him from the cockpit.

"See?" Matteo asks. "Hunky-dory, as bossman Hank would say."

Linda pulls Dave to his feet. "Come with me, dreamboy."

Dave stumbles after her. When he turns and looks back at Matteo, he sees Matteo isn't Matteo at all; he's Katie, wearing a sleep mask and oversized headphones.

"Katie," Dave says.

"Nope." Linda drags Dave to the cockpit, then props him in the doorway. "Stand here." To Matteo, she says, "Hit the auto for a second and come over here."

"Yeah, okay," Matteo says, and flips a toggle. "Whew. Feels good to get up." He stretches, then joins them, cracking his knuckles. "What're we doing here, icebreakers? Two Truths and a Lie? Name one—"

"Both of you, listen up," Linda says, clapping her fingers in front of Dave's face. "We're micro-sleeping. You know what that is?"

"Like microdosing, but way less cool?" Matteo asks.

Dave turns toward the cabin. "I saw Katie," he says. "I should check—"

"Assholes!" Linda shouts.

Both guys flinch.

"Yo, that was *loud*," Matteo complains, inserting his pinkie finger into his ear and wiggling it around. "If you were an archaeologist, you'd know hearing damage is no laughing matter."

"Anthropologist," Dave corrects.

"Audiologist, you fucks," Linda says. "We are sleeping. Right now. Our brains are so goddamn tired they're shutting us down, bit by bit. We're at the redline, boys. Doesn't matter what we do now. We're going to sleep. We can't stop it."

Dave peers at Linda's face, whose eyes are streaked with black. "Are you wearing mascara?"

"I want some," Matteo whines, and when Dave turns to look at him, Matteo blinks out of sight.

"Dave," Linda says. "Stay with me, buddy."

Linda is holding a basket, and Dave peeks inside. "There's a baby," he says. The blanket moves, and a tiny gray elephant unfurls its small trunk and trumpets. "It looks like my mom. It sounds like a kazoo."

Katie appears at Dave's shoulder. "It *does* look like your mother," she says, touching the elephant's little round belly. "What a cutie. Is it you, Dave?"

"I'm sorry," Dave says, beginning to cry.

"But, Dave," Katie says, "I'm happy now. Don't be sad. I got everything I deserved."

"We're going to die out here."

Dave and Katie look up to see a new Dave, cross-legged in the copilot's chair.

"You think?" Katie asks New Dave.

"Theoretically we're already dead," says another Dave. He stands in the aisle behind them, wearing a crisp white shirt and a blue bow tie. "Can I take your drink orders?"

"Where's the gas pedal?" Davy, small and delighted, sits in the pilot's seat, kicking his feet. "I want to make this thing *fly*."

# 6

Dave jolts in his seat. His face stings; his ears ring. Linda stands over him, hand raised to slap him once again.

"It's about fucking time," she says, breathing hard. "Listen to me, Free Willy. You want to go to sleep once we land? Go right the fuck ahead. But you're not getting off this plane before we do. For the next two hours, I'm making it my personal responsibility to slap your ass awake. Understand?"

Dave blinks at her. "Two hours?"

"Two goddamned hours. That's what you owe me. And Matteo. And Katie, too. Remember? She wanted you to get where we're going." Linda thrusts a finger in his face. "If you so much as blink one more time, I'm going to kick you in the balls."

He nods, swallows hard. "I'm going crazy."

"Welcome to the party."

"I'm so tired."

The plane lurches, then drops steeply. A moment later it stabilizes again.

"Mother*fucker*," Linda says. "Why do I have to be the mom, huh?" She grabs Dave's wrist and drags him in her wake, stopping en route to the cockpit to pluck a bottle from one of the duffel bags.

She cracks open the ammonia bottle and holds it under Matteo's nose. Matteo, gone limp at the controls, suddenly snaps upright. His skin is pallid, clammy with sweat. He looks wildly around for a receptacle. Linda hands him a vomit bag, then turns to Dave while Matteo fills it.

"Your turn," she says. She holds up the bottle. "Big whiff."

The sour bite of the ammonia cuts through his fog. It sharpens him, if only a little.

"Good." Linda turns to Matteo. "You trust the autopilot on this thing?"

Matteo nods weakly.

"Turn it on," she orders. "I want you both walking. Front of the plane to the back, then do it until I say stop. Okay?"

"Katie's back there," Dave protests.

Linda sighs. "Fine. Jog in place. Move your ass."

"If that dial right there goes down, you've got to—"

"Move!" Linda barks, and the guys start moving.

# 7

The remaining two hours pass slowly. But Linda's efforts work, somehow locating a fifth or sixth wind in each of the guys. When Matteo's voice comes over the speakers, announcing land, Dave can hardly believe it.

Linda releases a breath she's been holding for hours. "We made it."

"I feel about fifty years older," Dave confesses. "But we're here. We really did it."

The intercom crackles: "Oh fuck. Hold on!"

The plane banks a hard left, and Dave and Linda throw themselves into their seats and buckle.

# 8

"Here's the deal," Matteo says, half turning in the pilot's chair.

Dave and Linda have squeezed into the cockpit, which smells of sweat and bile and Red Bull.

"We, ah, don't have a runway," Matteo says.

"What?"

"I've circled the island three times now. There's no fucking runway."

Linda says, "Okay, but there has to be."

"There isn't."

"I'm afraid of heights," she says. "Plus sharks."

"The fall will kill you," Dave jokes feebly, but nobody laughs.

"Nobody's jumping," Matteo says. "We're too low."

"So go higher," Dave says. "This thing has parachutes, surely."

"Not an option, bro. We're flying on fumes. We'd just stall right out of the sky."

"So what *are* our options?" Linda asks. "Please don't say—"

"We're gonna butter the plane."

Linda's brow knits. "What the fuck is butter?"

"I'm gonna Sullenberger this shit."

"Is he speaking English?" she asks Dave.

"We're landing," Matteo clarifies. He gestures with his hands, simulating a plane skipping across water. "On the ocean."

Linda blanches. "That's what I thought you were going to say. Before 'butter.'"

"Can we do that?" Dave asks.

Matteo looks at the controls, then at the water, then back at Dave. "Is this a trick question?"

"He's asking if we're going to die," Linda says. "Are we going to die?"

"Probably. But that was going to happen anyway, right?" Matteo says. "But if you do what I say, then maybe we have a shot . . ."

# 9

Dave and Linda race around the plane, following Matteo's shouted instructions. Dave stows the duffels in overhead compartments; when there's no more room, he straps the remaining bags into seats. Linda handles Katie, buckling her body tightly into place. Then she returns to the front, where Dave's locking down the last bag.

"Linda," Dave says. "If we die . . ."

"Stop."

"It was cool to meet you. Matteo's right: you're crazy. But we wouldn't have gotten this far without you. I'm certain of it."

She snorts nervously. "I got us all the way to the end, just in time for us to splatter on the waves." The mental image sobers her up. "Goddamn, I'm scared," she admits.

"Me, too."

The intercom crackles. "I hope you guys are squared away. It's time." Matteo calls out for them to buckle in. "Heads between your knees. Wait! First make sure you see the exits. If we survive the landing, go right to them. Don't grab anything."

Linda grips Dave's hand as they buckle up, side by side.

"Okay, *now* put your heads down." Matteo's voice strains. "Cutting the engines . . ."

The persistent white noise of the engines suddenly ceases. For a moment, all Dave can hear is the low whistle of wind over the fuselage and wings. He looks to his right and sees Linda, eyes closed, lips moving, reciting something he can't hear.

"Descending!" Matteo shouts. "Here we go, folks!"

The whistle becomes a shout, then a shriek. The seats rattle in place. The last thing Dave notices before he bends forward is the windows: they flex against the pressure, bowing inward like bubbles.

Matteo's voice is faint over the cacophony. "Opening emergency doors!"

There's a sudden boom as the doors explode away from the plane. The cabin fills with biting wind. Linda's hair flaps against Dave's ear. He squeezes her hand tightly.

"Brace for impact!" Matteo's tiny voice cries.

Linda screams.

Time slows. Dave hears a whisper and raises his head to see Katie in the aisle. The seats around her snap violently back and forth, but she is unmoved, serene. Her hair rides the wind like a scarf. She wears a peaceful smile as she holds Dave's gaze.

The cabin lights go out. Light spills through the windows like rays of sun through a canopy of leaves. The horizon rotates at an impossible angle. All Dave can see now is the ocean, broad and blue and still, barreling toward them.

*God help us*, he thinks. He bends forward, then remembers that he doesn't believe in God.

# Apocalypse Radio

## I

Eli is relieved he can't feel anything below the waist, because he's almost certain the emergency brake is jammed right up his butt. He maneuvers himself into the gap between the passenger seat and Millie's seat, then goes to work on Millie's face, slapping her until her eyes fly open. She gasps loudly, gutturally, as if she's just been resuscitated after drowning.

"Oh, thank God," Eli moans, and slumps against Millie's shoulder.

Millie coughs, then shakes her head to clear it. "I wasn't sleeping," she rasps, then coughs again.

"Says you," Eli observes. "I was the one watching you fall asleep at the wheel. And then you just about murdered us both. What happened?"

Millie rests her head on Eli's. "I told you. I have narcolepsy."

"But you take things."

"Right, but drugs are temperamental." Millie clears her throat, which feels like she's swallowed sand. "Or brains are. Or maybe just I am."

"You can't drive anymore," Eli rules, like a skinny judge in a T-shirt.

"News flash," Millie says, peering at the hood, a crumpled

mess. The windshield is cracked, but not shattered, and one of the headlights points skyward at a jaunty angle. "I don't think anyone's driving this thing anymore." She looks down at Eli's legs. "Is the ebrake up your butt?"

"Could be. But how would I know?"

"Fair enough."

"Do we just sit here?" Eli asks.

"We're an hour from Cleveland, and it's the storm from hell out there, and I don't see anywhere to walk. Do you?" Millie winces. "Also, I might have broken something."

"Where?"

"I don't know. Can you break your neck from whiplash?"

"You can definitely break your neck from whiplash. Can you turn your head?"

Millie turns a little toward Eli, then a little more, then grits her teeth. "Fuck. That far, and then it's like there's rebar jammed through my spine."

"I don't think it's broken if you can turn it."

"Can you break your ankle from whiplash?"

"You can break your ankle from a fucking *car accident*," Eli says. "Is your ankle broken?"

"You have to look. I can't bend my neck."

"Left or right?"

"Left."

Eli delicately leans over the steering wheel, squinting into the shadowy floorboard. "I can't tell. How can you not tell? Can you—?"

"I tried moving it already. I don't think it worked."

"Okay. So, maybe broken."

"What about you? Are you okay?"

"Everything from here up seems tip-top," Eli says, gesturing at his midsection. "Everything from here down . . . well, again, how would I know?"

## 2

Despite the storm, night comes in sticky and hot. The Honda's air-conditioning flails at the heat while Millie and Eli sit sweating on the side of the highway.

"What's up with that?" Millie asks, jerking her chin at Eli's old MP3 player. It's in the floorboard, where Eli can't reach it.

"It's got sentimental value. That's all."

"It's a knockoff," Millie says. "I remember those. Cheaper than an iPod or a Beatboxer, right? And old, too. Why are you carrying that old thing around?"

Eli regards Millie carefully, as if weighing how much to tell her.

"I don't bite," Millie says.

"This is my second car wreck," Eli says. "It's funny, I'd have expected it to fuck me up. Going through this again. But I feel fine. I feel more in control."

"What happened the first time?"

"I was just a kid. I lived through a Disney origin story, you know? On vacation with my parents. First vacation ever for me, in fact. And, *boom*, twenty miles outside the city—Well. They both died. I didn't." Eli fiddles with his fingertips, picks at a bit of loose skin. "The car went off the road and down this incline. There was a lot of brush. Took all day for someone to notice the skid marks, I guess, and come looking for the car."

"Jesus."

Eli glances at the passenger mirror, angled so he can see the shape of the dead man resting against the back seat window. "Not my first time in a wrecked car with a dead body," he mutters. "Thought that would've fucked me up more, too."

"You're in shock, maybe."

"Maybe."

Millie pats Eli's knee, then, remembering, pats his shoulder instead. "So what's the MP3 story?"

Eli lets his breath out slowly. "That's the last recording I have of their voices. They liked to sing. It's my favorite song."

"It looks like it might still work," Millie offers hopefully.

"Do you have a charging cable from 1842?"

Millie shakes her head.

"Then it won't work."

# 3

Millie counts out pills from the pharmacy stash. "I don't know about you," she says, dry-swallowing two, "but I could fucking sleep."

"These won't work forever," Eli points out. "Trust me, I've got experience with this sort of thing."

Millie side-eyes him. "You forget who you're talking to, squirt."

"We'll find something on the radio. I'm sure of it." Eli snaps the radio on, then presses the Scan button. He frowns, then presses it again. "Does anything in this old junker work?"

"This old junker made the Kessel Run in—"

"Nope, nope, nope." Eli spins the dial manually, skipping over station after station of static before the first working channel interrupts the noise. "What's this?"

A classical song fades into silence. There's a long beat, and then the same song begins to play again.

"There's nobody there," Millie says. "It's just a computer on a loop. Keep looking."

The FM band is dead, but on the AM band, Eli finds a voice half-buried in white noise. He cranks the volume, straining to make it out.

". . . goddamned apocalypse, I shit you not," the voice reports coarsely. "Under any other circumstances, the FCC would be at my door already. That I've been on the air fourteen hours without the feds showing up tells you all you need to know, now, don't it."

"Who *is* this guy?" Eli wonders.

"My mom knew all sorts of cracked-up survivalist types," Millie says. "When we were running all those years, sometimes we'd stay with them. This one lady, real old, she had this 1960s-style bomb shelter buried on her property. Way up north in the woods. Michigan, I think? Maybe Wyoming?"

"Big difference between those," Eli points out.

"Yeah, well, we went a lot of places. And I was six." She continues: "This lady, she had a ham radio setup in her bunker, connected to this homemade antenna she'd strung up in a tree. We slept in that bunker for a week, and every night she'd come down and start broadcasting at three, four a.m. Just old songs, mostly. I think she figured if the radio wasn't going to play what she wanted, then she'd make it play her favorite songs. Old Peggy Lee, Doris Day stuff." Millie nods at the radio. "This guy's probably doing the same thing. Some crazy in an attic or a basement with an old CB."

"Did you hear what he just said? He said it's the apocalypse."

"Trust me. To a guy like that, a plane flying over his cabin is the apocalypse."

"Yeah, but . . ." Eli gestures at the empty highway. "I haven't seen another car since we wrecked." He lowers his voice. "The dead guy could be right. It's the end of the world."

"Well, if it is, you and I are screwed. You ever see that old *Twilight Zone* episode? We're the last guy alive with a thousand books to read, except we broke our glasses."

"I never saw it. Shh."

On the radio, the amateur broadcaster says, "Now, look, I've been listening to all the broadcasts I can find. The last one I just played, that one was from Greenland, of all places. But this next one, it's a little closer to home. This one's from right here in the US of A. Listen up."

There's a harsh click, and then a new voice comes out of the radio.

> *Can anyone hear me? Hello? Matteo, is this thing work-ing? I hope this works. Listen up. If you can hear this, this is an emergency broadcast. I— Look, I'm just going to come right out and say it, okay? Do not go to sleep. If you can hear my voice right now, stay awake. My name is Linda Russo. I'm an advanced practice registered nurse at Santa Mira Medical Center. If you're hearing me: Come to the hospital. We don't know if this is some kind of pandemic, or . . . an attack. We don't know. Again, this is an emer-gency broadcast. I have to go now. The hospital. Come to the hospital. Do not go to sleep. Godspeed.*

Eli looks at Millie, who looks down at the paper sack filled with pill bottles and says, "It's a good thing we have all of these."

"I'm scared," Eli says.

"Yeah. Yeah, kid—me, too."

Eli's hand finds Millie's and squeezes. She squeezes back.

# The Dream Warrior

## I

Dave doesn't know where he is.

The plane disassembles itself in the black of the sea, waters that just a few moments before were glittering blue. The dark around him is not quite complete; there's movement in its depths.

A spark of gold somewhere below him—below him? *above?*—pulls his focus, and twisted sections of the plane corkscrew past. He can't swim out of the way. He's still buckled in. A hunk of fuselage strikes his seat and sends him spiraling deeper. He looks left, but Linda's seat is gone. The whole front of the airplane is gone.

Matteo.

Linda.

A coldness rocks him.

Katie.

Dave struggles with the seat belt, but the metal clasp is dented. It won't separate. Above him, the surface light grows fainter.

*I'm going to die,* he thinks.

Then: *Maybe I'm already dead.*

He turns his gaze upward, hoping to catch one last sliver of sunlight as the world recedes from him.

And something sleek and dark slides through the water above.

## 2

"Dave, come on, come—Shit, I've got him! Matteo, I've—"

A face, blurry and distorted, slowly morphs into one that Dave recognizes. Linda wears a relieved expression.

"Jesus," she says. "I thought you'd bought it."

"What did you bring me?" Dave mumbles softly. Water leaks from his mouth.

"What did you say?" She tips her ear closer. "Say it again."

Dave coughs, his torso spasming as water rushes out of his mouth. Linda gets a face full of recycled seawater, but quickly turns him onto his side. She hits his back with the flat of her palm, and Dave feels for a moment as if he's swallowed the whole ocean.

Miraculously, Matteo is there, too, and as Dave recovers, sucking fresh lungfuls of cool air, he reaches for his friends' hands, gripping each of them tight.

Matteo drops Dave's hand and throws his arms around him. "Hijo de puta," he mutters. "We're not dead. I can't fucking believe we're not dead."

"We should be," Linda agrees, lying down on the coarse sand. "Instead, we're stranded. This is it, isn't it? Aristera. You brought us to a deserted island."

Dave groans as he forces himself upright. Matteo helps, a hand on Dave's back.

"Not deserted," Dave says, his tongue an abraded slug in his mouth. He turns and squints, his back to the water, then says, "We have to go there. That way. Through the hills."

"You can't possibly know—"

"I know," Dave says. "It was in my dream."

He starts to get up, but Linda puts a hand on his shoulder, holding him in place.

"Just . . . breathe a minute, okay? We were just in a plane crash.

Let's just catch our breath . . ." She closes her eyes and reclines on the beach.

This time it's Matteo who puts an end to it.

"I don't think so, crazy lady," he says. "We move. We move now."

## 3

Aristera, on any other day, would be beautiful. But to the three of them, it's something out of Dante's *Inferno*. They stagger across the sand, bodies bruised and battered from their collision with the sea, past olive trees and scrubby patches of tamarisk. Sand gives way to grassy hills; smooth planes of sandstone rise up in complicated formations.

"Is that a goat?" Matteo asks, pointing as something disappears into brush.

Dave follows a path downward, and the hills become the walls of a narrow valley. "Keep moving," he says. "Don't look at anything."

"Don't look at anything?" Matteo echoes. "Did you not hear me say I saw a goat? Goats, man! On a dead island. This is the craziest shit ever."

"Does anyone else hear that?" Linda asks, rubbing her temples.

Matteo pauses, listens. "I don't hear anything."

"I hear it," Dave says. "I've heard it before."

"Where?" Linda manages.

Dave looks back at her. She doesn't look good. Her skin is pallid, almost green. He remembers the feeling, lying there in the dirt, chained to a stake. The needles chewing at his brain.

"Doesn't matter," he says. "But we can't stop now."

After another hundred meters or so, Matteo takes a bad step

and shoulders into the rough soil wall. "Fuck," he says. "I hear it, too. I feel like someone put my head into a blender. What the fuck is it?"

"It's trying to stop us," Dave says.

"It?"

They start moving again. Matteo's adrenaline has dissipated, and he staggers from side to side; Linda moans, somewhere between a cry of pain and a sob.

"Keep moving," Dave urges. His back is on fire, his muscles screaming. He thinks he might have a cracked rib or two. "We can't stop. We've come this far."

He forges on, until the path narrows. The walls tighten around them, and Dave points at a slender crevice ahead.

"We'll climb there," he says. "It's just a few feet. We can do it."

He and Matteo hoist Linda up first, and as soon as her feet touch the ground above, she collapses with a cry of relief.

"It's stopped," she says. "Thank God, it's stopped."

Matteo goes up next, then turns to offer Dave his hand. Dave bites back a cry as his broken ribs grind against one another, and then he's up, too.

The three of them catch their breath.

"She's right," Matteo says. "I feel like I just evicted a bad roommate from my head."

But Dave ignores this and says, "Oh fuck. Are you guys seeing this, or . . . ?"

## 4

None of this should be here.

Dave reaches for Matteo's and Linda's hands without thinking, then steps forward, toward the mirage ahead.

"It's not real, right?" Linda asks.

Before them, the stage has been set for a funeral: Chairs arranged in careful rows in the grass. Immense floral arrangements on tripods. A lectern, draped in black cloth.

And at the center of it all, a gleaming casket, black with striations of gold strands.

"I'd like to leave now," Matteo whispers. His voice is tight, his words barely audible.

"My gun," Linda says, and turns to Matteo. "Do you—?"

Matteo pats his waistband. His mouth draws tight as he remembers putting the gun down on the copilot's seat. "I don't have it," he offers helplessly.

"Dearly beloved," a voice intones, and as if triggered by unseen strings, Dave, Matteo, and Linda all square their shoulders and stand at attention. "Please take your seats for the mourning."

Dave can't stop his feet from moving. As if programmed to do so, he and the others walk to the rows of chairs. Their hands separate, and they each drift to their own chair, far from the others. Matteo finds a seat in the back, Linda on the opposite side, somewhere in the middle.

Dave is drawn to a chair right up front.

The strange voice belongs to a figure who stands now at the lectern, gripping its edges with pale fingers. The stranger's face is veiled in black.

"Welcome, children of gods," the figure says. Its voice is smooth, dark, deep, impossibly refined. "Today we gather in this place of memory and grace to remember the soul of dear Katherine Maria Dowd."

Dave's heart slows to a dull thump as the stranger turns to the casket and slowly lifts its lid. Inside lies Katie, wearing the cornflower-colored dress she wore on her first date with Dave. Her hair is twisted into a braid and laid across one shoulder; her face has been tastefully made up, so richly pink she might still be alive.

"Katie, as she liked to be called, was taken before her time," the figure says.

Behind Dave, Linda and Matteo echo those words: *Before her time.* He wants to turn and glare at them, or perhaps plead with them, but he can't move. He's stapled in place, spine straight, feet nailed to the earth.

"Katie gave her life to those who cared for her," the stranger continues. "What a glorious heart she had. Even in her own darkest hours, she put those she loved first."

The figure's veiled face shifts slightly toward Dave. Though he tries, Dave cannot close his eyes.

"In Katie's final hours, her last minutes on this great planet, she felt lost. Tired, afraid. She believed hope was gone, and she looked to others, for once in her life, to supply her with that lost faith."

The figure is now staring at Dave. Dave is certain of it.

"She looked to you, David Torres, and you looked away."

*You let my baby die*, a new voice says, and Dave turns left to see Margaret Dowd, Katie's mother, staring at him accusingly.

*She loved you*, says Tracy, sitting to Dave's right, hands flat against her cheeks, pulling at her skin. *She loved you like I loved you.*

Invisible hands turn Dave's face forward again. Katie is sitting on the casket, legs dangling, ankles crossed. Her blue dress is tattered, her hair unkempt. Her skin has lost its color. Her jaw works left and right, unnaturally, and when she parts her lips to speak, gallons of seawater pour out of her mouth, drenching her dress.

*I only wanted to live*, Katie says, a strand of kelp dangling from her lips. *Dave, I told you I was scared.*

"No," Dave says. "It isn't my fault. I tried."

The veiled figure cocks its head. "Oh, but did you?"

"Yes. I really tried."

The figure raises its hands to the veil. "What a pity that's what you believe," it says, and then it pulls the veil back, revealing black eyes and pebbled gray skin. "You're not special, Dave. You're just like your friends."

The sight of the elephant beast snaps Dave's head back, but he still can't move his limbs. The elephant's trunk curls around Dave's neck, and Dave squeezes his eyes shut, hiding himself away from the monster's hideous, empty eyes.

"Don't hurt my friends," Dave says through clenched teeth. "You're my monster, not theirs."

"Oh, they see me, too," the elephant says, its breath hot and foul in Dave's nose. "But they see me their own way. Take a look."

The elephant spins Dave's head in a circle, oblivious to the laws of physics. In the middle of the funeral assembly, Linda, pinned to her chair, is screaming. Ruth Nelson stands over her in a disintegrating hospital gown, eyes bulging from pallid blue skin.

*You took advantage of me*, Ruth says to Linda. Her mouth yawns black, an endless void, as she grips Linda's face. *You let me die so you could benefit. So you wouldn't have to.*

"I didn't!" Linda shrieks. "I didn't, I didn't, I didn't—"

"She took a life to save her own," the elephant says. "That is how she sees me. That is who I am to her."

The elephant turns Dave's neck further. "And your other friend . . ."

Matteo's head is thrown back in a primal cry. His shoulders shake as he wails to the sky. A child sits in his lap, skin charred and blown away from muscle and bone. The little boy is missing an arm, missing a foot. His small body is folded in directions it shouldn't be folded. But he looks up at Matteo with one eye, with half his skull still intact, and just repeats one word, over and over:

*Why? Why? Why?*

"He works so hard not to remember that boy," the elephant says. "The boy who ran out of an empty house right after your friend pushed the bomb release button on his drone console. But the boy has never forgotten him. Through me, Matteo still sees him."

The elephant rotates Dave's head completely around, then says, "And you, of course, get me. *This*."

"Fuck you," Dave says. "Whatever you are, you don't belong here."

"Poor Dave. You have tried so hard." The elephant's eyes widen more, as if they are gateways to some cosmic hell. "You dare to walk beyond the veil. But you and your friends will die here, at the threshold."

Before Dave can ask what threshold the thing is talking about, an ambient tone thrums violently around him, the force of it like needles piercing his skull. Behind him Linda and Matteo scream; Dave feels a warm rush of liquid in his ears.

"Let us go," Dave groans.

"Oh, but we've only just started," the elephant responds, and as Dave looks on in horror, it begins to shape-shift, its face contorting until it's the face of Dr. Castaneda. The doctor's fountain pen juts from its neck. "Remember, Dave? Yes, you remember. You killed me. I was only trying to help you, and you murdered me. Murdered, Dave! And all they did to you was send you to the hospital for two years. I know you think about it all the time. I know you remember me. I know I'm the reason you take the pills."

"You aren't him!" Dave yells. "You aren't real!"

The elephant-Castaneda pulls the fountain pen from its throat. A fountain of warm blood mists into the air, coating Dave's face. Dave blinks rapidly, trying to clear his vision. The monster touches the pen to Dave's cheek; the nib is sharp enough to puncture his skin with even the faintest touch.

"How about your eyes?" elephant-Castaneda asks. "A fair exchange for the damage you've caused, wouldn't you say?" When

Dave doesn't answer, it continues: "Did you know that I was married when you murdered me? That I had three little children?"

"This isn't real," Dave says. "Isn't real, isn't real."

"Oh, this is real," the monster says.

Over its shoulder, Dave sees Katie, legs still dangling from the side of her casket. She looks at him sweetly, her big eyes filled with kindness.

"Stay here, Dave," she says. "All of this will go away if you just stay with me."

"She's not real," Dave cries. He cries out as loudly as he can, hoping the others will hear: "None of this is real! Hang on!"

The elephant-doctor slides the point of the pen upward, into the soft tissue beneath Dave's eye. Fresh blood courses down Dave's face; the pain feels very real to him.

"Just take my hand, Dave," Katie says, suddenly standing next to the monster. "That's all. We can have another chance. You owe me that."

Dave squeezes his eyes tightly. A stuttering carousel of memories projects on his inner eyelids. Katie's cold feet touching his toes beneath the sheets. Katie laughing at his homemade carbonara. The warmth of her body pressed to his, the two of them turning in a slow circle on the merry-go-round in Helena Ward Park. Skywatching from the roof of Katie's apartment building. Her lips, small and soft. Her eyes, so deep that they—

He opens his eyes and looks past the monster, at Katie.

"Stay," Katie says.

Her pupils are large black triangles, like the answer in a Magic 8 Ball.

"Stay."

"I won't," Dave says. Then, as loudly as he can, for the others, he shouts, "We won't stay! We won't!"

For all he knows, his friends are dead already.

"A pity," the elephant says, shifting away Castaneda's features.

"Though I am not surprised. Stubborn, insistent. You have always been both."

The elephant applies pressure to the fountain pen.

Dave feels it slip into his skin.

"I know the whale," Dave says, clenching his teeth against the pain.

There is time enough to see the elephant's eyes reflect fear, and then the first gong sounds. The sound is to the elephant what the needles were to Dave and Linda and Matteo. The elephant clutches its skull, which bulges.

The gong sounds again, its powerful reverberation washing over the island like a tsunami. The chairs around Dave are blown away. The impostor Katie is knocked to her knees.

"I know the whale!" Dave shouts, and when the gong rings out a third time, the force of it slams Katie's casket lid shut—

## 5

Dave pushes against the ground, raising himself upright. Behind him, Linda is on her back, gasping; Matteo is bent forward over his knees, shoulders shaking.

"Guys," Dave says, looking around. "It's over."

The casket, the flowers, the chairs—they're all gone. The three of them are alone in a clearing that looks as if it hasn't been visited by humans in a thousand years. The sun hangs high overhead, throwing tree shadows upon the three of them.

"Are we okay?" Dave asks. "We're okay, right? Is anyone hurt?"

"Look," Linda says. She's rocked onto her side, and points.

Far away, through gaps in the firs, a bone-white pyramid rises from the island. Dave wonders how he could have missed it before. The sight of it now does something to him, draws him up straight. He squares his shoulders without realizing he's doing so; he feels his breathing regulate.

"That's it, isn't it?" Linda asks. "Where you're leading us."

Before Dave can answer, a voice calls out to the group. Silhouetted on a ridge above them, a lanky figure shouts, "My friends! Hello! Welcome!"

Dave's muscles tighten as the stranger lightly hops from rock to rock, down to the clearing. On closer inspection, the man, who grins broadly at them, appears to be no threat. He holds both palms out, showing that he is unarmed, and then claps his hands happily.

"There are three!" he says. "Oh, we knew there would be one of you. But three! What a glorious day!"

Matteo coughs and spits blood into the sand.

The stranger's brow furrows. "You are injured," he says. He turns to Dave. "You've found trouble here."

Dave nods. "You could say that."

"The veil is not so strong here," the man says.

"Are you Russian?" Linda asks.

The man's eyes light up. "*S priyezdom*," he says. When Linda looks confused, he says, "Ah well. It was worth a try. Yes, madam, I am from Sviyazhsk. Small town. Not many people at all. Not so warm as here."

Dave looks at his friends. Linda's face is scratched, and she's bleeding from her right ear and her nose. Matteo's bruised, his teeth stained red. And Dave can feel blood beginning to crust on his own face.

"We need help," Dave says to the stranger. "Are you here to help?"

"Help," the man says, and pats his hands together again. "I am your emissary from safety." He points toward the pyramid in the distance. "You are all safe now. Come with me. Let's take care of your aching bodies. You must be tired, no?"

"Fucking exhausted," Matteo says, and spits again.

# 6

The pyramid is not their destination, Dave realizes, and that's a good thing, because none of them could manage the distance right now. Linda and Matteo lean on each other for support; Dave staggers along behind the Russian. Soon, the man leads them through a narrow gap in a bank of bushes and vines, then does a little fancy jig and says, "Ta-da!"

Linda's sharp intake of breath is all the man needs to hear. He chuckles and says, "Oh, friends, I remember how it felt to arrive here myself. Only days ago, but I felt like a starving man who stumbled into a feast. Much as you do now, I think!"

The ground slopes away beneath their feet, revealing a village below. Houses with terra-cotta tile roofs, their walls painted all the shades of sunlight a person could imagine. Pale pinks and watery oranges and lilac. On a nearby terrace, people wrapped in blankets sit around a flickering firepit.

"Refugees," the Russian says. "Like you!"

There are people everywhere, in various states of disrepair and dress. Moving among them are several elderly women in flowing robes, serving tea, applying compresses and salves. Newcomers file into the village through a gate and are handed string-tied bundles: blankets and sandals and things. Chickens strut between people's feet, pecking at sand and one another. A woman rests in the shade of a balcony, a baby pressed to her breast. Dave can smell food roasting somewhere, and his mouth fills with saliva.

"It's heaven," Matteo says. "I can't believe this is real."

"I can't believe we made it," Linda says.

"Most people think they're dead," the Russian adds helpfully. "You three maybe more than most! We saw your plane. It was quite dramatic! A scene from an action movie. Maybe one of yours, with that actor who is always trying to kill himself."

"Tom Cruise," Matteo says.

"Yes, yes," says the Russian. "I like the one where he goes to space and loses his helmet." He clucks his tongue. "A Russian would never lose his helmet in space, let me tell you."

## 7

"Same as you," the Russian says in answer to Matteo's question. "Everyone here had a dream, received a message. 'Come to Aristera.' Almost certainly more people received it, too, and did not know what to do with it, or did not have the means to come."

Dave looks at his friends, their faces freshly scrubbed, hair washed, eyes bright. They are wrapped in blankets, cradling steaming mugs. The last few days feel suddenly very far away from here, like a dream he's woken from.

"Yesterday a little boat arrived," the Russian continues. "I'm surprised it made the journey. It was patched with tinfoil in places."

"Where did it come from?" Linda asks.

"Tunisia." The Russian tilts his head. "I suppose it's too much to hope any of you speaks Arabic?"

Matteo shakes his head. "Sorry, man. Spanish and English is all I've got."

The Russian offers a smile to some people who walk past his hut, carrying bundles of straw. "Yes, yes," he says, "good to see you, hello." When they have gone, he says, "They were here before me, but they never say a word."

Linda looks at Dave, then Matteo, then says, "I have to ask . . ."

The Russian nods. "You want to know what happened."

"Do you know?" Dave asks. "Do you know what's killing everyone?"

The Russian inhales deeply. "You've seen it, yes? What did it look like to you?"

"Like an elephant," he says.

"Specifically, what elephant?"

Dave glances at his feet. "I was terrified of elephants when I was a kid," he says. "I don't know why, even now. They just creep me out."

"Elephants, man, how do they work?" Matteo jokes, but his voice is unsteady.

"What was it to you?" the Russian asks Matteo.

"Pass," Matteo answers. He makes a circle motion with one finger. "Er, come back to me."

"It was a woman for me," Linda offers. "A patient I . . . took advantage of."

"It takes many forms," the Russian agrees. "For everyone, the beast is something different. For one of the little girls in our village, it is an enormous cockroach; one crawled across her once as she slept, and she crushed it with a book. For one of the old men, it is a vulture; as a child, he saw it picking at the bones of his father when the search party found his remains."

"I bombed a house," Matteo says in a rush. "It was supposed to be empty." He buries his face in his hands. "There was a little boy . . ."

The Russian places his hand firmly on Matteo's shoulder. "All of us here are walking wounded," he says. "We are not heroes or gods. None of us is innocent. The beast preys upon our guilts and fears. The old man who sees a vulture? When he was a boy, he wished for his father to die. He is now eighty. He has lived with that guilt all his years."

To all of them, he says, "It is our guilt that makes us human. And to the beast, it is what makes us vulnerable."

"Why do I see an elephant, then?" Dave asks.

"I do not know. But Safet can help you understand. He will teach you what you need to know."

"Who?"

"Oh, you've met," the Russian says, getting to his feet. "Trust me."

Everyone stands, too, but the Russian holds up a hand. He touches Linda's and Matteo's faces and says, "Rest for now." To Dave he says, "Come with me."

The Russian turns away, and Dave shares a look with his friends.

"I don't know," he says. "But it's okay. I can tell."

"Be careful," Linda says. "Please."


# 8

"They trust you," the Russian says.

Dave follows the man through the village. "I guess."

"They are here. You saved their lives."

"We almost died."

"We all almost died," the Russian says. "Many arrived in much worse shape than you three. Very fortunate you are. With the plane . . . Well. I thought for sure you were dead. I thought all was lost."

"All?" Dave pauses, then looks ahead, toward the pyramid rising from the trees. It's closer than before. "Where are we going?"

"It's time you meet him in the flesh," the Russian says. "Safet. Now, let us walk in quiet. Prepare your mind. You are still on alert. But you are safe. Let your mind rest in that knowledge."

"But—"

"In quiet," the Russian says again. "Please."

Dave follows, and the pyramid grows larger.

# 9

At the doorway, the Russian—whose name, Dave realizes, he still hasn't asked—says, "I wait here. You go inside."

Dave hesitates, craning his neck to look up at the shining white structure. It seems to rise to the clouds, to touch the skies.

He has fifty questions for the Russian, but he just nods, takes a breath, and steps inside the corridor. His sandals echo on the floor, each step reverberating off marble walls. Torches are stationed every twenty yards, transforming the white stone into warm, pink slabs.

Dave pulls the blanket more tightly around his shoulders. Everything about this feels incongruous. Until an hour ago, he was wearing his security guard uniform, bloody and battered from the last several days of trials. And now he's cleaner than he's ever been, dressed in simple linen clothing, walking into . . . what, exactly?

Except he is safe. He doesn't know how he knows it. He just does.

The corridor terminates at a wooden door. There's nowhere to go but through. Dave knocks lightly on the door, but no answer comes. He opens it gently, then says, "Hello?"

On the other side, a staircase descends, lit with more scattered torches. Here, he finds illustrations etched into the walls and illuminated by the flickering glow. The scenes seem to become animated in the dancing light.

The first scene depicts a throng of people gathered on a beach, surrounded by rowboats and rafts. They are hunched and tired; some are injured.

The next illustration is a collection of scenes that depict a journey: the group leaves the beach, crossing fields and plains and groves toward a distant pyramid.

In the next, the group enters the pyramid and finds a room

filled with beds; they climb into the beds and close their eyes. Above them, swimming in a circle, is a pod of whales.

Blue whales.

*What did you bring me?*

Dave touches the largest of the whales.

"I don't have anything this time," he says. "Just me."

He keeps descending, until the stairs come to an end. Before him stands a heavy door, painted blue. The door is decorated with carvings that echo the drawings he saw minutes ago: Sleeping people. Whales swimming among clouds.

This time Dave doesn't knock. He opens the door, and his nose fills with the salty brine of seawater. He can hear water lapping gently somewhere inside a darkened room, but it's ahead, and there are no torches here.

Dave places his hand on a wall and walks slowly, waving his free hand in front of him. He can hear voices now, murmuring softly, and the sound of water grows clearer as he navigates the dark tunnel.

Soon flickers of orange appear ahead, and the tunnel bends one last time before opening into a large circular room. He stands still in the mouth of the tunnel, taking in the scene.

The room is lit sparingly, with just a few torches anchored to the curved walls. A series of rings are carved into the floor, each ring tightening as they lead Dave's eyes to the center of the space, where a round pool of water throws rippling light on the ceiling and walls.

The effect, combined with the flickering torchlight, is mesmerizing, a little unsettling.

The outermost ring holds beds, two dozen or more, each of them several yards apart from the others. There are people there, too, clustered in groups around some of the beds, whispering softly to one another, as if not to wake the others, who are in bed.

All the standing people wear masks, decorated with feathers, bones, wooden carvings.

Beside the pool, a man sits in a rickety chair. He looks up when Dave takes a step forward.

"Is that connected to the ocean?" Dave asks in a hushed voice, pointing at the pool.

Through a heavy beard, the man's face breaks into a smile.

"My friend," the stranger says, getting to his feet. He opens his arms, and Dave, bewildered, feels himself step into the man's embrace. The man grips Dave's shoulders and holds him at arm's length, studying him. "Oh, you look very tired, David."

"I . . . Yeah," Dave confesses. "I'm a little tired."

"I am so pleased you are here." The man turns, and in a loud whisper, says, "Friends! He is here."

Dave looks around the room, at all the shadowy, masked figures. They all regard him a moment, then return to their conversations.

"Ah, don't mind them," the bearded man says. "They have no foresight." He claps Dave's shoulder, then gestures to his chair. "Please. Sit. There's much to discuss."

## 10

Despite the exhaustion settling into his bones, Dave listens, rapt, as Safet spins his tale. The history of his order, he says, began centuries before, when the first of the dreamers were contacted by the whales.

"In those days—" Safet begins, but Dave interrupts:

"The whales—they're real? I thought they were just part of my dream."

Safet's smile is gentle. "We all thought that in the beginning," he says. "We made the mistake of not telling one another, afraid the others would believe us to be crazy."

Dave flushes with color. "That's *exactly* how I felt."

"But they're very real, and much like us," Safet explains. "Intelligent beyond our understanding. Generous of spirit. They serve as our protectors, but more than that, they also create the veil."

"The elephant said that word," Dave says. "Veil. But I didn't understand. Don't. I don't understand."

"A curtain," Safet says. "A barrier between our world and . . . *theirs*. For as long as we have lived on this world, the barrier has been necessary. Long ago, our ancestors battled the beast, and died. If not for the whales, you and I"—Safet presses his palm firmly to Dave's chest—"would never have existed."

"How long ago?"

"Longer than history records. And for a long time, the veil served its purpose well. Until recently, when that evil found a new way into our home."

"Our dreams."

Safet nods solemnly. "As a species, we have always been most vulnerable in our dreams. Now most of us have fallen already to the beast. Just a few were strong enough to fight, even fewer able to find their way here, to us."

"I still don't know why I'm here," Dave says. "Why any of us is here. This sounds hopeless."

"That's your fear speaking," Safet says. "But we are not weak here. Aristera is a special place. It's where the veil is strongest. Here is where we prepare for the coming war."

"War?"

Safet's eyes darken. "David, if you do not already realize we are at war . . ." He stops. "You have something many of us have: you have the ability to walk between waking and dreaming. It is a rare gift."

*Gift.* Dave chokes on the word. He remembers the sound Dr.

Castaneda made when the pen plunged into his neck, the gurgling sound that came from the doctor's throat as he fought for breath, even as the life gushed out of him.

"I know what you are thinking," Safet says, placing his hands on Dave's shoulders. "You carry it as a burden. You do not see it for the skill that it is. We all carried that weight until we arrived here. You cannot erase the things that came before, the good or the terrible, David. You can only use it to fuel your development of the gift. Let those fears be the mighty wind in your sails."

"It's so powerful," Dave says, his voice hardly a whisper. "How do you even fight it?"

"You've already defeated it. You made it here. That's a victory—"

"A victory! The thing gutted us. Everyone I loved is dead. It's taken everything from us!"

"Everything except you," Safet says, accustomed to Dave's pain. Dave realizes the man must have heard this story from everyone who arrived before him. "You still have *you*."

Dave paces around the pool, then realizes all the figures at the edge of the room are watching him. One of them, a woman whose face is mostly obscured by her mask, offers him a tender smile.

*I know that smile.*

"Safet," he says. "I . . ."

Safet nods. "Yes. She—all of us—were there. Watching. Helping."

"The whale asked me for things."

"Yes."

"I gave it . . . pills."

Safet laughs. "Yes."

He reaches into a satchel and withdraws a bottle of medication.

Dave's eyes widen. "Is that—?"

Safet just smiles.

"How long?" Dave asks, looking around the room at all the gentle faces. "How long have you watched?"

"You dreamed first in the womb," Safet says. "You don't remember, of course, but we heard you. We went to you."

"I didn't know."

"No."

"All the nightmares, the clinics, the studies—"

"All of it was necessary to lead you here," Safet says. "And now that you are here, you must rest."

Dave yawns. Suddenly, he's so tired he can hardly stand.

"We will talk more tomorrow," Safet says. "Or the day after. For now, you sleep."

## II

The Russian stands back, holding the door for the three of them. Linda is the first to step into the quiet building, set far from the bustle of the village. Inside, the room is deep in shadow, the only light coming through an open-air window shrouded in gauzy cloth.

Along each wall is a bed, tidily made, with thick blankets and fat white pillows. Lavender stalks, in little bottles on the windowsill, fill the room with a sleepy, pleasant scent.

"Are . . . Are you sure it's safe?" Linda asks.

Matteo turns to the Russian, but the man has already left.

"It's safe," Dave says. "No nightmares here."

"We can sleep?" Matteo asks. His eyes are rimmed with red. "No shitting?"

Dave nods. "Truly. Nothing will happen to us here."

"And we'll wake up," Linda says hopefully.

"We will."

"The fuck are we waiting for?" Matteo asks. "I call the window."

He strides across the room, then falls facedown across the bed. The curtains gently waft around him as a breeze stirs the air in the room. A moment later, Dave can hear Matteo's breathing deepen.

Linda turns to Dave. "Thank you."

"For what?"

"This is some *Lord of the Rings* shit," she says. "I didn't believe."

"And now?"

"Now . . ." She looks around, at the hand-painted illustrations on the walls. They're nearly identical to the etchings Dave saw in the pyramid. "Now I feel like a newborn." She turns back to Dave. "And you somehow convinced us. You brought us here."

Dave looks down. "Not all of us."

Linda steps closer, presses her palm to Dave's cheek. "I'm sorry," she says. "Whatever happens next, we owe it to her to survive."

"Whatever comes next," Dave agrees.

With that, Linda rises onto her toes and pulls Dave's head toward hers. She places a delicate kiss on his forehead, then rests hers against his.

"Really," she whispers. "Thank you."

Dave watches as she claims the bed on the eastern wall, waits until she's asleep. Then he steps outside. A ladder leans against the hut, and he climbs to the roof. He sits down, legs crossed beneath him, and looks past the village to the ocean beyond, watching as the sun turns the atmosphere to radiant pinks and purples.

High above him, where the sky has already darkened, he can see the first, faint glimmer of stars. He leans back, reclining on the roof, and watches as a satellite, or maybe the International Space Station, carves a steady arc through the dusk, floating past the constellations.

Ursa, the two bears.

Aries, the ram.

Cancer, the crab.

Cannis, the two dogs.

Cetus, the whale.

Dave studies the last one until he can almost see the great mammal, swimming in a sea of millennia-old light and shadow.

The sun disappears below the horizon, and Dave closes his eyes. Before long, he sleeps.

He doesn't dream.

# I Go to Sleep

I

The dashboard clock reads 4:11 when the battery fails. The headlights flicker, illuminating drops of rain like bullets, and then fall dark.

"Millie," Eli says. "You're not asleep, are you?"

"Fresh as a daisy." Millie pulls at her cheeks, stretching her eyes. "I'd actually be waking up soon, you know? Getting ready for work."

"What did you do?"

"Quality assurance. I worked from home. Whole team was on different schedules, so I could keep whatever hours I wanted. Four a.m., I was usually giving up on getting any real sleep."

"The all-nighters suck," Eli agrees. "But I guess they were good practice for this."

"Except my all-nighters had Netflix."

"Mine had *Minecraft*."

"*Minecraft*."

"There's this science guild," Eli says. "People all over the world meet up there and re-create old science things there. I was working with some people to rebuild the Beijing Ancient Observatory. You know it was originally built nearly six hundred years ago?"

"That's the nerdiest thing I've ever heard."

Eli shrugs, too weary to argue.

"Is he starting to smell?" Millie asks. "I can't even tell."

"Noses acclimate to smells pretty fast."

"There's this movie I saw once," Millie says. "Had Frodo in it, from *Lord of the Rings*—"

"Elijah Wood."

"Yes. Right. Anyway. He was a kid in school, had to give a report. I remember it really well because he did his report on smells. He was like, 'Did you know smells are particulate? So that means when you smell poop you're really eating it.'" She grunts. "The stupidest things stick in my brain." Millie stretches, trying not to aggravate her aching neck. "Hey, what was the song?"

"What?"

"On the MP3. What song was it?"

"This old Pretenders song," Eli says. "It's called 'I Go to Sleep.'"

Millie blinks. "I actually know that song."

"Seriously? It's old."

"What am I, fresh out of high school?" Millie asks. "I don't know it because of the Pretenders, though. They're a little before my time, too."

"I read the Wiki about the song once. It wasn't even a Pretenders original. It was by the Kinks, but they never recorded it. Technically every version of the song is a cover."

"I know the version by Sia, then, I guess," Millie says. She hums a few notes, and Eli looks at her, startled. "Sorry."

"No, I just—It's a very special song to me."

"I won't bludgeon it to death for you, then."

"No, I mean . . . would you? Sing it?"

Millie studies Eli's face, his eyes turned large and desperate. "Okay," she says. "I don't remember the words perfectly, but—"

"It's okay."

"I'm naturally tone-deaf."

"Please."

"You asked for it, kid." Millie takes a deep breath, then begins. *"When I wake up from my pillow,"* she sings, *"it's like you're here with me . . ."*

Eli closes his eyes, listening. When Millie finishes, he wipes his face.

"Thank you," he croaks. "You have a nice voice."

"Don't blow smoke up my ass." But she smiles. "Thank you."

A gust of wind whips rain over the windshield in a heavy sheet. In the distance, the horizon faintly glows.

"You think we're going to die here?" Eli asks.

"I think if we are, at least it's going to be easy," Millie says thoughtfully. "Everybody says they want to go in their sleep."

"Ironic, then, that you and I don't sleep."

"Yeah. Ironic."

"But I'm not ready."

"When I was small, I figured out that whatever my mother was doing, dragging us from place to place in the middle of the night, it wasn't going to end well." Millie runs her tongue over her teeth. "I think I made my peace with the bad shit way back then. A child shouldn't have to do that, you know?"

"Yes," Eli agrees. "I know exactly."

"I'm with you, though. I'm not ready."

She reaches across the gap between the seats and takes Eli's hand.

"Millie?" Eli asks, like a child.

"Sing it again?"

He nods. "Please."

Through a curtain of rain, the horizon is a faint wash of violet, then rose. As morning draws near, Millie runs her thumb over the baby skin of Eli's knuckles, then squeezes his hand in her own.

Softly, she sings again.

# Epilogue

Santa Mira is a ghost town. Street after street lay quiet as the sun appears to the east. Its light touches the rooftops of apartment buildings and shopping plazas, casts its glow on empty intersections and quiet playgrounds. An abandoned ambulance rests on the shoulder of an access road a few miles outside a graveyard-silent airport.

The Santa Mira Medical Center, its main building walled mostly in glass, catches the sunlight and reflects it like a gigantic mirror. The light floods the parking garage, the carefully maintained lawn and visitor benches, slides across the emergency room driveway.

On the sidewalk beside the ER doors, three bodies lie in an impolite pile: two young men, one woman. All of them have lain here for several days, the color drained from their pallid skin. Coyotes, emboldened by the sudden stillness in the city, have ventured down from the hills to gnaw at the corpses. Crows have picked at the bodies, removing gobs of flesh from their faces, their exposed fingers. But it has been long enough now that even the animals are not interested. The abdomens have bloated; the meat has spoiled.

One of the bodies, a young man, still wears a face full of broken glass. When he stirs, when he coughs, a pebble of glass is dislodged and skitters across the concrete.

He struggles to rise, and cannot, pinned beneath the other bodies. A confused, inhuman grunt escapes his throat.

The woman twitches next.


### 2


Between Providence, Rhode Island, and Boston, Massachusetts, a thicket of smashed cars blocks a highway. Tangled metal, exploded and then deflated airbags, shattered windshields. And bodies. Many, many bodies.

Behind the wheel of a crumpled Toyota Tacoma, a teenage girl, skin mottled, eyes clouded and dried out, blinks. She jerks in place, inadvertently hitting the pickup truck's horn, which rings out over the devastation. A wake-up bugle for the other dead, who stir in their vehicles, many of them pinned in place, unable to extricate themselves from the wreckage.

Thousands of miles away, a girl in a *Steven Universe* T-shirt, still wearing her gaming headset, lurches upright. The game controller falls out of her stiff hand with a clatter. Her video stream, still active, shows four hundred viewers, but none of them are alive anymore. They just have reliable internet access.

Around the world, in Luxembourg, Martin Faber gasps and sits up suddenly. The power in his apartment has gone out; all the food in his refrigerator has spoiled, but he doesn't notice the smell. He struggles to stand up, knocking aside his coffee table, sending the plastic TV dinner tray skittering.

For days, the projector in the Cine de Luz in Lugo has shined a blank light on the theater screen. The film flaps tirelessly as the reel spins. Alarico Morales's eyes snap open, and blink slowly at the empty white canvas in front of him. A moment later he stands up; one leg works well, but the other gives way beneath him, and Alarico takes a hard fall. The sound of his left ulna snapping echoes like a gunshot in the theater, but Alarico hardly notices. He rises again, one arm dangling limp, bent, and walks jerkily toward the theater door.

3

Deep inside Santa Mira Medical Center, in an operating theater, the body of Duane Bradley rests on a surgical table. Bradley, who had been admitted several days earlier with a broken rib, now lies decaying with his skull open, his brain shriveled and dried out from exposure.

Still, his eyes flutter beneath closed lids, then open.

He sits up, ragged flaps of scalp still dangling from what's left of his head. When he tries to climb down from the table, the table's unlocked wheels skid away beneath him, and Duane Bradley falls again. A fall is what put him in the hospital to begin with, but he doesn't remember. His brain doesn't process thoughts or pain.

He hits the hard linoleum floor, striking his head on the table's casters. His sawed-away skull is fragile, and shards of bone crack and scatter when he makes contact.

He doesn't grunt in pain, doesn't pass out. He awkwardly turns onto his sunken belly, then forces himself onto hands and knees, then stands, unsteady, and waits.

Several rooms away, Ruth Nelson, still tucked inside the large MRI machine, tries to sit up, and cracks her head against the chamber ceiling.

4

Eighty-three miles from Salt Lake City, the electric car rests in a culvert, where Argyle crashed it days before, trying to avoid what it registered as a human walking in the road. Argyle's main batteries were damaged in the crash; the backup has held on, though, operating in extreme low power mode.

Willem, wedged on the floorboard, suddenly flails violently. He kicks the gearshift. His head and shoulders are pinned in place by the misshapen dashboard, mangled from the impact.

"The car is nonfunctional, I'm afraid," Argyle says. "I have attempted to call emergency services, with no success."

Willem thrashes about, unable to free himself.

"Would you like me to call the registered owner, Hodan Ferris?"

Willem wails like a wounded animal.

"I'm sorry," Argyle apologizes. "I'm afraid I didn't understand that."

Far away to the south, at a now-abandoned resort in Costa Rica, Lee Jong opens his eyes. He floats facedown in a swimming pool. Pale green light dances on the tile below him, but Lee doesn't register any of it. He turns over and discovers a deflated plastic raft draped over him, tangled around him. He brushes it away, then stands up in the water. Palm branches and scattered leaves cover the surface of the pool; the storm that blew them there continues to sweep over the hotel. A gust of wind takes the raft from him and wraps it around the rails of the pool ladder. Lightning ripples through the clouds above; a fresh torrent of rain falls upon the pool, churning the water into spray.

Bloated and sloughing skin from his many days in the water, box office superstar Lee Jong wades toward the ladder.

From high above, the lightning creates beautiful, intricate

patterns in the charcoal cloud cover. The ISS passes by silently, too distant to throw a shadow on the planet below. Miroslava Andropov, wrung out from days of trying to raise Mission Control, wonders what it would be like to throw herself out of the station. How long would it take her to enter the atmosphere? How long to burn up on reentry?

All her comrades are dead, and she doesn't understand why, or how. Only that each of them has gone to sleep, and each of them has died without waking. She and Amir and Reggie had stowed the first two or three bodies in Node 3, strapping them down like cargo. But then Reggie had died, and then Amir, and then Sandie and Kurt and Ling, and Miroslava just left them in their sleep sacks.

"Answer me!" she shouts at the radio, but of course nobody answers. Whatever has happened up here has happened down there, too, and now Miroslava is alone, maybe the only person left alive, and all she can think about is her body and how quickly it might burn up in the atmosphere.

Would it hurt?

There's a scuffling sound from the corridor behind her, and Miroslava turns; briefly, hope flares through her exhaustion. But there's no one there.

The sound comes again, though.

Miroslava drifts toward the crew cabins. She floats just outside Ling's cabin. Again, a thump from within, the sound of fabric rustling against fabric. A faint sigh, or perhaps a moan.

"Hello?" Miroslava asks. Hesitantly, she opens the door.

# 5

In Aristera, it is late afternoon. In the village, Dave, Matteo, and Linda sit alongside other refugees and listen as the Russian teaches them the basics of lucid dreaming. Matteo frowns, not understanding; Linda pats his knee and assures him she'll help him catch up.

The pyramid's shadow falls over the village, a subtle promise of protection. The shade extends past the boundary of the village, its tip pointing roughly toward the distant beach where Dave and the others crawled from the sea, gasping but alive.

The water, turquoise in the afternoon light, laps gently at the sand. Water has no memory, someone said once; it has no interest in the affairs of humans, is ambivalent to the rise and fall of our species. But water has carried history forward, delivering war to distant shores, birthing evolution's first steps, slowly dismantling traces of the past in its depths.

Today the sea watches without judgment as a figure rises from its depths and walks slowly, unevenly, onto Aristera's beach. Clothing hangs from her body in shreds. Her hair is clotted with foam and kelp. Her skin bears the marks of fish teeth and turtle beaks. One of her ankles is broken and drags with every step.

Katie feels no pain, carries no particular thought in her dark, inactive brain. Her eyes are milky, but not so opaque that her oddly shaped pupils, like smudged black triangles, cannot be seen.

As if guided by an unseen navigator, Katie lurches up the beach, toward the faraway white pyramid.

# Acknowledgments

We owe a debt of gratitude to everyone who helped bring this project to life.

First and foremost, thanks to Rob Herting and Dave Henning at QCode, who weren't afraid to believe in our strange vision.

Thanks to Seth Fishman, who shepherded the novel to its home with St. Martin's; and to Michael Homler, for his expert editorial guidance as we carried this story from one medium to another. We're also grateful to Cassidy Graham, Eliani Torres, Rob Grom, Ken Silver, James Sinclair, Michelle Cashman, Paul Hochman, Katie Bassel, Sara LaCotti, and everyone else at St. Martin's who touched this book along the way.

Many thanks to Brian Kavanaugh-Jones, for his expert production of the audio drama and TV series. Mark Fischbach, for thoroughly inhabiting the role of Dave, both in audio and live-action versions of this story, and for making the character very much his own. Thanks, too, to Noah Gersh and Jamie Schefman at Salt Audio, who brought the podcast to life, and to Tess Ryan, who produced the podcast. Chris Ferguson at Oddfellows, who produced the TV series, and Corey Adams, our visionary TV director. We'd also love to thank the entire cast and crew of both the audio drama and TV series for realizing our weird little story so brilliantly.